GIDGET & GRACE

A dog, a girl, a love story

Also by this author:

Heartbreak, Healing and Happiness: Flourishing after a heartbreak
Grief, Grace and Gratitude: Transforming through your grief journey
Loss, Love and Lessons: Healing pet loss and grief

LARA CASANOVA

Gidget & Grace

A DOG, A GIRL, A LOVE STORY

Gidget & Grace: A dog, a girl, a love story

Author – Lara Casanova

www.lifeinthepink.com.au

lara@lifeinthepink.com.au

Editing and design by: www.authorsupportservices.com

Photography by: Real Moments Photography

ISBN: 978-1-922375-32-2

A catalogue record for this book is available from the National Library of Australia

To
My sweet Suzy
My girl

You and me always!

A sweet life, a sweet goodbye
1.5.2007 – 14.8.2022

and

All our fur friends!

"A dog is the only thing on earth that loves
you more than he loves himself."

—Josh Billings

Preface

Gidget & Grace is based on a true love story. It has its muddy feet in many love stories. Mine, yours, ours. Some true, some fiction, some daydreams, some unfulfilled dreams and all inexplicably intertwined to my/your/our life with my/your/our dogs.

Gidget is the doggy protagonist who has a collective temperament of all my soul dogs, of others I have met along the way, and of dogs who are waiting to come into my life and my heart and sprinkle their unconditional love and joy all over it.

Grace is the human protagonist, the one who loves all dogs but most of all Gidget.

I dedicate this book to my late sweet Suzy, a golden retriever. She passed at fifteen and throughout my written word is expressed her sweet disposition, her lovely, devoted nature and the precious deep human–animal bond we shared. It was mutual adoration – her and me always together. Suzy was the perfect doggy, maybe aside from her loud, enthusiastic bark, which was mostly to get my attention to throw the ball for her or to remind me I was ignoring her when I was talking with someone. She was by my side for so many years. We experienced the ups and downs of life together – break-ups, moving houses, changing jobs, losing friends and family – and through it all she was the sweetest and most devoted dog. I have such deep gratitude for the unconditional love we shared and for the cherished memories. While that love is no longer present as we know it, it is deeply embedded into my heart and scattered as paw prints throughout my life.

Then there is an echo through the story of Pippy, my current golden retriever, who is delightful but too much some of the time. Pippy arrived when Suzy was thirteen years old and basking in her senior years. It was instant mutual love. Suzy was the most loving friend to Pippy. Pippy would curl up next to Suzy and lounge in her arms. Pippy was always very rambunctious yet Suzy never barked or growled. She was unbelievably patient, kind and loving as a furry big sister. All was well until we lost Suzy, then Pippy started grieving and developing some undesirable behaviours.

We consulted a behaviouralist, and now, despite my initial reluctance to try medication, Pippy willingly takes her puppy antidepressant every day. Thankfully, this keeps her stable and happy and able to lead a normal and much less stressed life. For Pippy, the diagnosis of doggy ADHD presented as hyperarousal and overstimulation, fear of things like cars, reactivity to some dogs and a noise sensitivity toward trucks, rattly trailers and the noisy postie on his motorbike.

Pippy visits her behaviouralist regularly and we conscientiously practise all our training games to help her overcome her struggles. Anyone would know that living with a dog with these difficulties can be challenging. She is never trying to be difficult but just finds it hard to cope sometimes. As her protector, I have learnt to be more observant and patient of her needs. For her, often less is more. More rest and sleep is best for her rather than more activity to seemingly quell her hyperactivity. She has gifted me many lessons and we share a deep mutual love. Each day we grow a little more together on our shared journey and, simultaneously, our bond deepens.

Maxy, who was my first ever golden retriever, my soul dog, the love of my furry life, lived to fifteen years. He was totally devoted and by my side through thick and thin. Maxy had a strong and determined personality. He liked to do some chest bumping in the park just to alert other dogs that he was the boss and if that was accepted then everything was okay. He was a lover not a fighter but fiercely protective over me. He never got in a fight but definitely had a very assertive nature. We shared love, fun, laughter, frustration and loss. The loss and grief associated with his passing was profound and life changing for me.

I also have a fondness for Labrador retrievers and have had four senior rescue Labs to date.

Chelsea came to live with me at eleven years old and lived till she was the ripe old age of seventeen. She was the cheekiest and funniest black Lab of all with the waggiest tail. Her biggest talent was collecting things to eat. It was amazing what she would find on our walks. I never knew there were things like uncooked lamb chops, rainbow lollipops, whole carrots or bananas hiding deep in the neighbourhood bushes. She never learnt to use the doggy door, so we all froze with the door open at all times for her access. She trained me that dinnertime was at 5pm sharp or else.

Charlie also arrived at eleven years of age but sadly passed six months later from a spinal tumour. I hadn't planned on adopting a dog at the time yet a cousin tagged me on a Facebook post about him. As soon as I saw him, I was sold on his beautiful old face and knew he was meant to come live with me. He came from a domestic violence situation, not that you would know it. He was happy and, despite only being with me a short time, wormed his way straight into my heart.

George came at eight years of age. He was originally named Heart Breaker and fully lives up to his name. He was the stud dog from a breeder/show family but was never successful in performing the deed apparently. He spent a little time in the show ring and his father was a Grand Australian champion. He has the most perfect temperament, especially for wasting the time away from any donut bed in the house. He is the most chilled Lab, unless there is food of course, then he is gone following some strange person around the park continually pecking his nose at their thigh to alert them to his presence. He does the same to me whenever we walk anywhere, even down the hallway.

Then came Sonny, better known as Sunshine, who is as bright, happy and therapeutic as the sun. He is a timid chocolate Labrador who was surrendered to me as a foster, but once I caught a glimpse of his grey, wiry eyebrows as he jumped out of the car, I knew I was in trouble. My doggy George Clooney. Sonny needed surgery to remove many mast cell tumours followed by chemotherapy due to one tumour being a high grade. He didn't blink an eyelid as he traversed his challenging healing regime. He loves nothing more than snuggles right next to me. He spreads the word to all dog owners to have all lumps tested, regardless of their size or type, just to be on the safe side.

I wake up every day eternally grateful with a deep, warm inner glow for these furry souls and often walk down memory lane in my heart just to see the ones I have lost once again.

Our dogs are not all perfect pooches, and some are seemingly naughty, untrained or reactive, but they are all loving and pure and shower unconditional love at every possible opportunity. At the core of their being, all they really want to do is please. It is up to us as the humans to show and teach them how to integrate into our families, and we do this with an abundance of time, patience and love.

With the right amount of love, attention and training, I believe most dogs can transform. They all just want to be loved, protected and cared for. Once they feel safe they can let their true personality radiate. There is something really special about dogs. All you have to do is look deep into their big eyes straight into their soul and there it is – unconditional LOVE!

Dogs allow us to get in touch with our vulnerabilities and meet our beautiful tender side. This part of us often gets buried deep below and can be quashed by our busy lives where we often struggle to survive daily responsibilities and the endless to-do list.

Despite the state of the world there really is beauty everywhere. It's the big dichotomy. Dogs would be top of that list for me. They bring us back to the present moment, where there is no rush, where a simple leaf is awe-inspiring, where an extended sniff is the best part of the day, where every dinner is scrumptious, and a pat from you is it and a bit.

This is truly where life is lived fully, and dogs take us there almost instantly when we allow ourselves to stop, sit and see the world through their eyes and their perspective. Then we feel the love bubble upwards internally and we share it outwards for them, ourselves, others and the world.

Aside from my perfect pooches, I possess an unfathomable love of all dogs far and wide. I have been known to speak with dogs in many countries. I house a deep sense of needing to know all the dogs I meet are cared for by my standards (which is pretty unattainable most of the time). Possibly irrationally, I feel like I've been bequeathed this huge responsibility and have been sent to earth for just this purpose.

My life purpose… my legacy!

Working in the veterinary industry and volunteering at rescue organisations for more than twenty years has been a testament to that, as well as instigating many, often dangerous, doggy rescues, happily having friends' dogs to stay, helping neighbours' dogs out, and hosting weekly doggy play dates often with seven to ten dogs surrounding me in the kitchen.

Dogs really are my life, my passion and my purpose.

It is with that sense of purpose that I love writing about them and sharing and expressing what divine pure creatures they are whilst educating others about their physical, emotional and mental needs.

With this story, I hope to share just some of what I have learnt to help all doggies live a full life with love and enrichment whilst simultaneously telling a love story for your enjoyment and pleasure.

Gidget & Grace

    Essentially, *Gidget & Grace* is a version of my dogs and me, your dogs and you, your family's dogs and them, and all dogs in general. It shares the hope of all dogs to be fully loved, healthy and happy. It is based on the love stories we build on our shared life journey together, which also deepens our human–animal bonds and enriches our lives.

Contents

You and me always

GRACE

The love was palpable.

I felt someone touch my hand.

I saw a dog lying before me.

I tasted the salt of my tears.

I smelt a familiar doggy aroma.

Then, I heard a soft, tender, familiar voice echo quietly in the room. "Are you ready?"

Out came the quietest "yes" and a tear slid softly down my face as I waited.

"I love you."

GIDGET

"Mum, I'm ready. It's time. Just hold me till my last breath comes and goes. All I need is for you to be by my side. Like you always tell me, it's you and me always. I love you," I woofed softly.

I knew I had fulfilled my purpose – unconditional love – to the best of my ability.

I placed my head on Mum's lap and closed my eyes as I waited.

Hi, Gidget and Grace here

GIDGET

"Hi, I'm Gidget! Hi, I'm Gidget! Hi, I'm Gidget!" I woofed loudly. I am a golden retriever puppy.

Let me paint you a pretty picture. Big, brown, sooky eyes. Floppy, soft, bendy body. Smooth, silky ears. A big furry ball of fluff with a soft and snuggly coat. Paws bigger than my short legs. A tail with little feathers that wags deliriously. A mischievous smile. A big butt wiggle. A neediness. An enthusiasm and curiosity for life. A wet, busy tongue. An inability to sit still unless I'm snoozing. And small yet deadly needle-sharp teethies.

That's me.

I'm adorable and sweet.

I'm soft and cuddly.

I'm angelic and divine.

I'm busy and chaotic.

I hear a voice saying, "You are too much, Gidget." And I see a person running after me.

"Gidget... no! Gidget... come here! Gidget... stop!"

I ignore it, of course. I'm a puppy. What do I know? I plead ignorance.

They must be talking about someone else. Surely not me. I'm perfect. I'm the cutest puppy doing what a puppy does best and that entails licking, biting, chewing, jumping, smothering, twirling, zooming, digging, whining, and peeing and pooping, often indoors. That's just how I roll.

That's how I arrived and it's all I know. You see, I'm not a human and don't come with a manual detailing expected appropriate behaviour. I'm a free furry spirit looking to have some furry fun! It's for you to teach me how to be a dog who assimilates into a human world so we can all live harmoniously. My mum Suzy told me it's tough sometimes. She said everything is about communication, and communication without words is difficult.

Please be gentle and patient with me as I take some time to learn. My mind is young and busy and can't focus for long... in fact, sometimes not at all! Did I say my name was Gidget? Was that a bird? What was that noise? What was I saying?

"Gidget... focus... look at me," I hear in the background.

And then... crash... I'm asleep soundly on my back with all four paws in the air exposing my fresh, bare, soft pink belly skin. With my head twisted to one side, twitching lips here and there, I dream of running free, my midget paws paddling as I snooze.

And then I'm awake again and it's witching hour. From zero to one thousand in a millisecond... I'm back!

Witching hour is that hour first thing in the morning or just after dinner when everything about me is amplified and crazy. I just can't contain myself. We play the best games, with humans running all over the place away from me and towards me, often shouting, "No, no, no Gidget!" What a great game.

I love my home and this strange person who picked me up for the first time and looked in my eyes. She embodied a sense of protector and carer. That's my new human mum; they call her Grace. She has a soft voice and gives great cuddles. I trust her with all my furry heart already.

It's been a week in my new home and I am assimilating nicely, I think. Woof!

I miss my littermates and my mum dog. The humans called her Suzy. I called her Mum which came out as Woof. I miss so many things – the warm, snuggly, long sleeps lying entwined with my siblings, swarming around each other trying to be as close as possible, suckling from Mum as we juggled teats at the milk bar before we were introduced to solids, and swirling around a round dinner bowl like a merry-go-round, all in sync.

Mum Suzy told me about humans and how they take care of us. She explained very seriously that it is our purpose to take care of them, to make them happy and to really love them, teach them and gift them lessons about loving unconditionally. Over and over, she stressed that the most important purpose is unconditional love.

One day she sat me down and told me I was ready to go out into the big wide world and start my life journey and bring this purpose to fruition. I was mildly excited and wanted to please her yet I wasn't sure. I wanted to stay tucked up in her wing of safety and love forever with all my warm furry siblings. Sadly, she repeated often that it wasn't possible. How would I say goodbye and leave this snug nest?

I kept asking why and she kept saying you will know in time. You have a bigger purpose, she would say, that is yet to unfold to you, but when it does, I promise you it will be so bright and dazzling and it will all make sense. I had to trust her. I did.

Her words of advice were to wake up every day with a joie de vivre for life. An enthusiasm that is infectious and radiates to all the humans. She explained to me in more detail that my purpose is to shower my person with love and attention, to make them happy, and to provide unconditional love.

This purpose was drummed into me. Mum said that humans have more life issues and drama to deal with. She didn't explain why. She said we have solely them. I thought that sounds like a great life and I can't wait to make my people happy.

Mum painted a pretty picture and I hoped that my life journey would live up to that picture from the first mum I knew and loved so dearly and deeply. My doggy mum Suzy.

Oops, I forgot... Did I tell you I'm beautiful? That's what I keep getting told.

GRACE

Hello, I'm Grace. And I am Gidget's owner. Some would say her fur mum. I like to just say her mum.

Gidget came to me without any warning, long before she was due. I should have known she would arrive spontaneously, as really, that's how I like to live. We were destined for each other.

I was dogless at the time which is not a great state to be in when you love dogs. Dogs help keep us healthy, active and social. They create routine and structure and get you out and about taking daily walks and meeting and greeting people along the way who may become your closest friends.

But at a deeper level, you have something to take care of that is nurturing and loving. Dogs generally bring out the best in you. You have something to love purely and unconditionally. They love you right back. I had been really missing that.

Losing my last dog, Ernie the black Labrador, about six months ago at fifteen years of age was challenging. It was taking me some time to commit to adding once again to my fur family. Traversing the highs and lows of grief over the past six months had taken some courage.

I had said to myself I would enjoy some travel overseas while I had no commitments and that when I returned it would be time to add to my fur family once again.

I had dreamed of Paris and Rome and travelling around these charming cities and further outwards. I imagined immersing myself in the culture, learning the language at a local language school, whiling the hours away chatting with the locals and eating the local delicacies while patting the dogs that ambled past.

Each time I attempted to travel while I had Ernie, I spent the whole trip calling and checking on him, worrying he wasn't getting enough walks, missing him like crazy and wishing myself home.

So, I was preparing for overseas travel, not preparing for a new puppy.

Most people plan and prepare for the upcoming arrival of the cute furry ball of love. They spend weeks at the pet store getting beds, food, collars and so many other bits and pieces. They possibly wait months for the mum to come into season and then deliver the puppies and hope they are the lucky family to be selected. Families then start making the nest for their new puppy to come home to.

Not me. Sometimes I am planned and structured, and other times I am a little more impulsive or spontaneous – or irresponsible, my parents may say. But I operate from my heart, my intuition, and I know when something feels right or not and I decide based on that feeling. Sometimes my next move is right then in the moment.

To date, this has worked well for me. Learning to use my intuition, my inner wisdom, my sixth sense has allowed my life trajectory to be exactly where I want it to be even if I didn't know it at the time. At times, when I haven't listened to my intuition and life has taken me off course or I have thought my head knew better than my heart, I have suffered. When this happens, a familiar sense of anxiety or unease will awaken within me and I use this as a lesson to steer me back to a clear head space and a more desired path forward.

This has always been my guiding light and compass forward. It has removed me from jobs, friendships and many situations that have not aligned with my deepest and truest self. I want to live the most elevated version of myself with experiences galore to learn from rather than in a comfort rut just whiling away the time until I'm old, with a devoted dog or three by my side.

So, in operating at this higher vibration, I don't generally make detailed five-year plans or set goals, or sometimes I do yet I don't hold myself to them like cement. I'm flexible, I'm spontaneous and I am attracted to things that feel right. It's hard to explain. I may hear someone talk about something, watch something on television or hear a song and a warm glow presents from inside. It's like all my insides feel warm, happy, calm and enthused all at the same time and I know it's something I want to investigate. It feels like the right direction for me.

This percolates around inside, sometimes unconsciously, and then the universe seems to provide. Then, poof! Something new arrives or a situation unfolds that enriches my life, or a decision presents that allows me to leave something behind. This way of living elevates my life more than I could have planned or imagined.

This is exactly how Gidget came to be in my life.

The beach

GRACE

The weather outside was glorious despite it being only the start of spring. There is something about the first warmish day of the season that invigorates you and quickens your step, bringing you more motivation and energy. That was today.

My heart was calling me to the beach. I was being drawn to the sound of the waves and the feel of the sand under my feet. I dressed quickly and off I went, following my calling. The warm, light breeze stroking my face was just what I needed after a busy week. Earthing myself on the beach always grounds me and clears my head.

As I walked down to the sand, I could feel it squeaking under my feet and I felt a sense of gratitude ripple through me. Alongside that was a sadness. Walking without Ernie was very surreal. I came weekly, and I would describe it as a bittersweet connection as I remembered Ernie's paws running madly all over the beach leaving their imprints on the sand. Those paw prints and the buckets of sand that lined my back seat on the way home were sadly now only confined to my heart and my memories.

Ernie's presence somehow felt so close yet so far away.

Ernie was hilarious, cheeky, brave, bossy, cuddly, calm and a ball of love. He absolutely worshipped the beach. It's like he was set free as the leash slowly slipped off his neck. Each time he arrived was like the first time. He would run from one end to the other with his ears flying behind him in the wind. And each time, I would chase after him calling his name as he disappeared into the distance with the determination of a marathon runner.

Thankfully his recall was pretty good. Eventually, he would reappear on the horizon and return to sit in front of me for his piece of chicken before he turned and headed in the other direction and did it all over again.

Other times, he transformed into a triathlete and introduced the swim component as he headed out to sea, chasing birds overhead. Like a cartoon skit, you would occasionally see me stripping down to the bare basics, hoping I had on good underwear, and swimming after him to grab his collar and drag him back to shallow water. After we both emerged wet and dishevelled, Ernie would give a big full body shake and off he would go again, while I tried to gain my composure and dry myself off with towels offered by strangers on the shore who tried to hide their laughter.

Even as a senior dog he still had good energy levels and managed to swim and get up to all sorts of cheeky antics that made me laugh. He tried often to replicate his younger years when he would drop and roll in the biggest mounds of seaweed, totally disappearing upside down and then reappearing covered like a sea monster before he would stand up and shake, sending green bits flying off around him. He would run up the sand hills and on his descent build up so much speed that he would trip over himself and roll down the mound. A favourite was trying to steal food from beachgoers or attempting to steal the fishermen's bait and even one time some freshly caught fish from the esky.

Then there were the yuckier times. Once, as a puppy, Ernie vomited all over me in the backseat of the car from inhaling too much seawater – disgusting, but forever a great story to retell. As was the incident when it came out the other end like a fierce jet stream. Three sets of jet streams later he was loaded into the car. He really was a character.

As I walked slowly along the beach, I remembered his quirkiness and the joy he brought to my life. I looked up and saw a small young dog running somewhat awkwardly towards me in full floppy flight. It put the brakes on and stopped dead at my feet and sat. All the Ernie memories continued to flood in.

A big smile appeared on my face. It was a perfect puppy. I laughed loudly to see its owner running along behind like I had so many times and dropped to my knees to pat him.

The owner eventually arrived after scooping up a fresh puppy poo on the way and stopped, bending down with his hands on his knees trying to catch his breath. Without looking at him, as I was still immensely in awe of this puppy, he finally said, "Gosh, sometimes puppies are a handful. Meet Charlie. Oh... and I'm William, the servant to the puppy."

Charlie sat almost still aside from a slow side wiggle looking deeply into my eyes or maybe it was more my hot pink treat bag. I still carried one despite not having a dog, just in case I needed to entice a hug from a strange dog. Eventually, I dove deep to retrieve some small pieces of chicken and his little tail increased its cute little wag. With approval from William, I handed over the chicken and Charlie's sharp teeth scratched my hand as he tried his best to be gentle. He knew how to shake and how to drop, of course. He was a golden retriever puppy. The cutest ever. The breed I reminded myself I was going to get next.

Charlie stuck close by as William fell into sync and we walked together down the beach. Charlie was only young and didn't yet have the courage of the older dogs to go off exploring. He was slowly learning about his environment but he was still mainly underfoot. One thing he did know though was what the purpose of the hot pink bag was. Smart puppy dog.

William and I were talking as we laughed over Charlie's uncoordinated antics. He stumbled and avoided the potholes he had created in an attempt to dig his way to China. Sand flew everywhere behind him and his nose was covered in a wet sticky concoction of sand and slobber as he face-dived into the sand.

I imparted my knowledge of dogs, and more specifically puppies, and offloaded any advice my mind could muster to help Charlie and William build a solid foundation for their life together. I tended to do that often. It feels like my purpose is to look after them all so I often offered unsolicited advice, hoping it was warranted and accepted.

"Where did Charlie come from?" I asked inquisitively.

"There is a local registered breeder nearby called Golden Glow. Why do you ask?" he replied with curious raised eyebrows.

I started to feel that warm glow inside and a calm, sweeping happiness. Oh no, it can't be! I haven't done my overseas trip yet. The carefree lifestyle I was hoping for before I committed myself to another puppy had not yet been fulfilled. But yes, that familiar knowing appeared from within my heart and it knew what it wanted.

I focused back on the conversation until I heard him say, "I think there is one more puppy left." I was done... gone. Why had he told me that? Those bright Paris city lights faded into the depths of my mind, as did the spaghetti carbonara I was going to devour in the streets of Rome. These became a dream for another day as big balls of golden fur floated around like tumbleweeds in my mind and settled in my heart.

The warm glow inside heated up, and I knew life had somehow changed forever.

"What did you say the name of the breeder was again?" I asked tentatively.

"Golden Glow," he replied.

"One left, huh," I whispered.

With that information tucked up tight, William and I said goodbye. I was impressed he hadn't spent too long at the beach and he had mentioned the five-minute rule. This rule denotes the time you should walk a puppy depending on its age so you don't overwalk them and create joint or bone disorders. A dog's growth plates are not closed or fully formed until about eighteen months of age. As a golden retriever, Charlie was a larger breed, so it was important to take things slowly during his development.

He seemed a responsible dog owner as it was a quiet time of day and it wasn't too hot to have a puppy out to experience its first feel of the sand and the water between his paw pads. I respected him for that.

As he walked in the opposite direction, I yelled out, "Good luck and thank you for the furry love. I may see you again one day if I get a puppy." I laughed to myself and wondered what were the chances that would happen.

"Bye Grace, that would be lovely," I heard him say faintly in the distance.

Either way, he was very nice and we had a nice interaction. It also had not gone unnoticed that as well as being a dog lover, he was good-looking, classy and well-spoken. If I got a puppy from the same litter as Charlie, we would be furry related.

I had a mission now. I loved a mission... a to-do list... a new adventure. And when I committed to something, it had to happen quickly to ensure I didn't miss out. A little FOMO appearing.

Having just celebrated my forty-fifth birthday, I had a two-pronged feeling circling internally. On one side, there was this sense of freedom and being able to do what I wanted so not wanting to rush into anything. On the other, a small inkling of older age approaching and a hurry-up kind of attitude rippled through me.

At a conference many years prior, one of the lecturers made a statement that stuck with me: life is not a dress rehearsal; there are no second chances. Many years of self-development had reinforced that and I tried wherever possible to embody this and live life to its fullest.

Trying to please everyone, never saying no, burning the candle at both ends, displaying achievement junkie traits, trying to be perfect, impatience, rushing, drama, confusion and competitiveness only lead to anxiety and burnout. And often this can sneak up without noticing, especially if you feel you are superwoman and live a disconnected head-to-heart life.

I had come close to the edge twice. Never again.

I also had to learn that seeking excitement from the outer world never fulfils any void we hold on the inside. I learnt that only I could make myself happy and I couldn't rely on anyone else to do that job. I had tried that and it failed dismally when I lost what I thought was true love. Pierce was so far the biggest teacher in my life. A soul mate is not necessarily someone you spend your whole life with but someone who changes you at your soul level and teaches you the lessons you need to learn for as long as they reside in your life. Well, he surely did that.

That relationship had imploded around the time I left the corporate world. Talk about a life change. Everything fell into a heap all at once. Stephanie, my therapist, helped me navigate through the break-up and learn the lessons.

I had to learn that my happiness is my responsibility, not anyone else's. I had to learn not to blame others and take responsibility for my choices and my boundaries, or lack thereof, plus a whole host of other deep stuff.

I had to learn a lot and pretty much reprogram myself, as how I had gained satisfaction, reassurance and happiness in my younger years no longer worked. It was a big task and rolling around in the muddy waters of self-development was gruelling and life changing, but concurrently brought enormous rewards of internal peace and calm.

I had chosen to dedicate the rest of my life to being about presence, calm, relaxation, kindness, connection, patience, yoga, meditation, time to process, time for self, stillness, reflection, holding an inner glow, wisdom, peace, deep-embedded purpose and intuition. Essentially what I experience and resonate deeply as grace.

And to do it all with a set of furry paws walking beside me on the journey – perfection!

A furry meeting

GRACE

I arrived home and stepped through my hot pink front door, a colour I daringly chose when I repainted my house. Some people scoffed. "Wow! That is pink!" they would say as they entered my house. I never really knew if they thought it was brave or if they disapproved of it being so non-traditional. But all that mattered was I loved it. And I was quite happy to say just that to anyone who laughed disapprovingly. Life is about making the choices that suit you, not everyone else.

Returning home now after the beach visit, things looked the same and everything was where I left it only hours ago, yet it felt different. It's like everything had already changed and yet nothing had except for my state of mind.

I know from experience that a state of mind can quickly change everything for the better or worse. Our perceptions, beliefs, values and experiences can add to our state of mind. We can absolutely change our mind and change our state with the click of our fingers. I am a testament to that time after time.

Gidget & Grace

My home now felt different after this morning's simple trip to the beach and meeting a nice man and a squishy puppy. It felt more loving. I felt more loving, more connected, open, glowing and radiating. Essentially, I felt love.

I felt my heart leading me forward to where I was meant to be. I felt a purpose reveal itself and present the opportunity for a new life. Did I want to take it? Could I trust my intuition? Should I do a pros and cons list? Or should I just follow my heart?

So many questions swirled inside me until something larger took over and I leapt out of my head and into my heart. I took a breath and along with that came a trust sourced deep inside me that led me forward.

And with that, I reached for my phone and googled the number.

"Hello, Golden Glow, how can I help you?" I heard at the other end of what I anticipated to be a life-changing phone call.

"Hi, I'm Grace, I hear you may have one golden retriever left in your litter that needs a home," I blurted out.

"Well, actually we do," replied the nice lady on the other end of the phone.

"What is your address?" I heard myself saying.

It all happened very quickly. Later that afternoon I gently picked up the last puppy of the litter out of its mum's embrace. It was a little older than normal. A perfect girl. So fluffy and squishy. She had an owner lined up who had three small children but they had withdrawn at the last moment due to a family illness.

The puppy let out a little whine and I noticed she felt heavy yet floppy in my arms. I closed my eyes and held her tight, wrapping both arms around her and drawing her as close as I could as she wiggled around.

Instantaneously, my heart burst open with love and protection. Everything was right in the world in that particular moment. I could tell because my head, heart and soul connected. They felt in alignment, with no questions, no fears, just love. A tear of joy and connection surfaced and rolled down my face, followed by another in honour and remembrance of Ernie, never to be forgotten.

A happiness so deep was born as we hugged for the first time.

I was ready to take the life journey together with this beautiful furry soul. It always fascinated me that only yesterday my life was heading one way and today... voila! I loved the fact that we were capable of this if we let ourselves.

Now, I just needed to check with her. I stroked her head and I said quite simply and quietly, "Hey, beautiful girl, do you want to come and live with me? I will make sure you are looked after emotionally, physically and mentally. I will love you and take care of you forever. You will never be lacking for anything. We will go on the most loving of life's journeys together. I will move the earth for you and protect you at all costs. You will have a place in my home and my heart for your ever. My sweet girl, you and me always."

With that, a wet face lick, a big wiggle and a sweet whine sealed the deal.

So became Gidget and Grace.

And the love story began.

Puppy capers

GIDGET

"Did someone say dinnertime?" I woofed. After racing out from the kitchen and sending the rugs flying upwards, I slid down the hallway on my silky smooth, pristine paw pads to the laundry where my dinner was.

"I'm here!" I woofed and proceeded to drool all over the floor.

Meal times are one of my favourite times. As well as treat times, walk times, beach times, park times, hugs times and mum times. I suppose if I'm fair, all the times are my favourite times. Life is great. There's nothing to complain about here. But meal times when I fill my tummy are extra special!

My normal night-time routine consisted of dinner, witching hour, cuddles on the couch and sleep, interspersed with uncontrollable zoomies that led me all the way through the house and up and down all the furniture that I wasn't allowed on. I was faster than a speeding bullet and no one could catch me – or that's how I saw myself anyway. In reality, I was a small, floppy, uncoordinated mess.

I liked to chew on my toys, flipping them around like I would a possum if I found one lurking in the backyard and ripping out the fluff and squeakers imagining it to be the possum's gizzards and heart. In my mind, I was completely uncivilised and like a wild dog able to survive alone. In reality, I would not be able to survive on my own at all. I needed all the comforts of an indoor life, my licking mat every morning and my warm pink donut bed every night.

Sometimes I get confused and mistake one of Mum's things for a toy. Like her new expensive prescription glasses that one time. "They were Prada," she kept telling me with exasperation. Oops. Sometimes I'm not sure what is mine and what is hers. If I knew, I wouldn't take it. I guess you learn from your mistakes. I'll chalk that up to being a puppy and being pretty clueless right now. Luckily, she feels the same. She calls it an oopsie. Sometimes a major oopsie.

My purpose I remember is to make her happy and impart unconditional love. I intend to hold that promise forever. I had promised Mum Suzy. With each day that I miss her silky coat and warm snuggles, I remember I have a bigger purpose.

The purpose I have outweighs me spending time missing her, which enables me to carry on being happy and puppy-like. There have been a few more oopsies. I won't name them all. The most embarrassing was an underpants issue. Mum said we are not to speak of that as it's humiliating and I promised not to tell.

"Gidget, tomorrow we are going to puppy school," Mum said.

"Yay, how exciting," I woofed at her.

"When is tomorrow? How long away is that? Actually, what is puppy school? I'm not sure what that means but I'm up for anything. I am a fun, energetic ball of floofy enthusiasm soaking up the world." I continued woofing in a shrieking, high-pitched tone.

So, yes, sign me up for all and any new adventures.

Now, though, I feel sleepiness overcome me. Mum picks me up, takes me outside and stands me on the lawn. As she says "wees" I topple over and lie there, do a little wiggle on my back and wait. I'm tired, I want to sleep. Why are we outside again?

She picks me up, stands me on all fours again and says "wees" again.

I drop to the floor and proceed to show her my pink belly again. It seems like we stay out there for ages repeating this same silly routine every night. At some stage my insides feel warm and full, I smell an interesting smell on the lawn, my body goes around in a circle or two and I do a little squat. I then feel a sense of relief and instinctively move carefully so I don't step in the puddle seemingly created by myself.

I hear Mum jumping for joy saying, "Good girl, good girl, good girl!" As I begin to get all revved up for another game, wide awake now after all the entertainment on the lawn, she scoops me up and inside we go to my soft, pink, floofy donut bed. Here she speaks softly to me while stroking my coat and before the lights are even turned off, I'm nearly asleep.

As I am drifting off, I hear her say, "I love you, Gidget. It's you and me always," as she kisses the top of my head.

She says that a lot. If I could talk, I would say right back at you and tell her she is my world and that she is the best mum ever. Mum Suzy had it right when she said I was off to a new life journey that was going to be amazing. I never thought I could love someone like I did Mum Suzy but my new human mum, Grace, is very quickly winning all my love and trust.

Puppy school flew by quicker than I can consume a piece of toast, or at least the corner bit that I'm allowed that is laced with a strange-tasting, dark black spread. Sometimes I get lucky and it is a sweet honey spread.

I graduated with a certificate on the final night dressed up like Elsa from *Frozen*, struggling to pose for the photo with a wig of long blonde plaits and a blue robe trailing behind me. I was awarded the happiest dog in class because of course I was.

It was fun. I made friends: another golden retriever named Sammy, a pug called Winston, a dachshund called Audrey and an Irish wolfhound named Walter or Wally for short. He was enormous.

We looked like a bizarre eclectic bunch in the graduation photo.

Throughout the four weeks, I consumed many Kongs filled with yummy foods which allowed the humans to talk while we were distracted. I heard the trainer say, "Kongs are perfect for calming and mental stimulation as are licking mats." They were covered in peanut butter. Yum!

Mum stocked up and we went home with a goodie bag filled with all the things to keep me calm. I thought I was calm but Mum begged to differ.

I took all my puppy school tricks to big girl training soon after. This was where all the serious dogs were: the overachieving German shorthaired pointers, the slow and steady Bernese mountain dogs, the yappy Jack Russell terriers, the merry cocker spaniels, the enormous Rottweilers, the fiercely protective dachshunds – I wondered why their legs were so short – the basset hounds with ears that dragged on the ground – surely that wasn't hygienic – and the hilarious Labradors – and I thought I loved food!

Then there was me, the happy-go-lucky golden retriever, a people-pleaser by nature who was very happy to work for food or just really happy for anything. I knew every trick in the book. Just ask me. Bang! Play dead. Yep, even that one. I practise that one a lot when I'm feeling tired at training.

"Hey guys, let's start the training," I would woof to the class as we arrived. I was a little overenthusiastic.

Grace

Training became a weekly event, and every week I bribed Gidget into the car with a peanut butter licking mat. She wasn't a huge fan of getting into the car after a vomiting experience when leaving the park after she overindulged on too many treats. I was lucky she was a golden retriever so she was built to be pretty amenable to most things even if under duress. She seemed to come with a preprogrammed pleasing gene. This was very handy when it was switched to enabled.

"Hop up, Gidget," I would say and promptly deliver the licking mat.

Last week I asked the trainer, "So, if I use licking mats and other self-feeders will that help her calm down and stop her rustling up the whole house every night around witching hour?"

"Yes, it may help," she replied. This was quickly followed by "But…"

Looking for a simple yes without any buts would have sufficed and delighted me, and I unconsciously cut her off.

"I love her to bits but she is a bit of a handful," I said to the trainer.

I actually mention this to her most weeks looking for that magic cure to stop all the crazy puppy shenanigans.

And I always get the same response. "Yes, they will help but she is a puppy and this is all normal."

"Puppyhood can be treacherous and difficult," said the trainer. "Never underestimate it. Just remember… time, love and patience."

I was wondering though if Gidget was just a bit more than that. Or was I imagining it?

Seriously, some days I look at her and think she is too much. But then I look deep into her eyes and the love consumes me and all is forgiven and my patience is restored.

We are in puppyhood, I keep telling myself as I recall the Facebook meme floating around stating from zero to three months, they are an angel; from three months to three years they are like a Tyrannosaurus rex; and from three years on they return to being a beautiful angel. Did that really read three months to three years? No guessing what stage we're in.

"Breathe, Grace, only about two and a half years to go," I said out loud.

It's easy to forget what a puppy is like when you haven't had one for fifteen years. It's a massive adjustment to family life and your schedule, your sleep and your nerves, and it takes a huge toll on your patience. But it's well worth it. In fact, the love it brings to your life is extraordinary.

I know that deep down, I reminded myself. I always have.

Buzzy bee

GRACE

I opened the door quickly, excited to see Gidget and to prepare for our weekly training. I mentally prepared a list: licking mat for the car, poo bags, a mixture of treats, training clicker, lead, water bottle, extra water for the car, mat, and training manual. Phew! Each week I felt like a pack horse as we arrived, attempting to juggle all the gear while containing Gidget precariously on the end of the lead.

What would we learn tonight? Would Gidget behave? Would I get any more calming tips?

"Gidget!" I called. "Let's get ready for training." Nothing. Again I shouted, "Gidget, gorgeous girl, where are you?" Still nothing.

Quiet. That's not good. When a puppy is quiet you always know something is wrong. It's very strange she didn't greet me at the door. I walked around the house, my pace speeding up, and I could feel anxiety creeping in. That familiar type of anxiety that slowly takes over and you feel your muscles tense and your tummy go weak, and you start to feel lightheaded and unbalanced. You immediately start to think the worst what-ifs.

After scouring the house, I finally walked outside and saw my little girl sound asleep on the lawn. Phew. Disaster averted. How cute she looked. My beautiful Gidget really was an angel disguised in a fur coat.

As my heart rate started to slow down, I bent to pat her and wake her slowly, "Hey gorgeous girl, hello, wake up. Mummy's home."

Still nothing. What?

The worry started to build again. I rustled her little body and my anxiety amped up again double-fold as I realised she was almost comatose, not asleep. There was no movement and no response, but she was breathing. Thank goodness.

There was no time to think about what had happened. My sympathetic nervous system kicked straight into gear ready for action while an underlying sense of dread niggled away at my insides. I picked her up like she was the most precious cargo and walked as quickly as I could, grabbing my keys on the way. I lay her floppy body gently in her crate on the back seat of the car. Her chest softly rising and falling reassured me she was still breathing.

I could barely start the car as my hands were shaking uncontrollably. I couldn't hear her whining or see her jumping around trying to get a better view which exacerbated the feeling of worry swirling inside me. But somehow the adrenaline kicked in and I managed to push the worry aside and instead focus on getting help.

"Hold on, little girl. It's going to be okay," I said as I started driving.

Our local veterinary clinic, Princess Park Vet, is not far away. "Siri, call the vet," I announced towards my phone.

When the call connected, I let the veterinarian know I was on the way and they assured me they would be waiting for me to arrive. "Do you know what happened?" the woman who announced herself as Sally asked. I broke down in tears barely able to see the road.

"I have no idea. She's only five months old," I blubbered.

I cursed the road rules and broke the speed limit a little. How on earth was I meant to go fifty kilometres an hour while my gorgeous puppy was in the back seat struggling for life? It's unfortunate there are no pet ambulances.

After screeching to a stop outside the vet, and without even closing the driver's door properly, I opened the back door, unzipped the soft crate, gently picked Gidget up in my arms and hurried towards the front door. True to their word, two nurses were racing towards me to help. They took her out of my arms, told me to head to reception and then whisked her away.

I stood motionless for a moment. The sense of dread lingered as if awaiting further instruction. Tears overflowed.

Seeing Gidget so vulnerable with no life in her normally energetic and animated body was intensely difficult to process. The sense of love and protection swelled to a crescendo. But a part of me relaxed slightly knowing she was in good hands. All I could do was sit and wait. And I did. I waited and waited.

After what seemed like an eternity, I was called in to see the vet. All my emotions were released in the form of tears and relief as Dr Finn Ross said, "Hi Grace, Gidget is going to be fine. Just a bad case of a nasty bee sting. Little puppies can have a big reaction."

"We found the stinger on the inside of her mouth which had swelled up and started to produce hives," he continued. "Some animals can collapse from a bee sting like Gidget did. We gave her an antihistamine injection and we would like to keep her for a few hours to monitor her before she goes home."

"Thank you, Dr Ross. Of course I will be back for her later," I said as I let out a deep sigh of relief.

I nearly reached out to hug him as I was so comforted by his words, but luckily something pulled me back. He must have thought I was already an emotional mess and a hug would have only corroborated that.

Dr Ross had administered Gidget's vaccinations and he was a professional with such a kind soul.

Actually, I had known him for a long time. We had shared some intimate doggy moments over the years, specifically Ernie's last moments when he injected Ernie with the life-draining drug known by lay people as the green dream drug to take away his life and his pain and plunge me into my own. The final act of love.

His warmth and compassion didn't go unnoticed then or now.

"How are you, Grace?" he asked. "It's good to see you."

"I'm better now. Thanks, Dr Ross. What a scare. My hands are still shaking."

"Grace, please call me Finn. I am so pleased you have another fur family member. I always remember Ernie and his antics. Gidget has big shoes to fill. How are you coping after your loss?" he continued.

He showered me with care and patience, understanding exactly what I needed to alleviate the range of emotions whirling around my head after the bee sting incident. I always admired his innate way of producing a sense of calm and confidence. He was one in a million.

I reluctantly left Gidget as instructed and headed to the closest coffee shop where I ordered, sat, processed, cried behind my sunglasses, drank my coffee and thanked my lucky stars. I just kind of zoned out and stared into space, a sense of shock rolling through my body as it tried to regain some sense of emotional equilibrium.

My overwhelmed mind wandered around searching for some form of grounding. I could only think how much love I held for this little ball of floof. The day she landed in my heart she took it over and proceeded to change my life. I had not planned her arrival but I could not have expected life would take this wonderful turn. It was turning out to be an incredible journey of love.

This love was warm and cosy, and there was an openness and rawness inside it that allowed me to feel fear without any form of intrusion to the love. The dichotomy of emotions happily sat beside each other bringing a sense of bittersweet calm.

It was an attachment so strong that it was almost unhealthy, yet it was profoundly one of the deepest and most unconditional loves I had known, even though I had only known her for a few months. It was a love that was inherently changing me from the deepest parts of myself to be a higher and elevated version of myself. It was exactly the same love I had with Ernie.

"My sweet Gidget girl is going to be okay," I said out loud.

I also reflected on Ernie and his beautiful nature of hilarity and charm and how he warmed me with unconditional love. Ernie and Gidget would have loved each other.

I waited for two hours, downing three cups of coffee and an apple and cinnamon muffin while processing all sorts of emotions, before the call finally came to say I could collect Gidget. I dropped everything and ran.

It was only when I had her back in my arms on the couch at home where she snuggled into me and I stroked her furry body and spoke softly to her that I found myself fully releasing the build-up of stress and fear. The tears flowed – tears of fear, tears of joy and tears of love – but I kept them quiet so as not to disturb her.

A rainbow of emotions flowed through me.

Eventually, she opened her eyes and looked at me, and all I could say was "You will do anything to get out of training, won't you, Gidget? I thought you loved training."

Trying to inject humour into the chaos of the day helped me to release. Of course, that was a lot easier to do when I knew everything was going to be okay.

GIDGET

I looked up at Mum and I wondered what all the fuss was about. I just took a little snooze after a playful session with a buzzing bee or three! I'm just a bit drowsy now, but I'll be back to my normal self tomorrow!

"I love you, Mum. My protector. You and me always and forever," I woofed quietly before I drifted off to sleep to dream of life and love with lots of bees buzzing around the periphery.

Namaste

GIDGET

"Hello, hello, hello," I woofed to Mum right in her face. She always tells me I have problems with personal space, and that's mostly true.

It's a morning ritual, you see. I wake up and it's still dark but I need to make sure Mum is okay and had a good night's sleep. What better way to do that than to jump my front paws up and start licking whatever part of her body I can reach! It's a bull's eye if I get her face.

"What's on the agenda for today?"

Sometimes she welcomes my 5am enthusiastic salutations and other times all I hear is her telling me to get back to bed while she turns over and ignores me. So rude! Yet I do what I am asked... mostly.

Today is the ignoring type of start to the day so it looks like I will have to find something else to do. Let's see what toys are around for a little chew fest.

Aha, there's Mr Racoon, my favourite toy. I pounce on it with my front two paws and then scoop it in my mouth and chomp down hard. I throw it around with a flick of my head and it goes flying in the air landing on top of my back.

Mum and I like to play the find game with Mr Racoon. She hides it in a tricky corner of a room while I sit and wait then she gives the FIND command. Once I find it, I go running around the house in excitement like a sideways bucking bronco and usually jump on the bed with it for a quick chew. Then we repeat. The hiding spots become more difficult as I master the game, and Mr Racoon gets a little stiffer from all my dried slobber.

Oops, I just chewed off an ear. I better spit it out under the bed. I hope Mum doesn't notice.

"Hurry up, Mum," I woofed.

GRACE

I switch the lights on and say good morning to Gidget who is busy chewing her racoon.

"Gidget, where has its ear gone? Oh my god!" I said. "It's only 6am and you have already destroyed something" comes out with a side serve of exasperation.

It's not surprising. There are skins of toys all over the house that have lost their stuffing, squeakers and appendages. I stretch as I think about what today will bring.

"Okay, I'll get up. Wees time, Gidget. Let's go."

Saturdays are always a good day as I have the whole day to plan what I want to do and Gidget is always a big part of those plans. Maybe the top priority. You see, for me, it's all about her having a good life. If she is fulfilled and happy, my heart glows. I think that's a mutual arrangement.

During the week I work as an administration coordinator at a small privately owned yoga studio called Pink Peace Yoga. There are only three of us besides the yoga teachers. The owner, Fred, gave me the long-winded nickname 'Gorgeous Grace, the master organising yogini'. It was a mouthful only he could get out.

I work part time and it's pretty flexible, so I have plenty of time to entertain Gidget, look after myself and volunteer at Animal Aid, the local dog rescue, once a week. For me, variety is the spice of life and I feel enormously fulfilled living between my passions of dogs and yoga.

This was not always the case. Spending many years in middle management in the corporate world stole my soul. It took me years to notice I was spiritually fading away and a few more years to build up the courage to change the trajectory of my life.

Throughout the time it took me to do that there were many stressful times and the odd unannounced and frightening panic attack. I was wedged deeply in a comfort rut that was destroying my hopes, my dreams, my passions, my energy and essentially me. My fortieth birthday present to myself five years ago was leaving my corporate nightmare. The unwrapping of that gift has been sweet.

Around that time my friend Camilla convinced me to come along to a yoga class. She had been my friend since school and being a flight attendant she was in and out of the country a lot. But despite merging in and out of each other's lives for what seemed like forever, when we were having a together patch, we were inseparable.

She was a huge dog lover also and had various larger breed dogs flow through her life as her companions. Presently, she had a big, beautiful Bernese mountain dog named Teddy. He was only a few years old so young at heart like Gidget, but he was enormous. They were best friends just like us and we tried to see each other every week despite all our commitments. When we caught up, Camilla and I were like excited two-year-old dogs, talking, laughing, jumping for joy and sometimes crying. All we lacked was licking each other's faces – no need for that when a simple kiss will do!

Teddy was pretty strong-willed and often refused to get into the car to go for play dates. You could see Camilla trying to hoick this enormous bottom into the car and Teddy flatly refusing to have it.

Camilla met her now-boyfriend Ernest this way from an unsightly experience as he picked her up from the gutter after one of Teddy's refusals. Her foot had slipped and she went face first down using her wrists to stop her from losing her front teeth. He had rushed to her assistance from the other side of the road and picked her up, and love blossomed from day one. Thanks Teddy!

So, along I went with Camilla to yoga. I had dabbled in yoga before but I always found it too slow or too boring. My busy, unfocused mind lived up to the theory that people think over six thousand thoughts a day. Interestingly, about eighty per cent of those thoughts are likely to be negative. I thought I would be driven crazy trying to last a whole yoga class as I assumed you had to empty your mind and think of nothing. I didn't realise that was not the aim.

As the class started, we fell silent as instructed. As the class progressed I realised it was different this time. I didn't expect anything yet I felt connected and quiet in the Savasana pose lying on my back at the end of class. It reignited the part of me that felt true and pure like when I was a child. It produced familiar somatic feelings of safety, warmth and joy, and this was enough for me to know my life had been heading in the wrong direction. An epiphany came to me that there had to be more. It took a little longer to actually break away from my soul-stealing job and make the changes, but slowly over time I did.

I noticed myself transforming and slowly yoga became one of my daily rituals. I learnt when the thousands of thoughts struck me that I could almost sit behind my thoughts and watch them on a movie screen and not get taken down the rabbit hole with them, so to speak. I learnt to acknowledge each thought as it arose, thank it, and then come back to the anchor of my breath. My breath became my focus during the Savasana meditation. Rinse and repeat. Calm washed over me. I was hooked.

At the end of the class, we jointly replied "Namaste" to the teacher and I felt a peace wash over me. My soul felt at home.

I loved it so much that I became a regular attendee, so much so that the hundred per cent that I give to everything paid off and not long after I was offered the administration position at the studio. This led me to do yoga teacher training which I completed for personal interest but occasionally I have taught a few classes for practice.

The directors at Pink Peace Yoga are a lovely couple, Fred and Lilly, who hold their staff's happiness at the forefront of their priorities. Fred was a little older and had spent ten years as a monk in a monastery before he left, wanting instead to live in and experience the world. Soon after, he met Lilly who liked to call herself a carefree hippy spirit. She had long grey-tinged hair and was always dressed in colourful baggy clothes and rarely wore shoes.

The calm they exuded was infectious and their wisdom was irresistible. This drew me to them and I loved being in their presence.

"Just be true to yourself," Lilly was always reciting. "Be present" was another gem.

The studio is only three kilometres from my house, which was perfect for a quick visit home to see Gidget and give her a hug, a wee break and a treat or three before heading back to work.

They loved dogs. Fred told me when Gidget gets a bit older and more settled – if that ever happens, I thought – she can come in to work with me. Just patting her is like therapy for the heart so she would do wonders for all the stressed-out souls coming to seek a peaceful space and a lighter life. I secretly didn't know if Gidget would ever be calm enough to be therapeutic but it was a nice idea.

Life was unfolding beautifully for me and Gidget.

The park

Grace

"Come on, Gidget. Let's go for a lovely long walk this morning. We can go to a few parks, make a coffee stop along the way and see what else the morning brings."

"Let's go," she said back... or so I interpreted from her woof.

As we set off with her pink treat bag filled to the brim with treats, poo bags and a whole host of other paraphernalia needed on a dog walk, I admired how smart she looked in her hot pink harness and matching lead.

Gidget had come in leaps and bounds since finishing her level two training and was getting really good at loose leash walking. After about twenty minutes, we approached one of the local parks. It was a big beautiful green area with luscious grass that was kept watered and mown. There were plenty of bushes and freshwater creeks to explore and trails around the outside full of sniffs.

Lots of other dogs were pottering around the paths and consuming the smells. I knew how important it was for Gidget to get her daily exercise, not only for her physical health but for mental stimulation as well.

I had asked Camilla and Teddy to join us but she had only flown in from Bali late yesterday and promised Teddy she would have cuddles and a sleep-in. I didn't tell her that I thought Teddy would have preferred to be let loose in the park running amok with his friends, letting the wind flow through his ears, and bouncing through the creek at high speeds. I think she probably knew that anyway.

"Okay Gidget, are you going to be good if I let you off the lead?"

She was often adventurous and disappeared out of sight. She usually came back pretty quickly, but this always left fear in my heart that she would eat something she shouldn't or end up in a tricky situation or do an oopsie of some sort.

Life with a young dog was extremely eventful and I had to always be on guard to ensure her wellbeing and that of any small animals in the park. Being spring, we had to be extra careful there were no ducklings around the water areas. As yet, I wasn't sure if they would be loved or seen as lunch!

Once she chased a duck further afield before it flapped and took flight. Another time she hunted down a little sick bird stuck in the creek and sat by it contemplating. I suspect it would have been gone in one munch before long. A dead possum was found another time and I am sure she was seconds away from picking it up and flinging it in the air like her toys.

She was learning to stay closer and her recall was excellent for a young dog. Fortunately, the park was surrounded by a fence of greenery so we were protected from the traffic somewhat.

As I unclipped Gidget, she sensed her freedom, just like Ernie used to. Woosh! She was off, running like a mad thing around the park sideways and in circles, finally coming back to do a doggy bow at my feet with her tongue hanging fully out of her mouth.

One chicken treat and she was off again, this time recruiting a few other dogs to chase her. It was a game she loved, running whilst veering left to right, changing direction and dodging the other dogs as she ran even faster. The game gained more momentum as a few more dogs joined in. After they ran out of steam, Gidget came back and sat at my feet, bringing with her another golden retriever.

"Good dogs," I told them. "Who are you?"

Before I could reach down to look for a name on its collar, along came William from the beach. Gidget and Charlie stayed sitting in front of me like a pigeon pair.

"Aww. You found your brother, Gidget." I said. How delightful. I always wondered if dogs knew their siblings long after they left their doggy mum. A mutual face lick between siblings confirmed they did.

"Hi, Grace, nice to see you again. So is this your dog?" said William. "It looks like Charlie might have been an inspiration."

"Yes, well, funny story. Meeting you and Charlie changed the trajectory of my life," I said.

"How so?" he replied.

I proceeded to tell him the story of how Gidget came to be and excitedly shared the stories of her training and her oopsies – leaving out the underpants incident of course.

He was eagerly listening to me, maybe hoping to gain some tips. It looked like Charlie was as enthusiastic about life as Gidget, and the two of them had run off again to fire up all the nearby dogs into playing more games.

We looked over to see them sitting in the creek, panting and puffing like twins. Their extremities were cooling in the fresh water and their hot pink tongues were on full display. Chewing the fat on life, possibly.

"What do you think they are talking about?" I said to William.

GIDGET

"**S**o, Gidget, how've ya been? How's life with your family? My dad is awesome and takes me to so many places. And we watch football. I don't like it much but he gets so excited that he hands out extra food, often pizza, so I love that. I sit in the boat while he catches fish. I try and eat the bait while mostly getting told off. A few times I jumped out to have a swim when I wasn't meant to. We run along the beach to get fit he tells me but I always outrun him. And I sleep next to him on the bed. We have so much fun together. How do you think all the others are going? And Mum Suzy? I miss her."

Charlie finally drew a breath.

"Phew! Charlie, you woof a lot." I tell him all about my life with Mum and how much fun it is. I share the bee and underpants incidents. Coincidently he had the same experience – with the bee, that is. "We really are twins," I woof.

"I miss Mum Suzy too, but my purpose is to look after my mum. That's what Mum Suzy told me and that's what I'm doing each and every day. So should you, Charlie."

"You betcha! That's exactly what I am doing. She told me the same thing. I don't have a human mum though, just a dad. His name is William."

"That's interesting. I don't have a dad. I only have a mum. Her name is Grace," I woofed.

"Do you think we should go back, Charlie? I can hear them calling us."

"Nah, not yet," he woofed.

I secretly think he is a bad influence but he is fun and now I was torn between my brother and my mum. Charlie won this time and we sat for a little longer. As the cool water ran past our bodies, we talked about what we thought Mum and William might be talking about.

Grace

"Till next time, Grace. So good to see you. Maybe we can get the dogs to have a play date again soon." William said.

"That would be lovely," I said.

Little did he know how lovely I thought it would be. I had forgotten how nice he was. Gidget and I then left the park and wandered around the neighbourhood enjoying the start of the spring day and looking at all the nice houses, wondering if all the dogs had a good life like Gidget did. I hoped and prayed they did.

I am a bit of an animal empath if there is such a thing, and I felt I understood the wants and needs of all dogs. Every time I met one, I had to squat down and assess internally how the animal was being treated and cared for and if that was up to my extremely high standards. Sadly, it often wasn't. Where possible I tried to help.

Gidget was stopping to smell every second leaf as usual. This allowed me time to think how lucky I felt to be in such a good space in my life.

I held an inner calm, despite Gidget's antics. Everything was travelling beautifully and my days, although busy, were spent literally smelling the roses and living in the moment, appreciating the beauty of life amidst the chaos. I knew that had a lot to do with spending a huge chunk of my time in nature, surrounded by dogs, and immersed in yoga and meditation as a way of life instead of in the soul-sucking corporate world job that just didn't resonate with my heart.

"We're home, Gidget. It's time for some breaky and a sleep." She raced to the food cupboard and then stood next to her bowl. She started drooling. Again.

Gidget

"Sounds great, Mum. What a morning! I'm so happy to have met my brother Charlie again. Can we see him more please? Hurry up with the food please. I'm starving," I woofed. I was nearly out of energy and needed sustenance to carry on.

A coffee date

GIDGET

"**M**orning Mum, get up! I'm ready to go. It's that time again. You ready? You awake? Hello! Hello!" This was a typical ritual of woofs in my head as I went to stir Mum from her deep sleep with a big lick on her face.

Up she gets and I wait patiently while she makes herself clean and smell nice with the human shower routine that I don't really understand or welcome. Especially when I am dragged in there to join her. Today, I just sit on the bathmat and watch and wait. I then lick her legs dry.

When Mum gets the bath ready for me, I want to do a dive and dash anywhere but near the dreaded bathroom. As much as I love water, the whole bathing routine is totally pointless in my eyes. I prefer to be stinky. I like all the smells that cover me from yesterday's walk. I like saving my collection of smells for later.

Mum is a bit cheeky and conniving. She gets out the bright orange licking mat and smothers it with peanut butter. This gets me following her or, to be precise, the scent wafting off the mat.

I'm so distracted that I don't notice as she leads me to the bathroom. She suctions the mat to the tiles in the shower alcove and almost before I start licking, I am drenched in doggy shampoo. This keeps me busy while she washes, rinses, massages and sings. While I'm licking, I Internally wiggle a lot, desperate to go outside and add once again to my doggy smells.

She tells me I smell good. All clean.

"Yuck!" I woofed.

GRACE

Meeting William at the park had become somewhat of a regular occurrence and today was no exception. Generally, we planned different walks each day but lately had been returning to our regular park with a secret wish to see him. Of course, Gidget mostly wanted to roll around and get stinky in the freshly cut grass with her brother Charlie. I may have to wash her later, I think, to get rid of all those stinky things she has rolled in. I'm sure she loves her baths.

It sort of occurred organically that Will and I began seeing more of each other. Dogs are a great social talking point and they naturally draw like-minded dog lovers together. This is strengthened by the fact that our dogs were siblings.

"Morning!" I yell out in a high-pitched voice as I see them approaching.

Charlie and Gidget stop still, frozen in time. I love this part. They simultaneously lower to a play bow, face to the ground and butt high in the air. A second or two passes and then it's game on. They run full pelt towards each other, jumping all over each other and pulling each other to the ground, showing off their snarly teeth — or their scrinch face as I call it when they crinkle their muzzle and show their teeth. Then comes the zoomies, with Gidget and Charlie ducking and diving like crazy dogs.

William finally arrives laughing. "How's the morning? Do you fancy a walk after they have finished their play?"

"Yes, that would be great," I reply.

We had only hung out at the park until now. This was new, I thought.

Shortly afterwards we clipped the dogs back on their leads — Gidget showcasing her hot pink lead — and walked past the water fountain for a quick drink. With the water still dripping down the side of their mouths and down their neck furs, we turned to head out of the park. Charlie seemed happy to motor forward but Gidget had other ideas as she laid down and put on her stubborn pants as I call them.

She had a set of stubborn pants and a set of cranky pants and most likely a whole wardrobe that I hadn't met yet.

She was still puffing so we waited a bit to allow her to cool. Eventually I had to physically encourage her with some little gentle tugs and a pull on her harness handle to get her moving. "Come on, Gidget," I said repeatedly. Eventually, a piece of chicken luring her forward solved the standoff.

Gidget was trained to walk on the left of me but walking with Charlie was somewhat of a challenge. At first, they kept wanting to play and twisting themselves in the leads. They also caught William and me up and we ended up doing a dance of sorts trying to untwist ourselves.

This left Gidget so hyped up that she was biting and tugging at her lead, something she always did when she was overexcited. Finally, after these shenanigans had exhausted them, we found our groove with chats for us and sniffs for them.

He made me feel really comfortable and we nattered on about many topics like dogs, holidays, exercise, food and work. When the conversation turned to his favourite loves of football or fishing,

I gently turned the conversation back to something I was more interested in, but not before I feigned interest to make myself look more appealing.

"Do you feel like a coffee?" he asked.

Absolutely I did! I always said yes to a coffee. I had already had one before we left, so I hoped I didn't get too hyped up from the caffeine and mimic Gidget's hyperactivity.

We headed up the tree-lined street to Penelope's, the local café.

Penelope's was a quaint little coffee shop with French-inspired décor. Pink flowers framed the outside seating area with a black and white awning shading rows of chairs and small tables.

Inside, chandeliers hung from the ceiling over a deep green velvet couch that was covered with pink, red and orange pillows. One wall was covered in floor-to-ceiling bookshelves showcasing hundreds of books and a large black chalkboard highlighted the daily choices. On the adjacent wall hung a large life-sized black and white print of the Montmartre neighbourhood in Paris.

Penelope's exuded a special charm.

There was a sign out the front 'Dogs Welcome' with a large water bowl filled with clean and fresh water sitting on a black and white striped placemat. They had me at 'Dogs Welcome'!

I found many places around our city to be not so dog friendly. Even the local councils seemed to advocate for removing dogs from shared areas and reducing household dog numbers, whereas I feel they should be encouraging dog ownership and realising the benefits dogs bring to the elderly, the young, the lonely or really just anyone. Among a host of other things, dogs provide companionship, help you be more active, lessen stress and anxiety, teach responsibility and prevent loneliness. They can really change people's lives.

Volunteering at Animal Aid had deepened my understanding of these benefits.

"Hi Antonio," I said as we entered, looking around for an outside table. Antonio was from Italy and had been in Australia for a few months on a working holiday. He was younger than us, buff, friendly, European-looking and inquisitive in a nice, interesting way. I saw him every morning and he always asked about Gidget. He loved dogs and told me his family had a Saint Bernard at home called Bernardo and a cane corso called Sophia. Big dogs.

"Morning Grace. How's Gidget?" he asked cheerfully.

"Amazing as always!" I replied with a big smile as we headed towards the perfect table to fit us and the two dogs.

"Medium soy weak latte for me please," I automatically chanted to William.

Once I sat down, he passed me Charlie's lead before he went in to order. I hadn't mentioned that Gidget wasn't a great café dog. She was just learning and didn't yet have the focus to stay still for the length of a coffee.

A moment later I realised Charlie was similar.

I kept handing out treats to settle them, yet all they wanted to do was play.

Next thing, they were knocking over the chair behind us. I finally wrestled them to sit still and apologised to the nearby customers who were looking a little disapprovingly at the two young golden hooligans.

Gidget then landed with her front paws in the large tub of water and sprayed it everywhere, enjoying the cool on her fur.

When William arrived back, I pretended all was calm while feeling pretty stressed. I handed Charlie's lead back to him, feeling relief at only having to grapple with one dog. Gidget was enough.

"Why are they all wet?" he asked.

"Well..." I started to say before he interrupted.

"Coffee is on its way. So Grace, tell me a little more about yourself," he continued as he looked right at me.

Dogs feel challenged when they are looked at directly and that is how I was feeling. It was like William was trying to look deep inside me. I felt a little rattled so I tried to move my gaze to something else.

"Umm, what would you like to know?" I said.

We had shared a lot of superficial information yet nothing that intimate or anything that gave real insight into our personal lives. I felt a little vulnerable. He was being more forthright than usual.

I was a pretty open book but I sometimes overshared, which is rarely appealing. I had to play this right and juggle a balance between what he wanted to know and what I was prepared to share. Normally I was fairly difficult to rattle so I realised I must really like this guy to be feeling this way.

Did I tell him I had been single for five years or that I had never really known unconditional love except from Ernie and Gidget? Or that I was scarred by Pierce leaving so abruptly after six years? Or that I was left bereft for years after my dad's passing?

Instead, out came, "Me? What about you? That seems a good place to start." I laughed.

Deflecting. This was my defence mechanism. Redirecting a conversation away from a challenging topic or charged emotions with a mix of humour had always worked for me as Stephanie, my therapist, had pointed out some time back. I had perfected it when I needed it.

Stephanie had been a breath of fresh air after my last break-up and helped me untangle a mix of falsely held beliefs. She challenged my emotions and patched my broken heart. Pierce had really messed with my head and broken my heart.

She was about the same age as me, always dressed smart and professionally, mostly in black. I had my appointments at her house near the edge of the hills. The room looked out through a big glass window over her backyard, which was full of trees and greenery with a beautiful pool that glistened in the sun.

Often birds would be resting on the edge of the pool, flicking water over their backs. One time there was a brood of ducklings, twelve to be exact. I counted them while I was pondering a deep question Stephanie had asked me and avoiding facing the reality of my answer.

She had this calm and contained nature. She was able to be warm and accepting, serious and knowledgeable and, at the same time, humorous and light-hearted. I learnt an enormous amount during the time I spent with her, not least how to live a life true to myself, how to feel all my feelings, how to quell my anxieties, and how to be in the present moment.

I liked her most of all, though, as during our appointment her dog, Eddie, a small, scrappy, wiry-haired Jack Russell, would always crawl up onto my lap. He would snuggle in calmly and soothe me as healing tears fell to my lap. I'd pat him as Stephanie deconstructed my life.

I still visited Stephanie sporadically to work on any issues that presented, but I didn't see her so often anymore. Thankfully, I was finally over the break-up.

"Well," said William, "how about I share one thing and then you? We can take it in turns. How about three things each?"

"Okay, agreed," I said laughing. I supposed that sounded fair.

The next minute, out he came with, "I've been single for six months after a bad break-up."

Okay, so straight into the deep stuff, I thought.

"I've been single for five years after a bad break-up," I replied, feeling worried he may think something was wrong with me for being single that long.

But there was no reaction or none that I could gauge anyway.

"I have no kids," he continued.

With relief, I replied, "Neither do I. Just lots of nieces and, of course, Gidget." I looked down at her still fidgeting at my feet.

Lastly, he murmured, "And Charlie is my best friend."

To that, I replied, "Same with Gidget. It's her and me, my girl." I thought to myself instantly that he was a keeper.

He was charming and good-looking. I was often blindsided by that in a man, which often meant trouble. He had asked deeper questions but not followed up with any lingering conversation around each topic. Most likely just too early in our friendship, I thought.

I had joked after Pierce that my picker was broken. I still wasn't confident that it had been fixed. Only time and choices would tell.

We continued talking until it became obvious we couldn't contain the dogs anymore. We downed our coffees and left the café. We walked at a snail's pace as our furry friends overturned and sniffed every leaf. Finally, I stopped and said, "I have to peel off here. It's been such a lovely morning. Thank you for the coffee and the chats."

He looked at me with his dreamy eyes and said, "Yes Grace, it has been lovely, really lovely. See you soon?" he said more as a question than a statement.

With that, Gidget and I rushed off not knowing when I would see him again but hoping it would be soon.

GIDGET

"Mum, that was so much fun. I love Charlie. Can we see him again tomorrow please? I had such a good morning. I love playing in the water bucket. Thanks for all the treats. Follow me, Mum," I woofed as I took her to the laundry where my food bowl resided and started drooling to show her it was time for breaky.

A good morning walk always allowed me to relax and look forward to my breakfast. Then came the dreaded teeth clean that wasn't fun. I struggled to keep my mouth open as this strange stick circled around my teeth. Then finally it was time for a well-earned nap.

I sat down and fell straight into my doggy dreams. I heard Mum say, "Back soon, Gidget. Love you." Then off she went to do whatever it is humans do.

I didn't mind as I knew she always came back and that was all that mattered. Except that one time when she was gone for what seemed like an eternity before she returned. I was terrified she would never come home. Then I realised I must have dreamt it. She would never leave me.

Call me Finn

Grace

"Hi Grace," she said.

"Camilla, are you free for a coffee?" I said quickly.

"You sound flustered, Grace. Are you okay?"

"I'm not really sure. Penelope's at 1pm?"

"Yep, perfect," she replied.

Spending years on personal development still did not prevent me from feeling anxious when someone I liked didn't contact me for a few weeks.

It had been weeks – and still counting – since my coffee date with William. He didn't have my number, though, which excused his lack of contact somewhat. It seemed strange that we'd seen each other often at the park before, but now he seemed to have gone completely AWOL.

I tried to remain cool and cruisy but deep down I was feeling tense. I tried to shrug off the insecurities and find my strength of character. I was struggling.

Everyone always says it's easy to be confident and happy when you are single but it's not until you introduce someone else into the mix that your triggers get activated. It's in these circumstances you continue to learn more about yourself.

Bending down to ruffle Gidget's ears, I said, "Why haven't we seen him, Gidget?" No reply from there so I flew back into my head to search for some sense of grounding, wishing my mind to stop racing down a rabbit hole of questions and irrational thoughts.

There were a good few hours before I met Camilla, so I got myself up and grabbed my yoga mat to head off to the 10am yoga class. That would keep me busy until Camilla and I could talk it over and analyse it ad infinitum. I knew this never really achieved anything. Sometimes it made you feel better but other times it made you question things more, depending on the response from the person you were talking to.

Yoga always soothed my nerves and gave my mind a chance to settle. I had missed last week's class due to a minor chest infection and was feeling less balanced because of it.

Fred was in the welcoming area when I arrived. "Good to see you, Grace," he said. "Here for our practice this morning?"

"Yes," I said. "I really need it today."

"I really need it every day," he replied.

I was paralysed in thought momentarily as I always envisaged Fred being a picture of serenity, regardless of his external environment. Maybe it was the regular yoga practice that kept him so monk-like.

We nattered about the administration tasks that were on my to-do list and our inaugural Pink Peace Festival looming in just a few months. My weekly workload was amping up to achieve this upcoming deadline. A few more people arrived and our conversation organically ended.

Fred's unruffled demeanour helped calm me despite only talking about work. It was the vibration he radiated. I loved being in his presence. I always had. I already felt my mind clearing.

Call me Finn

My yoga practice had dropped off over the last couple of months despite being at Pink Peace a few days a week for my administration role. It ebbed and flowed depending on my commitments as it always had. I made a mental promise to up my practice to three times a week at least and to lock down a daily twenty-minute meditation practice again... no excuses!

I was excellent at meditating when something was wrong. It calmed my nervous system. But when things were going along swimmingly, I seemed to ease off, thinking I didn't need it. But my subconscious and intuition knew I did.

I would notice in my periods of abstinence that I was crankier. Gidget's cranky pants fit perfectly. This caused the mixed and unsettled emotions that could flip me from zero to one hundred per cent in a millisecond. Perimenopause didn't help either. Double whammy.

I learnt early in my yoga training that meditation calmed the nervous system and also changed the neuroplasticity of the brain. This enabled changes and positive effects on everything from memory, coping abilities, calmness, immune system, anti-aging, hormones and sleep to stress and anxiety.

Sometimes, though, despite knowing it pretty much had a positive effect on everything, actually committing to a daily practice was not as easy. Another mental note to self: just do it!

Being wrapped up in my thoughts, I nearly missed seeing Dr Ross walk in. I did a double take. I didn't think he would be a yoga-type person. He was a vet. For some reason, I didn't think the two were affiliated.

I loved that people always surprised me. And I reminded myself not to pre-judge people.

"Grace, is that you?" His familiar voice echoed around me as a vision of Ernie and his big black velvet coat flickered in my mind.

"Hello, Dr Ross," I said.

"Finn, it's Finn. Grace, please call me Finn."

I always found it difficult calling professionals by their first name. I was brought up in a traditional environment and my schooling had taught me to also be respectful, even if I was speaking with someone of a similar age. It was just a habit I suppose. He was a veterinary doctor after all, but maybe he was more modern than most of the doctors I knew.

Anyway, I decided I would call him Finn from then on.

"Finn." His name kind of rolled off the tongue. What a great name. "Nice to see you. I didn't expect to see you here."

"I've been doing yoga for years. I started when I was doing my veterinary degree as I found it helped me balance the deadlines, workload and stress. And now I continue to practice to help my work. I've only just started at this studio though."

"Yes, I understand that totally. Leaving the corporate world some years back, it was yoga that saved me and balanced me. It kept me from completely sinking into some sort of despair from all the stress," I replied. Oops... oversharing again.

"It's a great tool, isn't it?" he replied. "It also helped me enormously going through my divorce a few years ago as that was pretty traumatic on me and my kids, Charlotte and Oliver."

It felt nice him opening up to me. He asked how Gidget was and we spoke about her. He told me about Mortimer, his six-year-old basset hound. My grandmother had basset hounds and I remember her specifically talking about one called Albert.

I was very nostalgic as he talked about Mortimer and his antics. I noted especially his comment that they were the poster breed for ear infections. It's no wonder when their droopy ears with the heavy skin folds collect moisture and debris as they drag them around on the floor. They would scoop up all the dirt and dust as they manoeuvred slowly around on their short legs and big paws. I remembered my granny telling similar stories about Albert. He had to go to a specialist to help solve his ear issues. Sadly, they never did.

I loved their ears... so big and silky smooth and soft.

He explained how every breed had its own breed predispositions. He then told me that for goldens it was generally things like hip or elbow dysplasia, skin conditions or hot spots, thyroid issues, heart issues and cancers. Wow, that's a long and slightly scary list, I thought. I would have almost preferred not to know.

The studio room door opened and everyone got up to enter. Our conversation would have to wait for another day.

I found it interesting that people rushed into practice to claim the same spot each week despite the teacher explaining it's good to create change and place your mat somewhere different. It's healthy to be spontaneous and open to trying something new that puts you out of your comfort zone.

Today I decided to do just that. I followed Finn into the studio, placed my mat next to his and laid down on my back. Closing my eyes, I waited for those first few moments of calm to wash over me. As people assembled, I felt myself melt into stillness.

The ninety-minute class flew by. As I was packing up my things, Finn was still lying in Savasana. I was just about to leave when he sat up. "Well, wasn't that bliss?" he said.

"Absolutely," I said.

I wished him goodbye and said I was off to meet a friend.

"Till next time," he called out as I left.

As I drove to meet Camilla, I realised I still felt it odd that I had seen Finn at yoga. It was strange to see him as anything but my vet but it was a pleasurable experience nevertheless. He was a lovely man with a nice nature that always made me feel at ease.

I felt much calmer since my earlier call to Camilla. Yoga was a miracle worker.

"Camilla, it's so good to see you. How was your trip to Los Angeles?" I said as we embraced in a warm hug.

"Oh, you know, Grace, it was okay but I think I'm getting too old to be flitting around the world and Ernest gets sick of me taking off all the time. But I love the shopping and, secretly, the time away on my own. So I'm not going to stop any time soon.

Plus, he has Teddy to take care of him and I have him to take care of Teddy, so it works well for me at least," she said.

"Your life always seems like such an adventure. I am not sure I could leave Gidget so often. I'm such a sook when it comes to leaving her, and who would look after her anyway?"

"I would," she said.

"So, tell me, Grace, why the weird demeanour when we spoke earlier today?"

"Well..." I started to explain.

I told her about my coffee date with William and the dogs. I told her how I felt rattled that I hadn't heard from him and thought it might mean that I liked him.

She laughed and said of course that's what it means! She said she thought because I had been single for so long, I had forgotten how to do the dating dance. Dating dance, I thought. I just want things to be simple. No games. Just transparent, real and engaging.

We spent the next few hours deconstructing dating life in general and yakking about men, dogs, travel and, importantly, the array of colours in the new fast-drying nail polish range.

As part of my personal development, I had challenged myself to reflect on my job, life situation, men and friends – everything really – and ask the question, "Does this elevate me or deplete me?"

The challenge was not in answering the question but to be honest enough that I would actually take action on the answer. Often, I had hidden the answer from myself because the consequence of changing anything or removing anyone or anything from my life was too tough.

Camilla was definitely on the elevated list as she always lit up my life. I left feeling happy with a warm inner glow, almost skipping, and acknowledging my gratitude for her friendship.

We committed to meet at the same time next week. It was a regular appointment and one of my favourites.

As I hurried home, I was thinking about having left Gidget for a few hours. It was her walk time. Where would we go today? Her afternoon walk time was shorter than her big walk in the morning. Sometimes, instead, we had a play date at someone's house. She knew the routine off by heart – morning and afternoon, every day, rain, hail or shine.

Gidget

"You're home! You're home! Where the woof have you been? I have been waiting here for hours bored out of my head on my own. I finished the freshly filled Kong you left me hours ago. I barked at a few birds and checked the floor for any food.

"Yes, I have been asleep the rest of the time but don't think I didn't notice you were not here. I hate it when you're not here. I am a good girl. I didn't destroy anything. I never get anxious but I just want you with me.

"I know you have a full life and part of that is me, but all I have is you. I love you and only you. I'm just glad you're home. Is it time for us to do something together? I love that time. It's one of my favourite things."

I woofed all of this out as quickly as I could as I could tell we were in a hurry.

I could see Mum pull out my hot pink harness. Even though I didn't see colours the same as humans, I could tell it was bright. Mum loved it, which was all that mattered. I was a dog, not a fashionista, so I didn't have any preferences. I did, however, have post-traumatic fashion stress after the Elsa dress-up episode at puppy school. Thankfully that has never happened again – yet anyway!

Looks like we are ready to go. Woof!

As we left, I woofed, "Mum, will we see Charlie this afternoon? I miss him."

The ladies

GRACE

"Gidget, stand still gorgeous girl," I repeated as I tried to slip her harness over her head. "Please!" I begged as she took off for a zoomie using the furniture as a parkour course. Eventually, she came back, tongue hanging out and proceeded to roll on her back with her four paws in the air as if to say I'll be ready in a minute.

"Okay, are you ready now?" I laughed, finally slipping the harness over her head.

"I wonder if we'll see Charlie today?" I said to her as we left. I had almost given up on him as it had been four weeks and not counting. Well, maybe counting a little.

We headed up the street, turned right at the local servo down the road, then walked through the shopping centre and past the butcher where Gidget looked earnestly through the window. Occasionally a piece of sausage came her way when the butcher spotted her outside. We then crossed the road to the park, taking care to avoid the duck pond.

As always, I said, "Gidget, you ready? Are you going to be good today?"

No response. Her deep brown eyes stared deeply into mine and her toe-tapping front paws begged for freedom.

I unclipped her harness and off she ran straight towards another golden. It was Olive. I should have known from all the barking.

Olive's mum, Polly, was a family friend who lived nearby. Olive was a beautiful dark-haired golden with a soft and silky coat and a soft and sensitive nature. She was scared of loud noises and suffered from a thunder phobia that kept Polly home and up late with any storms.

She had tried everything from calming collars, counterconditioning, behavioural therapists, natural therapies and supplements to thunder shirts, doggy noise-cancelling headphones and medication. Finally, this helped ease some of her anxiety. She also loved to bark up a storm in excitement. We often had to talk over the carry-on or spend time distracting her to be able to hear ourselves. She was loved despite her quirks.

Gidget was nearly two now and had settled remarkably over time. I kept telling Polly and Camilla or anyone who would listen that I never thought she would settle but one day she just seemed to grow up. I'm not saying she was perfect. Rather, she was perfectly imperfect, just like most humans. I loved her unconditionally to the moon and back despite any of her oopsies. It was easy really.

Last time I saw Dr Finn he said the same. Goldens were still young at heart until about five years old, so I could expect even more settling over the next few years. That excited me but I didn't want to wish away her youth.

"Hi, Polly, so good to see you. How are you both?" Following Polly came two ladies who looked familiar. I had seen them before and smiled at them from a distance but hadn't talked to them.

Polly introduced me. "Grace, this is Susan and Paula."

Susan had goldens all her life and was heavily involved in clubs and managing Facebook groups. She had two golden boys. The older one was called Hudson and was a big thirty-eight kilogram strong, happy and enthusiastic boy. He carried toys around endlessly in his mouth or at least the skins of the toys after he had destroyed them. He particularly enjoyed a game of tug-of-war. He was perfectly trained and walked to heel beside her with no lead required.

Snowy, the other one, was a few years younger and looked like a bloodhound. He had big droopy eyes and jowls that sagged downwards imitating those of a bloodhound. He followed Hudson around everywhere like glue, trying to play with toys that Hudson promptly stole from him. Susan was a wealth of knowledge, I was told.

Paula's golden girl, Shelly, had a noise sensitivity to loud traffic but was the happiest and prettiest girl. Paula told me she was a regular at the dog park every day without fail. She told me she would often sit in the afternoons and watch the comings and goings while Shelly would rest at her feet. Shelly was a hunter at heart and spent time chasing ducks in the creek beds. In the evenings she chased possums up fences. Besides Shelly, Paula's other love was her weekly bridge game.

"Nice to meet you both. This is Gidget. She can be a bit of a ratbag sometimes. But she is the sweetest thing most of the time," I said. I didn't have an inkling then of the profound friendship and influence these ladies would have on my life.

I always found it interesting how life could change overnight. You never knew what was right around the corner. How a stranger one minute could become a best friend forever. Or how a friend could become a lover. Life was marvellous.

We all stood around chatting as Susan handed out endless treats. The dogs would run away and soon after return to Susan's feet and look for more. On the last return, they brought another golden with them in a sea of fur flying towards the sky and glimmering in the sun. Gidget and he ran to me instead of Susan and sat at my feet looking eagerly at me and puffing madly with their tongues out.

"Charlie, where have you been?" I said. "It's been ages." William sauntered over slowly behind them. He looked healthy, fit and still as good-looking as he was when we shared coffee a few weeks back.

My heart fluttered. Hoping I wasn't blushing, I could only manage a quiet hello. I was still a little annoyed at him, albeit most likely unjustly.

"Hi Grace, how are you? It's so nice to see you," he said, disarming me with his charming, deep, attractive voice.

Absence makes the heart grow fonder must be true, I thought. I didn't recall the effect he had on me as being quite this strong.

I told myself to act cool.

"Hi, William, how are you?" I asked. "Gidget has missed seeing Charlie." I introduced William to the ladies and their dogs before he had a chance to respond to my loaded comment.

"Hi, ladies, what beautiful dogs. Can Charlie join in with the group play?" he asked as he bent down to give them all a pat and ruffle their ears.

"Of course," they chimed in together with cheeky smiles. Polly looked at me with her eyebrows lifted while Paula flicked her hair back.

To remove myself from a potentially awkward and embarrassing situation, I took out my iPhone and snapped some photos of the dogs playing. With a few quick keystrokes, it was uploaded to Facebook with a simple spiel: Golden Doggy Love.

I often posted on the local golden retriever page called Golden Love. I loved sharing Gidget's adventures and also looking at others' posts. The ones matched with music were particularly captivating and time wasting. I had met many cyber friends through this Facebook page who ended up being Gidget's playmates.

The Ladies

Occasionally, we went to some of the beach events where you are surrounded by a haze of something like fifty to seventy golden retrievers. Gidget always sported a hot pink rashie to separate her from the rest. She was a fashionista at heart always in pink, although I'm not sure she loved it as much as I did. Nevertheless, she willingly lifted her head up so I could slide it on her as she waited for the calling of the sea.

All you could hear at these events over and above the woofing echoing out to sea were people calling their dog's name, sometimes frantically as they tried to pick which one was theirs out of the bunch of look-alikes.

It truly was doggy heaven and I was in my element there.

Dogs were my life. Goldens, and Gidget more specifically, were my entire purpose. I felt I was completely encircled by my tribe when I scrolled away for hours on this page. I would leave sprinkles of comments here and there and often had to wish myself to stop to turn the light out late at night.

"Grace," William started to say before he was interrupted by the ladies.

"Bye Grace, bye William." Polly, Susan and Paula left at the same time. We had been there for an hour playing. "See you tomorrow for a play?" asked Polly as she winked at me.

"Yes, of course," I replied.

"Sorry William," I turned to say to him, hoping he hadn't noticed the wink.

"Would you like to walk together?" he said.

"Yes," I said. Now I had him to myself, I wondered what he would say or, more specifically, if I would find out where he had been.

Gidget

"That's a big yes from me," I woofed. "Let's go! Let's hurry!" I looked at Charlie and he gave me a butt wiggle and a body nudge to indicate he felt the same, but just a gentle nudge so I didn't tip over.

We waited for our harnesses to be slipped over our heads and then picked up the pace until Mum and Will said simultaneously, "Slow down."

Things were too exciting though.

"Charlie, did you see that leaf? Wait, let's go back and sniff the one we missed. Did you smell that bird poop? Is that curry I smelled going past on the Uber Eats motorcycle? I think I smelt a cat... no, wait... maybe it's a possum... wait... let me get a better whiff." I rattled on and on in a woof as my nostrils waivered in and out.

There were so many smells and they were overwhelming some days, especially when it was windy. For a dog, the best part of the day is the walk, the ability to take in the environment. The pure, innocent enjoyment of the day for us dogs is the walk.

"Tell me everything, Charlie. What's been happening, bro?" I woofed at him along the way.

$\mathcal{P}aris$

GRACE

"Gidget, Charlie, let's go!" we yelled simultaneously. William started to tell me more about his job. He was the Chief Financial Officer for a Parisian fashion company called Latouve. They were not fully high-end fashion like Dior or Chanel but on the hopeful verge of breaking into the famous luxury market.

The head office was in Paris but they also had an office in the eastern suburbs of Adelaide. I found that weird but the founder of the company was brought up here and went to a prestigious private boys school in the area. Adelaide with its charm and charisma was his home. William was schooled there also.

His job sounded lavish, impressive and important in what I had always seen as a flamboyant, classy and fancy industry. It almost seemed surreal and fantasy-like to me. Like in the movies or a TV series. It was very different to my seemingly quiet girl next door life. I felt spellbound yet mediocre in comparison.

I loved Paris. I had only visited once many years ago. I often dreamed about strolling at dog-sniffing pace along the Champs-Élysées. I dreamed of sitting on a park bench in the Bois de Boulogne, listening to the birds chirp and people-watching whilst patting every dog that walked past. It made my insides warm and glow. My intuition wanted to visit, but my finances and logistics were not on the same page. Yet.

I always loved to hear people's stories and learn about their careers, their goals, their achievements and their obstacles. William's story was one of luxury and charm. I was fascinated with it and possibly with him too. I was captivated by his storytelling of his life.

He talked about the spectacular fashion parades he attended, the outlandish styles, the copious bare skin and the extended long lunches. He would meet talented designers while the French champagne flowed generously. He had even attended Paris Fashion Week as a thank you for his efforts in his Chief Financial Officer role.

William had worked with the company for a few years and had negotiated a contract to work from Australia. He explained that it was difficult to secure this type of position without being in Paris but it was working for everyone involved. They said he had the qualifications and personality that were perfect for the role. He loved his job with its variety and spontaneity and the travel it required.

As he was talking about his job, he explained how a few weeks back he had received an urgent call to fly to Paris to attend some meetings. Something about a merger with another larger French company. He had to literally drop everything and go overnight. He had packed, organised Charlie's things and dropped him off at his mother's. Twenty-four hours later he flew out to Paris. He spent the next three weeks schmoozing and diligently labouring.

Gidget landed at my feet with a tennis ball. "Where did you find that, Gidget?" I asked.

She always seemed to find tennis balls and then it became an endless cycle of frustration. It would start with her dropping the ball at my feet, looking at me as if to say throw it now. NOW. If I didn't, she would bark at me. If I did, she got all overstimulated and became a bit manic, which only amped up the cycle.

I didn't like throwing tennis balls especially. When Ernie was growing up, I used to throw a Frisbee for him every day. He loved it. He would run with so much vigour to catch it, sometimes doing flying twisty leaps in the air. He would catch it perfectly mid-flight, then deliver it back to me and drop it at my feet with a toe-tapping routine waiting for the next round of fun. I loved remembering him and all the energy he had in his youth before the greys and the slowness arrived.

A few years after Frisbee chasing at the age of two, he jumped up for a catch, mimicking an athlete or as much of an athlete a black Labrador can be. He caught it perfectly mid-flight yet landed awkwardly and just stopped and looked at me. He lifted his back leg and just stood there balancing precariously on three legs, tripod-like, trying not to topple over. The Frisbee was hanging from his mouth as he let out a little whimper. Help.

Unbeknownst to me, throwing a ball or Frisbee endlessly is one of the best ways to rupture a cruciate ligament. It is the stopping and starting, the running while changing direction, the continual little tears progressing over time to one big tear.

After hobbling back to the car, we drove straight to Princess Park Vet to see Dr Finn. He had surgery the following day and then a three-month recovery loomed after that. I can barely remember it. I must have blocked it out as it was a pretty traumatic time.

Gidget woofed loudly, which I interpreted to mean, "Throw the ball, Mum!"

Charlie was oblivious to the ball antics; he just wanted Gidget's attention.

I picked up the stinky slobbery ball and put it in my bag while I clipped on her harness. She started grabbing the leash in her mouth and tugged at it, a sign of her overstimulation.

Finally, she calmed down using a treat game and we exited the park to start our walk around the neighbourhood. Only then was I able to focus back in on our conversation.

"So," William said "that's why you haven't seen me. I didn't have your number to call you. If I did, I would have. I really enjoyed our coffee. I felt like I just disappeared. Would you like to go out to dinner with me? Anything except French food."

"Yes," I said quickly, maybe too enthusiastically. It's a date, I thought to myself.

I felt relieved there was a perfectly valid and rational explanation as to why I hadn't seen him. At least I hoped it was. I still tended to spend time worrying about nothing. Thankfully, this time, the reality had turned out to be completely different to the story I concocted in my head.

I settled into enjoying the walk. We fell into a comfortable pace with the dogs walking nicely on their leads. They stopped at the kerb after a stop command. Good dogs. My trainer said that the more modern way of training was to stop at the kerb but not make them sit. Allow them to decide if they sat, dropped or stood, as long as they didn't move. It made sense. Old habits die hard as I asked for the sit again.

Charlie and William followed suit. I'm not sure he had done as much training as Gidget and me but he was willing to learn from us and happily mirrored our commands. Charlie, like Gidget, seemed to do anything for treats.

Later that day, as I sat on the couch with Gidget snoring on my lap and exhaling hot air all over my belly, I called Camilla. We debriefed the chat with William. I told her how I dreamed of going to Paris and how I was tremendously jealous of his life. She reminded me meekly that she visited at least three times a year.

That didn't help. Now I was jealous of both of them!

I asked her to tell me more about it – where she stayed, who she knew, where she shopped and ate, pretty much everything. Camilla loved being the centre of attention and could while away hours with these types of questions.

When the conversation drew to a natural close, I looked down to see Gidget had wiggled into a new position with four legs in the air. She was now breathing hot air right into my face.

Hanging up the phone I quietly said, "Dinnertime, Gidget," so as not to startle her.

GIDGET

"Finally!" I woofed. I flipped myself upright and leapt off the couch like a furry gymnast. Did someone say dinner?

That was the best dream. It was of the most enormous steak and I think I was drooling in my sleep. In the dream, I made Charlie sit next to me and watch as I inhaled it. I apologised to him after but secretly I was not sorry. There was no way I was sharing and when he tried to take a little nibble, he understood what my soft growl signified.

I heard Mum often say that you never stop a dog from growling as the growl is a warning sign. If you stop the growl a dog may go straight to the bite. She was so right; my growl is my voice and as such it is a warning sign when I'm not comfortable or don't like something.

Charlie had obviously learnt that also as he took a step back pretty quickly when he heard my pathetic grrrr. It was a great dream, despite this.

"Thanks for the fabulous walk with Charlie. I love him!" I woofed. "Where did that tennis ball go that I found? One minute it was there and the next – poof! – it disappeared. It took effort to find it buried under a tree and it smelt fabulous – like dog spit. I had carefully covered it in my spit to disguise the original smell. All that work and then it was gone."

Sometimes Mum really doesn't understand me. I think back to Mum Suzy and I remember swiftly it's all about keeping the humans happy. We are a different species and the human–animal bond is all about learning to understand each other. Learning things like needing to wear a pink rashie must just be part of that.

"To the laundry," I woofed, drooling on the way.

Festival frolics

GRACE

Pink Peace Festival was only days away. It was being held over a three-day long weekend at a big local park just outside the city. We expected a big turnout and had advertised accordingly to attract the like-minded tribe we were seeking.

The last few months had seen me preparing madly for this event to come to fruition. My to-do list had blown out exponentially. My part-time role organically grew to an almost full-time one in under a few months and I was just keeping up.

Thankfully, yoga classes were at my fingertips. I only needed to exit my office and turn left at the studio at the scheduled time and I was promptly in Savasana ready to clear my mind.

I was speaking daily to yoga teachers, spiritual guides, reiki masters, meditation teachers, massage therapists, jewellery makers, artisans, henna artists, sculptors and many more gifted individuals, along with arranging all the logistical things like sites, electricity, toilets, schedules, food stalls, marketing and advertising, and trying to plan everything meticulously.

Everyone seemed to have something to fuss over. They either didn't like something or wanted something different. Working around everyone's individual needs and wants was exhausting.

But I loved it. This kind of adrenaline derived from a big project with lots of things to arrange always kept me energised yet exhausted – a dichotomy really. I had learnt I could not live this way for long periods of time, but in short bursts it kept life and me fully engaged.

Fred and Lilly were fully invested in making this event miraculous. They spent even more hours than me to ensure it was all planned to perfection. Fred kept explaining how a daily meditation practice brought laser-pointed focus and energy galore. He was walking proof of that.

We checked in daily on the final preparations. We navigated the to-do lists with surprising ease and arrived at a mutually desired result in a timely fashion. It was like clockwork working with these two. Fred, calm and cool as a cucumber, keeping us sane. Lilly eccentric and colourful. She called in all her creative talents and friends she had met along the way. As for me, a doer and organiser by nature, I was ticking everything off the lists with steadfast enthusiasm.

Three more days to go. The calendar was marked with a big number three in pink.

Despite the busyness, I still made sure that Gidget had her daily morning and afternoon walks. It was a ritual never to be missed, even if I had to rise way before my body desired.

Earlier in the year, I completed a questionnaire at a yoga seminar asking us to list the three most important things in our life. The things that were non-negotiable. The ones that brought us eternal joy, helped us feel in the flow, brought us to the present moment and were most valued by our heart.

For some, this question was tricky. For me, it was simple.

Guess what was number one. Gidget!

This also extended to helping all dogs or dog owners wherever possible to make the dog's life more enriched. Second on my list came seeking peace and trying to achieve a calm and joyful existence. Third was making connections with like-minded people.

Fundamentally I wanted to make a difference and give something back to others or more specifically to dogs' lives.

With Gidget sitting at number one priority, it was pretty easy to make sure we never missed a walk. She really did come first. If she was happy, that happiness flowed up the leash and found its way directly to my heart and resided there in the form of pure joy.

Some of our adventures may have been shorter during this busy time, but they would still consist of a run or a sniff fest, a visit with doggy friends, a chase of the ball or just whiling away time sitting on a grassed verge doing some relaxation training exercises. All followed by Gidget having a lovely long daytime snooze while I continued with my to-do list at Pink Peace.

I used to feel guilty leaving her alone during the day but I was likely projecting human emotions onto her. I learnt from our trainer that it was good for dogs to have a peaceful and uninterrupted sleep. This kept them balanced and happy. They needed twelve to fourteen hours a day.

If they don't get this sleep they can become agitated, overstimulated or stressed – just like people really! So, after her walk, I could leave her happily for four or five hours. Around lunchtime, I would drop in for a quick hello and give her a licking mat or a Kong for enrichment. She would then happily rest and regain her energy until I returned home from work.

We had fallen into the nicest of routines, something dogs love. It helps their physical, mental and emotional wellbeing.

During the set-up period for the Pink Peace Festival, I had managed to fit in many more dates with William. We had also fallen into a nice routine. William, Charlie, Gidget and I were enjoying hanging out together.

William worked a lot. He was always busier than me and attended lots of social functions for his job, mostly in the evenings. Networking he said. He loved it.

What torture, I thought, standing around drinking endless glasses of wine, sharing shallow conversation with people you didn't know about the colour of the latest maxi dress or stilettos, or discussing finances with the sole intention of winning them over and attaining their business. All with no doggy friends present. I did love hearing about it afterwards with Gidget asleep on my lap. It seemed he was a natural born charmer and made for this role.

I was more of a homebody. I liked to socialise but it normally came with half a dozen golden retrievers attached to me, long conversations about how cute they were, coffee, pants covered in fur, pockets full of liver treats and poo bags, and sand everywhere.

Despite our different social natures, we got along well. I was enchanted. I still wondered if that was a healthy way to feel. I was not yet sure what I brought to the table for him. I was a natural reflector of situations so I was sure it would all be revealed in time.

Latouve took up a lot of his time. When he finished work, though, he was totally focused and in the present moment with me and the two dogs.

We shared lots of walks, dinners and coffees. We would hang out together solving the problems of the world. Or mainly the problems of dogs which was high on the list of conversation topics for me. He didn't seem to mind.

He would share a bit about Latouve and the latest fashion styles and couture appearing in Paris. This always made him sound more desirable somehow. I often had to pinch myself to make sure it was real. I was dating this handsome man who loved dogs, who had Gidget's brother and who flew to Paris on a whim to fulfil his exciting and glamorous career.

I wondered when I would get asked out on that date. The one that involved a long flight, a passport and a little black dress. I could handle socialising if I was in Paris. That would be totally acceptable.

Well, so much for that dreamy thought pattern. The next thought that flew into my mind was who would look after Gidget? How could I ever leave her? How would she react or cope without me? I didn't know if it would be possible for me to leave her.

I was sounding like a helicopter mum in my head. Maybe I actually was. I realised as I was getting older that I didn't need to justify myself to anyone. I was quite happy with the way things were. Especially in relation to Gidget, my sweet girl.

Despite how fascinating William's life seemed, he appeared mesmerised when I spoke about the Pink Peace Festival and how it all worked. I wondered if it was because of the way I light up when I speak about my passions. I feel like I am internally radiating and externally animated with a sense of importance, of purpose, of passion, almost like a male peacock with glorious train feathers impressing others with the array of colours and iridescent eye feathers. Dazzling, I would joke.

When the pink tape was cut on the opening night a few days later, William was by my side. He gifted me two dozen pink tulips in a crystal vase to congratulate me on my achievement. The only thing that would have made him look more attractive is if he had two furry kids by his side.

Walking around the event and checking in on the stallholders was my form of socialising. It was disappointing there were no dog stalls, however. The closest thing to a dog stall was Anton the sculptor. He had garden art pieces, including two rusty iron dogs. They would look amazing next to my water feature. The one Gidget frolicked in.

William searched for my hand while he looked at me with a knowing. He knew exactly what I was thinking. We both knew they would mine before the end of the weekend. I stood next to Anton and whispered in his ear, "Please put a sold sticker with my name on these." He laughed to indicate his acceptance.

I felt an internal tug. Every time I went out at night without Gidget, I felt a deep urge to hurry home to her. No matter how hard I tried, I couldn't seem to shift it, despite knowing she would be curled up on my bed warm as toast snoring the night away.

She was normally asleep by 8pm every night anyway unless a possum was chanting mating dance rituals in the backyard.

I contemplated looking at my home cameras. Sometimes that made me feel calmer, knowing she was safe and resting. Other times it made me want to race home for a cuddle. I could never decide.

At the information booth, Fred and Lilly were engaged in an animated conversation with an English couple.

"William, can I leave you here for a moment while I go and check in on the reiki master, Gabriel?" I asked.

"Of course," he said. He loved seeing Fred. He found his lifestyle a most interesting one that was so far removed from his own. To William, extremes were always appealing.

Gabriel confided that David was his real name. He changed it when he left his banking career and transitioned to a more holistic lifestyle. It was a more fitting name, according to him.

Gabriel's site was beautifully set up. We had planned it together scrupulously.

A light blue and white rug led up to the opening of a crisp white glamping tent. Loose white flaps over the tent were held open by white ties with a big bow on either side.

Flickering pixie lights in different colours lit up the entrance to the tent. These circled around to the top of the tent and were drawn right up to the point in the centre high off the ground. They showed off the outline of the perfect tent structure and enticed people in.

As I stepped inside, I was instantly drawn to the sense of calm within. The serenity soothed my heightened nervous system. The lavender smell wafted past my nose. Divine.

Although minimalistic, the space radiated cosiness yet openness. A white-covered deck chair with a colourful crochet rug thrown over the back sat near a small table. It held some candles and books, which instantly caught my attention.

I loved adding to my self-development library and I spied a book, *The Saint, the Surfer and the CEO*, by Robin Sharma, one of my favourite authors, that I didn't have. Note to self: one to buy!

In the far corner stood the most elegant white leather massage table. This was the special spot where patrons could rest while Gabriel would go to work using his magical hands. With gentle movements, he would guide the flow of energy through their body, reducing stress and promoting healing.

Around the tent were vases filled with different coloured roses. A few eclectic pieces showing his alternative nature added to the ambience.

Gabriel looked up as I approached. "Hi Grace, thanks for visiting and thank you for arranging my special space. It's wonderful. Do you have time for a session?"

"Gabriel, your tent looks spellbinding. I would love that but I have to check in on all the other stallholders. Raincheck? I heard you had some concerns with Gloria, the massage lady next door. Want to tell me more?"

I broached the subject gently, as I had heard from other attendees that he had been complaining to them.

"Well, yes, I didn't want to complain. I am sure the clients probably love it but it's a bit disrupting to me. All the loud clanging of the Tibetan sound bowls and the deep chanting is distracting," he said.

Before he finished, I heard the rich deep tone of what I envisaged was a crystal sound bowl. This was followed by a long deep Om that seemed to last forever. Excellent lungs, I noted. The sound travelled from Gloria's tent next door.

Just when I thought it was over, I heard the clang of a gong, so loud it rattled the tent walls and vibrated through my chest. I personally found it hypnotising and delightful. I wanted to race next door, wish myself on the table and be the recipient of Gloria's massage treatment. I winced, feeling Gabriel's likely annoyance.

It took me thirty minutes of pandering to calm him. I promised more suitable neighbours next year. After agreeing to refund some of his stall attendance fee, he finally seemed content. He wished me on my way, almost shooing me out of the tent.

It was interesting to see how people reacted to situations and what triggered them, how they dealt with these triggers, and then what calmed them down. Learning this was part of the job, and negotiating a calm outcome was another necessary skill.

I knew that no one got through childhood unscathed and most people housed deep, often unconscious, triggers. Many people do what they can to create an awareness and consciousness of their triggers, to better understand where they originated from and how to minimise or even eradicate them. All in the quest to be a better version of themselves and to live bathed in self-love. Like me.

Others try to ignore what is going on and try to survive as best as they can, often using activities, busyness, overworking, overexercising, substances or addictions to distract themselves. Some people live in the drama believing they enjoy it. Some blame others and play the victim, doing anything to avoid facing their emotions or the reality of what is happening deep inside. They have no awareness or consciousness of their triggers. Sadly, they may be prone to self-loathing. Also like me at one point in time.

Stephanie had taught me that when I faced my fears and my emotions and challenged my deeply held beliefs and values, I could work to heal my past hurts and clear stuck emotions to live a lighter, more authentic life and be more present and free. She was absolutely correct and most of the time this now worked for me – I reiterate most of the time.

There was no right or wrong way to live. I had learnt to observe rather than judge people and, where possible, to learn from them and allow everyone their own journey. Their journey for them is where it needs to be at that moment in time.

I was not sure how William fitted into this theory. What were his fears, his triggers, his hurts? Was he conscious and aware? We hadn't discussed these topics. This was unusual for me as I often got into the nitty gritty of life with people pretty quickly. It fascinated me. He, however, seemed to always steer me away from these conversations.

"Guess who?" I said, placing my hand over his eyes. He was sitting on the bench enjoying a lamb yiros, garlic sauce trickling down his hands and onto the ground between his legs. He had found the only non-vegetarian stall at the event. It smelled delicious.

We wandered around and observed everyone looking relaxed. The air of peace was contagious. The beautiful energy had rubbed off on me and I noticed William had slowed down his walking and his talking – a common symptom of unwinding and basking in the present moment.

I bumped into a few dogs with their owners. I dropped to my knees to greet each one, give them a chin rub and hand over some liver treats to win their affection.

Everything seemed to be running smoothly and it was most enjoyable. I felt myself relaxing until I heard a gong sound in the distance. I grimaced. As an empath, I again felt Gabriel's likely frustration.

GIDGET

I stole a toilet roll and sent it unravelling down the hallway – a trick I remembered from puppyhood. I chased after it for Mum to clean up later. I also loved eating cardboard, ripping it up into little bits and then scattering it everywhere like white snow sprinkles.

I peed on all the bushes outside, sniffed a few leaves, chased what looked like a rat, took a drink and brought half the bowl back inside, dripping all over the hallway. I jumped up on the counters looking for any lingering crumbs.

Finally, when I was out of antics to entertain myself, I lay down and succumbed to another sleep. Making sure I got my twelve to fourteen hours a day was never a problem.

Laying there with Gertrude the giraffe, my new favourite toy, I was happy but concerned. Normally, I slept with a few toys but it was toy washing day. All my toys had spent the morning circling around the washing machine while I looked on earnestly to ensure their safety.

Now they were all lined up on the clothes line. Earlier I saw Mum sneakily take a few to the rubbish bin, but to be fair they were skins only. One was Ecci the Echidna, my second favourite toy. Gone but never forgotten.

I rolled over, allowing my legs to reach to the sky, paws free-floating in space, exposing all my bits. I wondered if Mum had spied my night-time capers on the cameras. I lounged in my special pose in case she was still watching.

I threw her a golden retriever clown smile. The smile where the corners of my mouth are pulled back and upwards, looking like a big smiling clown mouth but a lot cuter and less scary than an actual clown. Yuck! They scared me.

And I waited half awake, half asleep for Mum to come home.

Mortimer's big ears

Grace

The deep, voluminous vibrations of the gong penetrated my body. Such a primal sound.

I turned to look over my shoulder sensing it had come from directly behind me. To my surprise, I noticed a beautiful and very long tan and white dog with his ears dragging on the ground.

My gaze trailed up the lead to see Finn holding the other end. I had an inkling it could be him.

"Hi Mortimer, it's nice to meet you," I said. It was a bad habit that I often forgot to acknowledge the person and was more captivated by the furry soul with the waggy tail at the end of the leash.

I followed it quickly with "Hi Finn, Mortimer is insanely adorable. Look at those enormous basset ears and big droopy eyes. What a cutie."

"He is pretty special, Grace. To me at least. I heard you put this all together. It's so lovely. Are you enjoying your night?"

"It's beautiful," I said. "I couldn't be happier." I looked down to see Mortimer pulling at the lead stretching for a piece of garlic-covered lettuce lying on the ground just a few inches from his reach. Finn was trying to contain him without much luck. He looked a little agitated but with an air of patience. Mortimer's legs may have been short but he was still over thirty kilograms, I guessed, and seemingly full of strength.

"Sorry Grace, I must go. Mortimer has other ideas. I hope you have a great night. See you soon, but hopefully at the studio, not the vet clinic," he said with a smile.

Holding on tight to the lead he turned to go following Mortimer's big dumbo ears.

William looked at me. "Grace, who was that? Why didn't you introduce me? I felt a bit awkward," he said.

"Sorry William, it all happened so quickly I didn't get a chance. I was just about to introduce you."

"Hmm," he kind of gruffed.

Well, that was weird, I thought.

I wasn't sure why I had ignored William when Finn arrived. William had never got grumpy with me before like that and I wasn't sure his reaction was warranted. Why didn't he just introduce himself, I wondered.

I didn't want to spoil what was such a perfect evening so I apologised, put it out of my mind and continued with our enjoyable night.

Later that night when I put my weary body to bed, I found it difficult to go to sleep. My earlier contemplations went round and round in my mind relentlessly, just like Gidget chasing her tennis ball.

I must remember to meditate daily was my next line of thought. I would be able to get to sleep if my mind was calmer.

Be more like Fred popped in next. Maybe I will meditate now. No. It's much more productive to just overanalyse all night trying to come up with explanations that would likely never arrive, I thought sarcastically.

Gidget could hear me fossicking around and I felt a big wet lick on my hand which was hanging out of the bed. "Hop up, Gidget," I said and rolled over to cuddle her, hoping a serene night's sleep would follow.

Gidget

Mum, what's going on? It's the middle of the night. I love you but some dogs around here want to get some beauty sleep! I get up and stretch into an easy downward dog followed by an upward dog as Mum calls them and slowly walk over to the bed. I plant a big lick on her hand. That will calm her down surely.

Shall I pretend I need to do a wee in the guise of wanting to chase possums in the backyard? That always works. She would get up dreary eyed, open the door and stand in the cold repeating like a mantra, "Hurry up, Gidget, it's cold." One time, she even sat on the outdoor couch to wait and woke up when the sun rose. I slept under the stars that night. I loved the outdoors.

Tonight, though, I'm not sure I can be bothered. I hadn't seen Poppy the possum for a while anyway. Had she moved away after all my yapping and hullabaloo whenever she appeared?

In my own mind, I was a scary beast. But when I looked in a mirror, all I saw was a floofy, sooky, cuddly dog. Mum added to that picture with all the baby talk. And she didn't help the portrayal of my ferocious dog persona with all her snuggling and cuddling and kissing.

"Hop up, Gidget," I hear. On command, I hop up in one bound and lie down next to her. All sorts of smells are wafting off her. Lamb... mmm... my favourite. And strange dog smells. Basset hound I'm guessing.

Gidget & Grace

My smell is excellent. I passed smell school with flying colours. I learnt that we have more than three hundred million olfactory receptors in our nose. Humans only have about six million, so our sense of smell is significantly more sensitive. I was told I could smell human fingerprints that were over a week old. Wow. I should be known as Inspector Gidget!

Last week I smelt a tiny piece of something under the fridge. Mum spent ages telling me to stop pawing. Finally, she got fed up with me and moved the fridge, and lo and behold there lay the culprit. A tiny piece of ham. Debacle sorted. Apology given.

She clearly had forgotten about the smell school certificate on the fridge. Outstanding, it read!

We had been spending lots more time with William and Charlie. He was my brother and best friend. I was adjusting to them being around more and sharing Mum's time and energy. In the early days, every time Mum and William hugged I jumped up to try and break them apart. Charlie followed suit and would jump up also. It was a game to us.

My overstimulation would switch on, and I would wiggle and push and shove. But I never showed my teeth cause I was a softy at heart.

I had learnt with the handover of treats to let them be. Instead, I harassed Charlie for games. We would tussle around or I would lick him from ear to ear creating a strange sticky, wet mohawk hairdo. He loved that.

William was a bit of a pushover. I had mastered the sad eye routine and it worked on him every time. Charlie had told me about it and we practised it together and learnt quickly that treats followed soon after.

Training taught me a behaviour rewarded is a behaviour repeated. It's considered the gold standard for positive reinforcement training, and a powerful method for shaping or changing a dog's behaviour in a kind and gentle way.

That's what we did. I am a positive reinforcement trained dog and proud of it!

I have a certificate to prove that too. It's on the fridge right next to the smell school certificate. I showed Charlie the other day but he just woofed and said I knew he couldn't read.

We practised clicker training and ingested an enormous amount of treats each session. Before I was even a year old I had at least a dozen tricks under my belt – marching, playing dead, rolling over, saying prayers, spinning, weaving between Mum's legs – alongside mastering loose lead walking and all the normal common commands like sit and stay. I was a straight-A student.

I missed training and showing off my skills. I had mastered all the levels so that was it for now unless I was going to be something like a show dog or a highly trained sniffer dog.

Mum told me I had calmed down a lot. A combination of training and just getting older helped. I miss my crazy younger days and all the antics but being more settled did feel more relaxing and soothing. Instead of Mum always saying, " Gidget, you're too much," she now said, "Gidget, you are delightful." I liked that a lot. She felt calmer and spoke more softly. I just wanted to please her.

We were experts at manipulating and influencing the flow of treats, food, hugs, pats and outings. It was so easy. Mum told me she loved me so much that she would do anything for me and that she was a pathetic human when it came to being strict with me or being able to say no. But now that I knew this, I regularly used it to work in my favour. I taught it to Charlie too as I guessed it would work the same with William. It did, of course.

After finally sending Mum off to sleep, I rested my head fully. I allowed my third eyelids to close over as I was sent off to a blissful sleep next to my mum, who I loved endlessly.

Biscuits

Grace

"WOOF!" A deep and loud bark – very loud for a girl dog – echoed down the hallway from the front door.

"Who's here, Gidget?"

Visitors could never arrive unannounced. I certainly didn't need an alarm system or even a doorbell. What a waste of two thousand dollars it would have been when I already had a Gidget bell.

Polly, Susan and Paula were at the door. Their dogs were bursting at the seams to come inside and making a racket. Four dogs on one side and one on the other stuck to the screen door made it almost impossible to wedge the door open. With some cajoling, we moved the dogs so the door could be opened.

Down the hallway they raced, sliding around the corner into the kitchen and almost landing in a heap at the corner. It was the usual scene at every play date. While they were tugging away at each other, we removed their collars for safety reasons as they were always up into each other's necks. The ladies sat while I put the kettle on.

We had bonded at our first visit. Park plays had turned into house visits for coffee and biscuit play dates. The dogs loved each other and our human relationships continued to deepen as we spent more time together.

Biscuits for the dogs and biscuits for the people were laid out on the counter. Sometimes they came with extra slobber if we weren't quick enough to stop Gidget from jumping up and giving them a lick or devouring a few. The girls just laughed.

Some of the dogs were slow and inflexible, not even able to jump over a hose in the backyard, while others could go from four on the floor to four on the bench in one spring – and devour all your tuna salad! Gidget was the latter.

They all asked the question at the same time. "So, how's William?" It was almost an interrogation, with a stream of never-ending questions in cheeky voices. Mostly from Polly, wanting to live vicariously through me and my romance, but they were all overexcited waiting for my response.

Polly was happily married to Steve with two daughters in high school. Sarah and Peta were good kids. They loved Olive. They were literally the perfect white picket fence family. And with a beach house on the coast. We didn't really hear any cheeky antics about her children, which was good for Polly but not so good for our entertainment. Steve seemed like a perfect husband, despite being on the golf course too often apparently.

Susan spoke about her three girls all the time. She secretly named Sam, Betsy – who would only answer to Betts – and Clara the three rascals. All were under fourteen and, just like Gidget, had selective hearing. She often said she was managing a madhouse with the three kids, the two young dogs, her husband, Bruce, and his useless brother, Harry.

Harry stayed most weekends, and every weekend he drank beer with Bruce in the man cave he built for them at Susan's request so she could escape their tomfoolery. It had two spare beds to accommodate both of them after a night of binge drinking.

I thought she was remarkably calm considering the stories she entertained us with about the crazy situations they ended up in.

Paula, on the other hand, was meeker and came across as a little anxious, Shelly was being trained as her therapy dog. As long as she wasn't hunting ducks or possums or surrounded by loud noises, she fulfilled this role brilliantly. Paula was single with no children. The timing had never worked, she told us once. I felt she was still shielding a broken heart from her previous relationship.

"So, girls, what's been happening?" I said, deflecting the conversation away from me. I was more interested in what was happening in their lives. I did like to talk about my life but had spent hours chatting with Camilla yesterday where we debriefed everything that had been going on with William.

They didn't really notice my deflection technique.

Sometimes we are bursting to share our point of view, our opinions and our thoughts, and to seek connection. It takes patience and strength to actually actively listen and not forge a question or sentence in our head while someone else is talking. I have learnt much more about my friends when I just relax my lips and relax my tongue as they say in yoga practice. I laugh when I hear this and then take the advice and dive into silence.

Susan jumps in like she always does. "So, do you know what Bruce did this weekend?" This didn't surprise me as it was the way most of our coffee dates started out. Sometimes I loved to hear about the latest situation. Often, I felt it was like a record going around and around with no solution to the problem. Just an opportunity to vent and perhaps to entertain.

She continued. "Harry and Bruce had too many beers and one thing led to another. They thought it would be wise in their tipsy state to fix the fairy lights in the room as I'd requested, so they climbed onto the pool table and while Harry was balancing on the edge, he accidentally stood on one of the balls. The yellow one, he told me, like that really mattered. Anyway, he slipped and fell off the table winding himself and breaking his wrist." She laughed. "Then Snowy and Hudson licked him all over while he was rolling around in pain waiting for the ambulance."

I laughed loudly, shaking my head. She was about to continue her story when I glanced over to see all the dogs had ventured to the snack cupboard. They stared expectantly at the door and then back at me. I took this as an opportunity to break from the conversation and deliver the treats.

The dogs all knew the drill. They had to wait for their name to be called. With each name, they moved their head forward to take the treat. Snowy was pushy and tried to edge into the others' space. Hudson was a little snappy happy and I told him to be gentle about five times before he took the treat nicely. They were the youngest ones of the pack so I excused their behaviour.

The next minute, Paula jumped in with a "Guess what?" which was unusual. She was bursting at the seams to share something. Susan looked a little miffed with her story being interrupted.

"What? Tell us," we all said enthusiastically, thrilled to see her light up like this.

"I spoke to Golden Glow yesterday!" She waited for our reaction. We were all quiet but our facial expressions must have said it all.

"And, well, I will be adding a puppy to my family in a few months. Another little girl. She was born last night and is identified by a hot pink bow. I have named her Wilma."

We were all so excited and started screeching and jumping up and down. This excited the dogs and they started to do zoomies around the kitchen, nearly bowling Paula over. Susan willingly gave up on finishing her story.

If it was after 5pm we would have cracked the French champagne but considering it was only 10am we agreed another cup of coffee would suffice. We were excited.

When we got over the puppy hysterics, Polly said "Well, not much is different in my life. It's just travelling nicely and everything is good. Grace, you still haven't told us what's happening with William. Tell us all."

It was then I thought I should share. I could only deflect for so long.

GIDGET

"**M**um, hand the treats over. We are all starving. Please don't embarrass me," I woofed.

She saunters over, like a dog slave to me, Gidget the queen of the house.

I was mortified when I didn't get the first treat. I clown smiled like us golden retrievers do and knew mine was to come. I had to wait for my name and hope that pushy Snowy didn't steal mine.

I heard Mum talking about William and Charlie. She told the girls it had gotten quite serious. It had been nearly two years now... an anniversary imminent.

I saw Charlie a lot. So many play dates and late nights while Mum and William chatted about the things they found interesting. Which was me, of course... well, mostly. Sometimes they watched movies or cooked up a storm – mostly Thai food – and on occasion left us at home while they went out without us. Disgusting, I would woof on those nights. We like going out too.

Last night I heard William say, "Grace, I would like to take you out to dinner tomorrow night. There's something I want to talk to you about." He was much more serious than usual.

Mum told me he had a serious job but at home he was quite jovial and always rolled around on the floor with us. He had to brush himself down with the sticky roller afterwards to de-fur head to toe.

Mum seemed thrilled and enthusiastically said, "Yes, that would be lovely. I can't wait."

This morning, I found her doodling engagement rings on a notepad. She is lucky I can't talk; her secrets are safe with me. When she finished, she folded the piece of paper up neatly and put it in the pink book she called her journal.

She was always writing in that thing. I wondered if it was about me. Surely, I was the most interesting thing in her life? What else would she write about? If only I could read.

I ran outside to do a few more zoomies. I didn't want to know any more about anything serious with William. I wanted to have some doggy fun. Mum would share with me in time. She shared everything with me. I was surprised she didn't call me her journal or her therapist.

I was fur sure a good listener.

Inner niggles

GRACE

"Gidget, you really are my confidante and my best friend. I can tell you anything."

I always shared everything with Gidget as she was the only set of ears that I knew would keep my secrets locked in the vault and one hundred per cent confidential. I was able to share my innermost thoughts, my desires, my hopes and dreams, my irrational thoughts and the things that scared me most.

She never judged!

She was like a little furry therapist who would sit and look at me as I talked with animation about whatever I was saying. I would notice a head tilt here and a head tilt there. When the tears arose, she would place her head on my lap and look up at me pleadingly, showing the whites of her eyes. The best thing was that she didn't present me with an enormous bill after I left like Stephanie did.

I hadn't been to therapy for a few years now and noticed that things mostly had been flowing smoothly since Gidget and William had come into my life.

Most of the time William was engaging and charming, caring and fun. It was only the odd time he had been a little gruff with me. The first time I remember was at the first Pink Peace Festival. Like that time, I had continued to sweep the seriousness of any of these situations under the rug as I didn't want to upset our status quo.

He seemed to enjoy things more when it was just the two of us. Despite being a social character he was always a little on edge when I was talking to other people, especially if they were male.

He had been like that when I was chatting to Finn that time at the festival. Jealousy maybe. It had been a hard topic to broach with him. We had chatted about it, but he seemed to like to deflect any hard questions. I knew the signs as I often used the deflection technique too.

It wasn't so bad. I was really happy most of the time.

I was excited about our dinner tonight. I racked my brain wondering what he wanted to talk to me about. Surely it was too soon for a proposal. Did I really want that anyway? Did I really want that with him?

Was he Mr Right or only Mr Right Now? Maybe he wanted to discuss moving in together. We did stay together most nights anyway.

There was a niggling feeling deep down this train of thought. I couldn't put my finger on it, though. I pushed it away, not wanting to face the reality of anything changing our current situation. I was surprised to realise though, in that moment, I felt some ambivalence. But Gidget, Charlie, he and I worked well together.

I pulled into Camilla's driveway and beeped the horn. We were going to Friday morning yoga class together followed by coffee at Penelope's. I loved our time together as she was my favourite person after Gidget. She still couldn't believe she came second.

As I waited I saw Teddy run out the door with Ernest close behind. He nearly tripped over the hose trying to stop Teddy from escaping out to the front yard. Too late.

Teddy, who was the same age as Gidget, had matured. He was quite lazy, but when he saw an opportunity to hightail it up the street to find his favourite sniff tree, he was off. He had an obsession with this tree, likely because it was surrounded by possum poop.

Ernest yelled, "Hi Grace," as he ran after him up the street in his boxers and a pink I Love Rome t-shirt.

"Let's go, Grace," said Camilla as she laughed. "Ernest will sort out Teddy. He hasn't had a walk for a few days as I was in Singapore. Obviously, he is busting to get out."

We chitter-chatted all the way to Pink Peace. Knowing we would fall into silence at yoga we tried to get all our gossip out in the car trip. She told me all about her latest travels and the duty-free handbags she had bought back.

She asked if I wanted one of the high-end name brand bags sans the duty. Of course, I told her. Handbags and high heels were my most loved accessories. Not that I got to wear the high heels much as they didn't really suit a Gidget lifestyle. They were really just eye candy in my wardrobe. Truthfully, most handbags were covered in crumbs of liver treats, even the good ones.

I didn't tell her about Williams's dinner invitation, thinking I would save that for coffee after yoga. We needed more time than just the car trip to yoga to sort that one out.

Still laughing about Ernest and his Rome t-shirt running up the street, we walked into the studio. Immediately we bumped into Finn while taking our shoes off outside the studio door.

Aww... Finn. I thought he was so lovely. Every time I saw him, he asked about Gidget and shared some stories about Mortimer or Morty as he nicknamed him. His smile was so refreshing. He was different to William. William was engaging and charming whereas Finn was more grounded and authentic whilst also being charming and kind. I really enjoyed seeing him at yoga out of the vet clinic setting.

With Gidget in the family, I often frequented the clinic. I had seen him only last week after an incident with Gidget chasing

Poppy the possum. Her agile body sprung as high as it could but she managed to slam into the fence. Upon landing, she lifted her back leg and, on closer inspection, I noticed she had also taken some skin off near her eye – most likely from a stick protruding from the bush she tried to scale.

Finn had said it was only a minor injury. He applied an orange stain that identified any scratches or lesions, assuring me moments after that she had not done any permanent damage. I had driven there picturing her getting around the neighbourhood with a pink pirate patch on. He checked her leg and paw also and I was relieved when he said it was just a minor sprain of the ankle and nothing to worry about.

"She is much more accident-prone and busy than Ernie was, isn't she," he commented.

I remembered Ernie's cruciate ligament incident and the three months of rehabilitation. What a hassle it was keeping him confined while trying to keep him entertained and provide enrichment. But he bounced back like nothing had ever happened.

Beautiful Ernie, the other love of my life. I had pictures of him everywhere around the house. I often spoke to Gidget about her predecessor. He was present in spirit.

Everything felt right in the world as I lay in Savasana at the end of the class with Camilla on one side and Finn on the other. I kept my eyes closed and basked in the space in between, devoid of thought, filled with joy.

I could have stayed there forever. Then I heard the familiar chime at the end of the class. Loud enough to hear and soft enough not to startle you out of Savasana. Next to me, I could hear a soft and quiet snore from Finn.

We slowly woke our bodies by wiggling our fingers and toes. We came to a seated position, bringing our hands to our heart in a prayer gesture. To end the class we chanted three Oms and said "Namaste", which means I bow to you or the light in me sees the light in you. It could be used as an expression of appreciation and respect towards others or yourself.

When I first started yoga, I found this gesture strange. Slowly I stopped worrying what others may have thought of me and I found the respect in the gesture. Now I loved honouring myself this way at the end of class.

We rolled up our mats and I heard Camilla say, "Finn, do you want to join us for coffee at Penelope's?" Camilla knew Finn as he was Teddy's vet also, and she raved about his care and compassion just like I did.

I was kind of excited she had asked him. I really liked his company and yet was kind of annoyed as I liked having Camilla to myself to debrief life with her. Especially considering the impending dinner invitation conversation that I had planned to have with her.

Gidget was great to talk to but with not being able to speak or verbalise anything I never received any substantial advice other than a head tilt. They say that dogs have the IQ of about a two-year-old child so I'm not sure what her advice would have been anyway, except maybe I should definitely go if it included food.

"That would be great. See you there," he replied.

As I walked into Penelope's with Camilla, the first thing I saw was Mortimer pulling Finn forward with his ears dragging behind him. I was in heaven that Morty was joining us. I think I was more excited to see the gorgeous long floppy-eared dog than I was to see Finn again. I mastered the seating arrangement so Morty was right next to me on his fluffy rug.

I didn't talk about my dinner date until Camilla and I got back into the car. I unloaded quickly to allow her time to assimilate all the information and provide the perfect advice before we arrived back at her house.

Camilla being Camilla, pretty chilled almost to the point of being nonchalant, just said "Grace, don't overthink it. Enjoy it and follow your heart. He's a great guy. Just make sure to call me tomorrow and tell me all about it."

I promised her I would do just that as I dropped her home. I watched her slink in the front door before Teddy could come bustling out to leg it up the street and hang with his possum tree again.

GIDGET

"Mum, where have you been? It's been ages," I woofed with another sniff. "Mum, you've been to yoga, haven't you? You appear more relaxed. And mmm, you saw Finn, my vet. He is a lovely vet by the way, aside from the odd needle or the cold thermometer up the you-know-where wazoo. I'm not sure what that is all about but he has excellent treats and the girls there always love me up."

Sniff, sniff... I can smell basset hound. It's the ears, I think. "Can I meet him one day? Play date? Please Mum!"

All of a sudden, I felt a zoomie coming on. Mum always laughs when I do these. They're hard to explain. It's like I get really excited almost to the point of frantic yet with an undertone of euphoria. A surge of emotion rises and soon after the zoomie starts taking over my body.

It allows me to release pent-up energy. I ensure furniture is used on my zoomie path for added effect. I change directions as much as possible, ears flapping, as I move swiftly around the room with much determination. Then I drop, panting, with my tongue hanging out exposing my three black birthmark spots. I feel so much freer.

La Bella

Grace

It felt strange getting ready to go out. I mostly wore black yoga pants accessorised with flecks of dog hair. Searching the wardrobe to find something appropriate to wear was a novel event.

I usually depended on my mood to help me decide my outfit but I didn't know what mood I was in. Was I in jeans and leather jacket mood? A pretty dress and pink bow mood? Or a maxi dress and cardigan mood? I finally settled on my newest pair of blue jeans, a fresh white shirt, a black velvet jacket and a pair of black high heels. I finished the look with the mandatory pink handbag, tipping it upside down to ensure any liver treats were expunged.

It had been a while since I last applied any makeup. Normally I just went au naturale but I felt like tonight warranted some effort. Layering my eyelids with eyeliner and a charcoal grey sparkly shadow felt good.

After finishing off with a dark pinkish lipstick, I touched my lips together to spread the lipstick. I looked in the mirror to see it had covered most of my front teeth. I never knew how to prevent that but cleaned them up and blotted a tissue on my lips. I used to see my mum do this when I was little. It seemed to remove the excess for now.

"Ready," I said to Gidget.

I gathered my things together and tried to quell the nervous energy I was feeling and the butterflies floating around my tummy and rising to my chest.

Gidget probably thought she was coming. I needed to make her a Kong. This was a creative way to distract her from my leaving and encourage her to dismantle it rather than slam the fence for possums, especially when it was dark. It was also an excellent form of enrichment. I filled it with dog biscuits finished off with a dob of peanut butter to seal the opening.

I was thinking about the night ahead while Gidget was drooling. I was meeting William at La Bella, a local Italian restaurant. William said it had won a few local awards and was stunningly authentic in its food, atmosphere and service.

He had drinks beforehand at a bar in the city for an account he was looking after. This always seemed to happen when we went out and I usually had to meet him somewhere. It would be nice to arrive somewhere together but tonight, I tried to quell my agitation. There was something important he wanted to talk to me about. This took more of my focus. It left me uneasy yet excited with anticipation.

"What is so important, for heaven's sake?" I asked Gidget.

She looked at me with her 'hand over the Kong' look while handing me her paw.

I liked surprises when I arranged them for someone else and received all the accolades. Not so much when they were directed my way and I had to be the centre of attention. I wasn't very patient so waiting on edge rattled me.

I handed over the Kong and Gidget ran to her bed and flopped down, tilting her head to the side and extending her lengthy tongue to scoop out the goods. She started with the best bit, the peanut butter. She usually finished them quite quickly so out I dashed, leaving a light on for her and the TV for company. As always, I said the obligatory, "Back soon, Gidget. I love you."

I understood what William meant the moment I arrived at La Bella. It was lovely. The waiter swanned over to me to greet me at the door with a casual yet friendly, "Buona sera, Signorina." I always wondered why we didn't frequent more French restaurants. William told me that despite loving French food he was inundated with it at work. His other great love besides Thai food was Italian food. He cooked a lot of both.

He was currently mastering gnocchi with a ragu sauce. The sauce was excellent and the meat was so tender it just melted on your tongue. I didn't have the heart to tell him his gnocchi was not yet quite as fluffy as the traditional Italian restaurants in Rome. I didn't complain though – I hated cooking.

The waiter led me to our table. I didn't see William anywhere, which was no surprise. My phone beeped with the arrival of his text, "Be there in five." Like clockwork. I chose the chair facing the door. I liked to see the activity and the comings and goings of all the different people in a restaurant. One advantage of being there first was you could choose your seat.

If Gidget were here, she would have sat on the other side of the table facing the kitchen. I could imagine all the scrumptious smells wafting through the air to line her nostril hairs.

True to his text, five minutes later he arrived looking business-like in a dapper black suit, accessorised by the pink and white diagonal-striped tie I had bought for him months earlier. He looked so handsome and turned heads as always.

It was normal for him to receive this attention. He oozed an air of confidence and moved with a sense of elegance. When he spoke, he sparkled, his whole being jam-packed full of charisma. I felt proud and only occasionally a prickle of jealousy arose if the head he was turning was one of a gorgeous younger girl.

"Hi Grace, sorry I'm late," he said. "You look beautiful."

It wasn't often he saw me all dressed up with my hair down and wavy. I had it cut and blow-dried that afternoon. Plus, wearing a face full of makeup likely helped with making me more attractive. It was nice feeling more girly for a change. It was strange not to have my furry attachment at my side, yet somehow I still managed to spy dog hair on my clothes.

I flicked my hair back and accepted the compliment. I had struggled with accepting compliments for years. Thanks to Stephanie I could now just say thank you and truly let the compliment sink in.

I was feeling calm, energised, happy and joyful all at the same time. I was only a little on edge awaiting his chat.

"So, Grace..." he said.

Straight into it.

"I spoke to Claude from Paris, the CEO at Latouve, at some length this week. He has offered me a once-in-a-lifetime opportunity. A promotion, more money, a different role. But it's based in the heart of Paris."

He stopped for a minute before he continued, sporting a big smile. "Claude said they would pay for all relocation costs and move me into a lovely apartment in Montmartre. It's in the 18th Arrondissement, which you might know as the painter's neighbourhood."

I could see the enthusiasm he was poorly trying to suppress while trying to explain the situation slowly and calmly so as not to upset me too much. I could see straight through him. I knew how much he wanted this just by his facial expressions. He was fully transparent.

To live in Paris with all his social networking and sense of adventure would light up his whole personality. He would shine. I could tell he was trying to assess my feelings on the matter before he continued.

I was still waiting to hear the whole story. My facial expression was likely pretty bland. Unreadable.

I was blindsided. Paris seemed exciting. I had always wanted to go to Paris. I literally had dreamed about it in fact. But for him to live there. What would that mean? This was crazy.

Despite having a high-powered, interesting job, he had opened up a few times and confessed he thought something was missing. He never quite seemed settled and was always seeking more. I wondered if this was what he needed to satisfy him. Would this be the solution to his void?

We were different in that way. I was happy with a simple life of dogs, peace and connections. Smelling the roses, so to speak. I liked going to yoga during the week, having regular coffee meet-ups with Camilla and hanging out with all the dogs I could find.

I had once tried to climb the corporate ladder. I understood its seductive appeal but only until my insides screamed at me to stop and, instead, to look within and find a more creative, productive, purposeful and passion-driven existence. Essentially, I sought a heart-opening career where I felt entirely fulfilled and authentic, and not stressed out to the max.

I felt my heart sink and a sense of confusion ripple through me. My hands began to shake a little. I slowly put them on my lap so they were hidden by the table.

"So," I said. "What does that mean for us?"

"Well, it looks like I'm moving to Paris. Come with me!" he said.

Oh wow, I thought. I had not expected this. He had decided already and now he expected me to go along with it. Just like that. He made it seem so simple. A stream of thoughts did laps around my head. A romantic fantasy rushed in like the rom-coms I loved so much until one second later reality hit and I spoke.

"What? You mean move there with you?"

"Yes," he said enthusiastically. "Why not?"

I think he really thought I would just say yes and pack my pink suitcase full of my possessions and jump on the plane, beret in one hand and a Paris guidebook in the other, trying to feel all Parisian. Most girls would.

"Are you kidding?" I replied, raising and emphasising the pitch on the last syllable.

Really? Does he not know me at all? A holiday would be nice. We could travel over together for a romantic getaway and stroll around Montmartre and visit the Eiffel Tower, Sacre Coeur and the Palace of Versailles. I imagined us holding hands before relishing a warm buttery croissant and sipping a cup of tea at a café with black and white striped awnings.

A permanent move, however, was another thing altogether.

There was a Gidget to consider. There was a Charlie to consider. Had he completely forgotten about Charlie? Why didn't they even come up in the conversation?

By the end of the night we, or rather he, had realised two things. He was going to Paris and I was not going with him.

It kind of overlayed the night with an awkwardness. We had lost something.

We had yet two other big things to consider. Would we break up or have a long-distance relationship? And what would happen to Charlie?

To be honest, my heart was sadder about Charlie being abandoned. Not because I didn't have feelings for William, but because dogs don't really understand. Sometimes they adjust easily to big changes in their lives and other times it is traumatic for them.

Camilla's dog Violet who she had before Teddy was a prime example of this. I shared this with William, only to be told, "He'll be okay. He'll adjust." He stopped abruptly but I was sure he was about to say, "He's just a dog." He knew what my reaction would be to a comment like that.

I thought he was bonded strongly with Charlie. Obviously, the opportunity to advance his career and move to his dream job on the other side of the world overshadowed the importance of the human–animal bond and commitment he had made to Charlie.

I wasn't so sure Charlie would be okay. But it looked like sadly we would find out soon.

Truthfully, I didn't really understand. To me, a dog is a dog for life from a puppy to a senior, for better or for worse, for richer or for poorer. Holding their paw as they transition to another realm came to mind like a mantra to me.

I would move heaven and earth for Gidget.

I understood people were different and that it was not my place to judge. I heard Stephanie's voice echo in my head as I often did. She really had made a difference to my thinking.

People need to do what they need to do. You can't plan for everything and you have to take the opportunities that feel right and readjust and realign as you see fit. That was where William was right now. I just thought it was sad he hadn't even mentioned Charlie as part of the decision or the planning until I mentioned him.

Camilla's dogs Violet and Daisy were a beautiful pair of dogs despite living up to their reputation as crazy chocolate Labradors. They were inseparable and closely bonded to Camilla. When they were about six, we were at the local park playing ball with Violet while Daisy played chase with an English springer spaniel. Suddenly the spaniel darted across a nearby road with Daisy in hot pursuit. While the spaniel had a near miss, sadly Daisy was struck by an oncoming car.

No one saw it coming and the car came out of nowhere. Just a tragic accident. At first, we didn't think it was too serious, yet looks can be deceiving when you consider what can be happening underneath the outer layer of skin and fur.

She held on for a few days at the emergency vet after receiving some serious internal damage and internal bleeding. Over the next few days, it became obvious they were not able to fix her complicated issues. Her body started to shut down. Camilla, Violet and I said our goodbyes late one night. While a thunderstorm was raging outside, we held Daisy's paw and watched her take her last breath.

Violet was different after that. She spent months camped under a chair in the bedroom only to be coaxed out for dinner or to do her business. She became nervous, shy... scared even. She became wary of other dogs and reactive to loud traffic.

Amy, the behaviouralist we engaged, said it was grief. It lingered for some time. Thunderstorms became a nightmare and everything seemed to be a struggle. About eight months later, with a concoction of behaviour therapy, natural supplements and medication, she regained more normality but was never quite the same. The trauma had shaken her. It was heartbreaking. She lived a long life to fourteen years of age, sadly though almost a half-life without her loved sibling by her side.

This recollection scared me. I didn't want grief for Charlie as he mourned William.

"When are you leaving?" I asked.

"In two weeks."

I was in shock, and all that came out of my mouth was, "I will take Charlie," thinking to myself there was no other choice. I surprised myself but was not really surprised at all.

"Excellent. I thought you would," he said.

He casually followed it with, "Please, Grace, can you still think about my proposition. We could work out something else for the dogs. We would be amazing together in Paris."

Despite everything, a little part of me wondered if he could be right.

GIDGET

Like always when Mum arrived home, I pounced all over her. Mostly she was thrilled when I was all bouncy and loving, often getting on the floor with me and rolling around, playing and tussling. Not tonight though.

Something was different. She seemed distracted and distant. She knelt down to pat me telling me she loved me so much, yet I could feel a sadness oozing from her. She didn't want to play. Instead, she just sat and patted me. She mumbled off a whole lot of other words I didn't understand, except for the odd 'William' which I knew. I just continued to nuzzle against her and cover her in wet sticky licks and fur.

Eventually, she laughed and said, "Gidget, that's enough."

My job here is done, I thought, as she ushered me out the door to do a late-night wee – the ones I loved best as it was always an opportunity to see Poppy the possum.

As I headed outside, I saw Poppy resting on the top of the fence, quietly enjoying the stillness of the evening. I couldn't believe it. Time to go into stealth mode! I crept forward, lifting each leg one at a time ever so slowly and placing it back gently on the earth to prevent being noticed. Who was I kidding?

I already felt triumphant. But just as I got ready to leap and lunge, to slam the fence and catch her, I felt a little tug on my collar. I looked up to see Mum.

"Gidget," she said, "remember the last time you hit the fence you had to go to the vet because you hurt yourself? We are not doing that again."

"Mum, you ruined it. I had her!" I woofed.

She dragged me back inside, clipped on a lead and then outside we went again, this time with me in disgrace. I had to do a wee on the lead as I couldn't be trusted. Humiliated, I looked around and Poppy was nowhere in sight. Gone again. So close. That Poppy was my nemesis.

I'd get her next time, I thought, as I dozed off to sleep shortly afterwards. I always got her in my dreams.

In limbo

GRACE

I walked around in a daze. He wanted me to go to Paris. What an opportunity!

Even to be asked, to be wanted by this man, was kind of special. When I focused solely on that, I thought there's no reason I wouldn't want to go. Living in fantasy land momentarily, my mind relished in the thought of living the Parisian lifestyle with a handsome man dressed in a nice suit, speaking snippets of French, seeing the sights, basking in the culture, flaunting the fashion, strolling the streets, and eating the culinary delights that everyone always talked about, especially the macarons. Bliss.

When I thought about it like this, I could feel a yes on the tip of my tongue – a longing, a desire, a long-held dream to venture there for a season or a lifetime. But was my train of thought for the right reasons?

Then my mind went into overanalysing mode – normal when I had a big decision to make – swaying between the good and the bad, the sixth sense and the desires. The confusion overwhelmed me. I didn't want to make the wrong decision and regret it for eons after.

I tried to ignore my sixth sense somewhat before I totally dismissed the idea. I wanted to live in this fantasy of William and me in Paris for a little longer before reality came crashing down. Was I letting go of my love story too quickly?

So I asked myself the hard questions. Did I love him? Yes, I loved him. Was I in love with him? That I wasn't so sure about.

Did I want to spend my future with him? I was unsure. Some of the time we spent together was amazing, yet those inner niggles were still there rattling around just below the surface.

Then I asked myself if I would leave the dogs behind for this guy.

I was pulled back into reality hearing Gidget bark at a plane roaring overhead, much lower than normal.

Then my sixth sense snapped me out of it. It was bellowing internally with a roaring no. It was like a hard slap across the face. It echoed throughout my physical, emotional and spiritual body. Of course not. And that was it. It was a done deal. Decision made.

There was no way I would leave Gidget. I also had Charlie to think about because William clearly hadn't catered for him in his decision-making process.

The decision was made right as I heard the phone trilling.

"Hello?"

"Grace, it's me. I know I threw this on you suddenly and it may seem impulsive. I really do want you to come and live with me in Paris. We can make this work. We can work something out for the dogs. Maybe they could stay with my mum. All I know is I love you and I want you beside me."

I cut him off as I didn't want to hear much more of the fading love story that was coming crashing down. I didn't want to start the overanalysing process all over again.

"It all sounds amazing in theory, Will, but I can't come to Paris with you. I'm sorry. I have a good job here and there is no way I could leave Gidget and now Charlie. I want you to follow your dreams and I wish you all the happiness but I will be staying here. I can't come with you."

Our conversation went on for a bit longer. Finally, he accepted my choice but I'm not sure he understood. He thought I placed more value on the dogs than him. Maybe I did. Maybe for good reason.

We had agreed Charlie would come over for a few more sleepovers without Will as we planned to transition him to moving in permanently.

The phone call ended. A few tears fell yet I felt a sense of peace and calm. I knew that I had honoured myself with absolutely the right decision for me.

Sadly, knowing something is right doesn't alleviate all the sadness. It can still cause anguish – another one of Stephanie's gems.

Gidget

Life was different with lots of emotion. Charlie began to stay most nights and there was a lot less of Will around our home. I sensed it was permanent. My senses never let me down.

I sensed a sadness leaching from Mum. I gave her the sad eye treatment and extra licks and rested my head on her lap a lot more.

It was confusing as I was excited also. Life was amazing with Charlie around more. Charlie... my brother, my best friend, my playmate. I turned on extra zoomies and Charlie loved to join in.

I didn't see William much at all anymore. To be fully furry honest I wasn't too fussed about him. He did play with us sometimes and rolled around on the floor with us but having Charlie and my mum to myself is furry fabulous.

We all slept on the bed together as Mum seemed to need some soothing. Doggy Mum Suzy said to always keep the humans happy, so I did a few more silly zoomies, fell at her feet and turned upside down. Then I got up and did a little toe tap in front of her then climbed on her and just sat there. She finally laughed and rustled my head. I was always able to get her to laugh. Task completed. Charlie just looked at me and woofed, "Well done Gidget."

Mum Suzy would be proud.

I eventually lay on the carpet near the bed with Charlie and started planning in my mind how the logistics would work now Charlie was here more. Who would get fed first? Where would the extra food live? Was there enough room in the pink treat bag for treats for two dogs? Did we have enough Kongs? All the important stuff a dog must consider. All based around food of course.

As Mum turned off the light that night, she patted me on the head and said, "It will all be okay, Gidget." She then turned to give Charlie the same pat. "You, Charlie and I will be great."

She didn't have to convince me. I fell asleep listening to Charlie doing soft little doggy snores right next to me with our tail feathers touching.

Au revoir

GRACE

Today was the day. William arrived with Charlie as he often did but this time with all his belongings that hadn't already made it to my house. He also lugged a full BBQ chicken – bribery if needed. This was the permanent transition.

Gidget literally jumped for joy as they ran off down the passageway out to the yard, tussling each other on the way.

I had to stay strong in my decision. I was never good at goodbyes.

Watching the dogs playing chase outside just like any other day, we hovered in the hallway and just looked at each other. His flight was later that night then voila, he would be gone. Just like that.

He took a step closer and drew me into a strong embrace.

"Grace, I will miss you so much. If you change your mind, I'll organise a ticket for you. Any time, any day, baby. I love you," he said.

I melted into his arms but couldn't fully relax. I couldn't speak. I was so confused and overwhelmed with emotion that I stepped out of his hug soon after and shrugged. I didn't know what to say or if there was anything else to say. I knew there was no real solution to keep everyone happy. To return his embrace fully would break me. I felt I had little choice. I now had to protect myself.

The dogs bounced back and he looked down. "Charlie," he said, "be a good boy. You will be so well looked after and Grace loves you. I love you too buddy. Have lots of runs and rolls at the park for me."

William saying goodbye to Charlie as he did a head tilt was more upsetting than the hug. I could feel the tears well. With that, he gave me one last look, turned his back and left. I watched him walking away from me. I was surprised to feel a swell of relief washing over me. It was unmistakable. Not what I had expected. And then I burst into tears.

Despite the initial relief, the next few months were a haze of sadness, anger and grief. It all flowed inside me with a million questions arising. Most of them had nothing to do with William leaving and more to do with a whole host of other events in my life that I had long since tried to forget but clearly had not dealt with.

This situation was clearly the catalyst for my newfound emotional state. It was like the cork in the bottle had exploded and it let the entire contents spill out and into my body, flooding it and swishing around, making it a challenge to find a clear head and a stable inner self.

I understood what grief did. I had read about it. I had studied it. It was similar to when Ernie died. Back then I had tried to keep the cork stuck in the bottle. Now I felt the grief would overwhelm me.

But, as they say – I always do wonder who 'they' are – feelings wait for you. They wait to be felt. You can't escape or outrun them. They hang around in your body to be processed in the form of emotional or physical symptoms or pain. They can often manifest in disease or illness if left undealt with.

Understanding these things in theory was much easier than actually figuring out what to do about them in reality. But I was doing everything I could to heal, putting into practice techniques I had learnt from Stephanie such as meditation, journaling, sleeping well, eating well, speaking to others, drawing, dancing and exercising. I did all that.

Stephanie would say, "Just meditate, Grace." Her words reverberated around while I tried to find ways to procrastinate. I seemed to be happier getting stuck in my head with a barrage of thoughts trying to find a solution instead of actually doing what I knew worked.

When I felt like I had no other choice, I would surrender. I would sit in a meditation or partake in one of the other healing activities and presto, I would feel a little better.

Just take one day at a time, I kept telling myself.

People say it takes time. I knew that not only did it take time but it took time and work, a combined effort. Without the work and just allowing time, you could be sitting in the same place years later waiting for the cork to burst, holding everything inside and creating havoc internally.

I promised myself again I would devote myself to do the work, like when Pierce left. That was torture. He really did break my heart. This was another level. A new awakening of healing needed to be done to clear my inner vessel. It never really stops. It's a continual learning about self, opening to an awareness, healing the layers, creating new opportunities, feeling the feelings, letting things in and washing things out.

Stephanie told me about a five-step process called 'In the Pink' to help heal grief: 1. Awareness, 2. Responsibility, 3. Feeling, 4. Forgiveness, and 5. Acceptance. I took an inner oath to put her process to work.

Gidget and Charlie were having a ball being together 24/7 and when it was time for a rest they spent hours at my feet gazing into my eyes. I kept writing in my journal. I kept trying to process the conundrum of feelings that exhausted me.

I was in my own world enveloped with a shield of grief. It felt like I was wearing a big woollen coat done up tightly and I was tucked up inside protected only by myself. I was struggling to survive the world. In fact, it was almost like I was alone in the world sorting through the deluge of inner chaos.

One day the phone rang and it was Camilla.

A part of me was secretly hoping it was William. Then the other part of me wondered why I was hoping for this considering the relief I had felt upon our initial separation. I continued to be swamped by confusion.

"Okay Grace, that's enough," exclaimed Camilla. We haven't seen each other in weeks. You're coming to yoga today."

I begrudgingly got up and got dressed. Camilla was a force of nature when she wanted to be and there was no arguing with her when she set her mind to something.

For Camilla, despite being an avid yogi, yoga was more about the physical than the spiritual. She didn't really understand my need to go inward and ponder life. She was more of a let's-just-go kind of girl. Her solution was to have another glass of champagne. She was always upbeat and looking for the next fun thing to do. Sometimes I wished I was more like her. Most times though I loved the introspection. It was an inner adventure of sorts. I usually maintained a balance.

Besides work and walking the dogs, I hadn't been going out much or doing anything fun despite the onslaught of invitations from Camilla. I was immersed in my inner world and most of my time was spent on healing.

Fifteen minutes later I heard her car pull into the driveway. 'Video Killed the Radio Star' was belting out from the radio. She knew this was one of my favourites. I had only just pulled up my yoga pants, covered in dog fur as always. Now double the amount of fur was floating like tumbleweeds around the house. When she walked in something shifted. Instantly I felt different. I thought it was about friggin' time.

"Let's go," I said, feeling more alive than I had in months. I almost felt frisky!

She seemed thrilled and her smile implied she felt she had her friend back. Her eyes revealed it all. She reached down to pat Gidget and Charlie then grabbed my arm with one hand and my yoga mat with the other, and pulled me out the door before I had even done up my shoes.

GIDGET

"Charlie, Mum looks sad," I woofed.

"Woof," verbalised Charlie. He was a boy of few words but full of love and fun.

Despite Mum's blue mood, she always found time for us. She told us we were her guardian angels. She said often angels came in the form of four paws and a wet nose showering everyone with unconditional love.

I was fully starting to understand our purpose as Mum Suzy had explained to us way back when we were little whippersnapper pups. I never really understood it until now. Feeling her sadness and being able to carry some of the heaviness for her or at least lift it and create some joy amidst all the sadness had made it clear. It also made our bond completely unbreakable.

Charlie had fitted in without a glitch. It was like the smoothest transition ever. All my concerns about the food quandaries were quashed instantly. Mum said the same. One night she said, "Gidget, it's like he has been here forever. I was a little worried about how he would fit in. I hope you feel the same." I licked her all over, implying a yes. Charlie joined in the licking before we both busted a move into a zoomie.

We only had one minor stoush. It was sardine-related and a serious offence in my eyes. Charlie tried to lick my dinner plate. I tried to tell him but he didn't listen. He edged closer and closer and, when he put his big unwanted nose on my plate, I let out an almighty growl, baring teeth and all.

He backed away quick smart. He was a bit of a sook. Sardine juice is high value and treated as gold in the dog world. And no way was I sharing that.

After he backed away, I went straight up to him and gave him a big lick, as if to say sorry mate but you know… He licked back thankfully. And slowly his tail started to wag again.

He never tried that again. The smart boy only had to be told once. I established myself as head of the dog house after that, as it should be. I was here first, after all.

Mum learnt to walk both of us together. At first it was a struggle as we often did our twist the lead dance routine. Alternatively, we put her in the middle of a stretch machine as we went different ways for a sniff. Somehow, with lots of lamb treats and an enormous amount of patience, she taught me to walk on the left and Charlie to walk on the right.

Occasionally, we still did the little dance to keep it interesting for her but mostly we behaved beautifully. We only pulled if we smelt something delicious ahead like cat poop, scraps of food, a banana skin or berries that had dropped off a bush. Mum reminded us not to pull and how costly and prolonged an exercise it had been when she pulled her rotator cuff muscle that one time. Another oopsie.

Happy fifth birthday

GRACE

"Happy birthday to you, Gidget and Charlie," I sang. I couldn't believe how quickly the last five years had flown.

We never found any other siblings from the same littler despite putting out a Facebook post in the Golden Love Facebook group. They only needed each other and their little furry group of friends.

I had finally emerged out of my post-break-up blues and arrived at the acceptance stage. The last stage. The stage where you begin to move on. Finally. Along the way, I had cleared out other grief that was stuck deeper. I was feeling lighter and more joyful than ever before.

William, I assumed, was living the life and climbing the corporate ladder in Paris. I was happy in my simple life here at home. I would much rather be throwing a doggy birthday party covered in slobber than sitting in a boardroom with a view of the Eiffel Tower devoid of fur.

I hadn't been interested in looking for a new partner. I was content being with my friends and my dogs. I was independent and comfortable on my own. I didn't need anyone but understood that the right relationship could add to your life. For now, I was happily single.

Preparing for the party had been fun. I issued pink and blue invitations. I selected some dried beef jerky and chicken loaf treats at the local pet shop. I picked pink and blue bows from the haberdasher and spent endless time choosing dog toys. I made up doggy party bags and human sandwiches.

Covered in morning slobber, I said, "Time to get up. It's breakfast time!" They stopped instantly and looked at me. It's like the word breakfast made them freeze in anticipation for the excitement to come moments later.

Gidget had her top lip all caught up in her teeth as if to say "huh". The next thing they jumped off the bed and ran to the laundry. When I arrived a few moments later I nearly slipped on all the drool that was pooling on the floor. Fur, slobber and drool were part of everyday life with this gorgeous duo.

Polly arrived first with Olive and the kids. Olive, being a sensitive soul, came to the door timidly. Polly tried to drag her over the threshold but Olive had to have a big sniff before obliging. Finally realising where she was, she ran down the hallway with Gidget and Charlie, looking like three bucking broncos.

Sweet Polly handed over a pink and blue striped bag and inside was a hot pink chew toy that looked like a watermelon and a pale blue toy that impersonated an elephant. Underneath the toys were two blocks of hazelnut chocolate. She knew it was my favourite as we had devoured more than a few blocks together over the years.

Finn and Mortimer arrived next. Morty's short legs carried him leisurely over the step while his ears dragged along leaves from the porch and scattered them inside. He stopped to give his head a shake before continuing to join the others.

Morty had become talented at pretending he was a golden retriever and had easily become one of the pack over the last few months. He loved collecting all the treats the goldens dropped as he was closer to the floor. Finn and his lovely persona had been spending more time with us and obviously Morty always came along.

I had decided I was going to get my own basset hound one day and call him Fred. I have a feeling Finn suspected this as it's probably why he pulled from behind his back a soft toy that looked exactly like Morty. It was almost true to real-life size. He was wearing a little red vest. I wasn't sure if it was a dog toy or a doorstop, but I told him how much I loved it and placed it high up on the buffet out of the dog's sight.

Susan turned up in a bit of a flap with Snowy and Hudson. Both shoved their way in past the door before it had hardly opened. Whoosh... they were gone to find the others with leads still attached. They were no shrinking violets that's for sure. As soon as Susan put her first foot in the door she said, "Do you know what Bruce and Harry did last night?" All I could reply was "What?" and pretended to listen while I was trying to direct doggy traffic up and down the hallway. I would ask her to repeat her story later as no doubt it would have a funny side to it.

Susan came with biscuits and a homemade apple and cinnamon cake. She was a great baker and, despite having an exorbitant amount of food prepared already, I still secretly hoped she would bring something sweet today. On top of the cake was a golden retriever cake topper with two dogs, one in a pink skirt and the other in a tuxedo. Next to them stood a big number five.

All of a sudden two more dogs burst into the crowd. This time it was Shelly and Wilma. I didn't even see Paula arrive as I was so busy with barista duties and food prep while directing doggy traffic.

Wilma was a lot younger and her energy was electric as she rustled all the others up. Dogs were going everywhere. She crouched and ran, jumping over Olive who wasn't quick enough to get out of the way and body-slamming into Snowy. They both fell over then started mouth-playing. Legs were thrashing in the air. I noticed Paula placed a package on the counter. I would open it later.

Gidget, Charlie, Olive, Snowy, Hudson, Shelly, Wilma and the token basset Mortimer. What a sight. What a delight! It was a party with an extra serving of birthday craziness.

Taking the coffee orders and passing the food became a challenge while also trying to manage the chaos. Wilma jumped from a stationary position on the floor onto the kitchen bench. She managed to take a big corner bite from the apple and cinnamon cake before being hauled off.

Snowy took out Polly who landed on the floor. Shelly was barking at the kookaburra perched on the fence oblivious to the bedlam. Hudson took every toy out of the toy basket and scattered them all over the lawn refusing to share any. Mortimer pretty much just scoured the floor for food, his ears getting trodden on by Wilma as she flew past. The others just followed each other around and around.

Gidget stood out beautifully with her hot pink bow and Charlie looked handsome in his royal blue one. The birthday duo. The gracious hosts – always fun and hilarious. I was so proud of them. It had only taken a millisecond for Charlie to find his place in my heart right next to Gidget. Both sat alongside Ernie who resided there always, their paw prints scattered all over my heart.

After about half an hour the frenzy started to calm down and we could finally hear ourselves.

Susan repeated her story again. Bruce and Harry had gone out and had a few drinks at the local pub where they played competition darts. Apparently, Harry had got into a tussle with one of his opponents who accused him of cheating and not tallying the scores correctly. Harry wasn't necessarily the fighting type but he was fastidious about darts and not one to drop any slight against his character.

"Do you want to go outside" was what was heard next apparently. So they all trailed outside and Bruce found himself trying to stop an all-out brawl in the carpark. Luckily for all of them there was only one shove and no punches thrown. Harry had been pushed and landed in a yellow rose bush and spent the rest of the night removing thorns from his behind. Unable to move easily and in prickly pain, Harry eventually conceded to lose the game by two points.

Susan had laughed when she told the story but with an undertone of exasperation explaining she was so over living with her husband and his idiot brother as she described him. The only bonus was that the two of them walked the dogs often, took them to the park and wasted hours kicking the footy while the dogs sniffed and pottered around.

We were all unanimous in wanting the dogs to have the best life with plenty of environment enrichment and stimulation. Having extra hands to help gave Susan more time to manage her 'unruly adult kids' as she called them.

Later, when Susan and Finn had left, Paula looked at Polly and then back at me and said, "So has Finn asked you out yet?"

"No. What do you mean?" I said. "We're just friends."

"Hmm," Paula murmured.

"Really, we are. Plus I have only just gotten over William, like two seconds ago. I think I would prefer a date with Mortimer," I answered.

The girls continued to try and convince me he was interested. We had known each other for ages. He was Ernie's vet and now Gidget's and Charlie's. It was only recently we started seeing each other as friends at yoga and now at doggy play dates. It was way too soon for anything more.

Somehow, I got them to drop the conversation and instead got them cleaning up. Soft toys were scattered everywhere, some with their stuffing and squeakers ripped out. The dogs had been having way too much fun!

As I cleaned up, I had to continually step over Gidget who was asleep underfoot. I was thankful that there was some apple and cinnamon cake left for dinner. Having a quiet moment, I opened Paula's package and inside were two beautiful dog collars, one pink and one blue, both with my phone number on them.

Along with that was a silver bracelet that had been engraved with the names Gidget, Charlie and Ernie. All separated by a little love heart. I felt the tears well as I slid it on my wrist and I drew Paula in for a big hug. I was so grateful for my life, my friends and my dogs. What a beautiful gift... what a beautiful friend... what a beautiful day.

As I drifted in and out of sleep on the couch later that night, I noticed the new blue elephant had already lost an appendage. After bingeing another Netflix series with the dogs on either side of me, I realised I had completely missed two calls on my iPhone.

Before I got up to go to bed, still half asleep, I hit voicemail on my phone and listened to the messages.

The first was a gabble of words from Camilla. "Happy birthday, beautiful doggos. So sorry we missed the party. Only flew back in this afternoon from London, a bit jetlagged. Ernest was going to bring Teddy but they spent the afternoon at the emergency vet. A torn ACL, can you believe it? So he's booked in for surgery on Tuesday. Speak tomorrow!"

I winced at yet another ball-chasing injury.

The next message rolled straight on before I could gather my thoughts.

"Happy birthday, Charlie and Gidget. It's me, William. I miss you and love you all. Call me, Grace. We need to talk."

My interest was piqued.

GIDGET

Snuggling near Charlie, I woofed to him, "Wow buddy, that was the best birthday ever. How cool is it living here with us."

"It's great, Gidget" he replied woofingly.

I was the happiest dog ever. This was the best birthday. I was still full of life and vigour at the young age of five. Us goldens really don't even start to settle till after that age.

I sensed Mum was happy again after a dark time. I could always gauge her emotions. They were like vibrations emitting from her. It had been hard trying to cheer her up, sometimes with no luck.

Everything felt lighter and easier, happier and more joyful.

I hope nothing ever changes. I want things to stay exactly as they are now... always and forever... Mum, me and Charlie.

Mum often chanted that nothing stays the same forever.

But I was a dog. I didn't get intrusive what-if thoughts like humans did. I just went along with whatever was happening right now. Void of thinking about the past or worrying about the future, I felt calm and present for whatever arose.

For now, reaching out to touch paws with Charlie, I allowed my third eyelids to close over and drifted off to sleep. I was hoping to dream of my party and relive all the fun again. I think Charlie must have been doing the same as I could feel his body doing little jerks and his paws looked like they were running in his sleep.

My beautiful brother. I love him so much.

Retreating

Grace

It had all happened in an instant. They asked me and I said yes. That was only a week ago.

Fred and Lilly had invited me to go on a yoga retreat. Despite doing a lot of yoga and being quite involved with the studio and teaching the odd class, I had never been to a retreat. I had always thought about going somewhere warm like Bali or maybe at a stretch even India and immersing myself in a retreat, the yoga practice itself, the culinary delights and the culture of the country.

We were leaving early in the morning.

Today, packing to go away was a hard task. Much harder than I anticipated. Especially with Gidget and Charlie at my side acting like ratbags wanting to remove things from my suitcase as soon I put them in there.

Like sister like brother, Charlie loved stealing toilet rolls and running away from me. The paper became strewn down the hallway and often twisted over and around their bodies as they initiated the chase game.

Today, the contents of my makeup bag became strewn down the hallway. Gidget stole a pair of pink underpants and wouldn't give them up when I finally reached her, I tried not to laugh as I picked everything up again and again.

Deciding that I really needed to get on with my to-do list, I declared, "Okay, I'm the human here. I must be able to outsmart them." With that, I walked to the kitchen, smothered two licking mats in peanut butter, lactose-free yoghurt and wet can dog food and placed them on the floor a few feet apart. That fixed that issue... at least for a moment. I guessed I had about ten minutes of peace. I continued packing while listening to the squelching noise of a dog's delight.

This dream had finally come to fruition. I was going to Bali! Having Fred and Lilly by my side made it easier to say yes. They arranged the airfares and accommodation. Fred told me we were staying in lovely villas and we each had our own pool. They overlooked the sea on the east side of Bali a few hours from the airport. It sounded stunning.

They went regularly, so they knew all the local spots well. I particularly wanted to visit a water temple with tiered fountains, gardens and stone sculptures of mythical creatures spouting water into bathing pools. I was told you could swim in the sacred water and then sit in a café with scrumptious cakes and tea while taking in the ambience.

The retreat was at a local resort, which had a beautiful outdoor studio open to the elements with a wooden floor and thatched roof. You could see way out over the sea to all the surrounding areas and even see the active volcano Mount Agung peeking out in the distance through the low coverage of clouds. My insides started to swell with excitement.

Fred's son, Tommy, was going to look after the studio. He knew nothing about yoga and instead had dedicated his life to surfing. He had a small business called The Surf's Up. Teaching everyone how to surf would be his legacy, he always told us.

He wore his long blond hair tied back and was usually found in board shorts, a ripped t-shirt and thongs. He had a few tattoos of surfing-related paraphernalia splattered around his strong physique and wore a black leather chain around his neck with a shark's tooth on it.

The typical surfie.

When he wasn't surfing, he could be found lounging around with his dog, Bert, reading all the surfing magazines he could get his hands on. His beach house had a verandah looking right over the water. Before his full-time surfing life change, he had been CEO of a large corporate entity and travelled the world, with surfing only a side gig. His old career had funded his surf change. He now was gloriously calm and peaceful and totally fulfilled, compared with previously being stressed, anxious and totally unfulfilled. He was living his dream and for that I had an enormous amount of respect for him.

These days he was completely engrossed with surfing and Bert.

Tommy spent a lot of time overseas chasing the waves and Bert would be shuffled to Fred and Lilly's. Bert was a black flat-coated retriever who loved the water and also loved Fred and Lilly, so he had the best life.

Secretly we were all a little worried about leaving Tommy in charge – Lilly mostly as Fred didn't seem to worry about much at all. How would Tommy go running the studio and what would we come back to? But we didn't let that worry stop us from looking forward to the trip.

I had been somewhat perplexed about what would be best for Gidget and Charlie. Should I get someone to come and stay with them or should I send them elsewhere? It really should have been easy but it became a massive dilemma in my head. With the help of Susan, as she was such an expert, I decided to leave them with Camilla. Teddy had recovered from his cruciate leg surgery and had returned to normal walks and activity. He had healed beautifully, Dr Finn told Camilla.

She had assured me Teddy would welcome them and he would love to show them his possum tree up the street. I was really hoping they wouldn't escape out the front door unaccompanied.

I had to stop myself from worrying about all the what-ifs before I had even been shown the emergency exits and asked to fasten my seatbelt. I was much more of a helicopter mum than Camilla which worried me. She had the week off work and I was only gone for five nights. Surely nothing disastrous could happen in that time.

Camilla, used to getting up at all hours, opened the door cheerily at 4.30am when I dropped the dogs off. They both raced in with hardly a goodbye followed by their bags, beds, licking mats, leads, harnesses and all their other must-haves. They almost needed a bigger bag than me. After a big hug from Camilla, I was off to my first retreat. I tucked the worry somewhere deep inside and waved goodbye.

Finn had called me and wished me bon voyage and a safe trip. How nice, I thought. He reassured me that he was there if there were any issues with the dogs and he could help Camilla out if needed. This helped ease my worry as I got back into the car and directed my thoughts to my flight and travel plans to arrive safely at the resort. It was time to think of me and this lovely holiday experience I was about to embark on.

On the way to the airport my thoughts diverted to the voicemail from William. What could he want to talk about? I thought we had said everything we needed to say. It sounded more like he actually had to address something rather than just ask how Charlie was.

I was still irritated that he could just leave him. But Charlie had a great life with us so maybe it worked out for the best. I loved him like my own despite only having had him for a short period of time. I decided to put it out of my mind until my return. Surely it could wait until I got home.

Truthfully, I still felt a little vulnerable around him. As soon as I spoke to him his charming voice could take me to another realm. One where I forgot about reality and his imperfections and imagined he was a prince on a white horse coming to finally take me away and fully commit without any guffs or jealousy.

In hindsight, I admitted to myself he did seem to get somewhat cranky at times. He had been constantly late for our dinners, using work as an excuse, and he did have jealousy issues. Despite all this, I didn't really notice it at the time as his charisma, charm and good looks masked it all. It was not until I had removed myself from the situation and took the rose-coloured glasses off that the raw truth emerged.

I was stronger now, I hoped. But I still felt it best to try and ignore his message for now. I hoped he would not call back. But then if I was really honest with myself there was a part of me that hoped he did.

Bugger, I thought as I was interrupted...

"Welcome to Bali, the island of paradise. Ladies and gentlemen, this is your captain speaking. Please remain seated until we taxi to the gate. Thank you for flying with Bali Airlines."

These words were music to my ears. They sounded so enticing... tantalising in fact. Like the start of a new adventure. We had arrived and I felt fully present for my week-long relaxation and healing journey. I looked over to Fred and Lilly and they smiled. They looked like they had shredded every piece of stress. Not that they carried much but they seemed floppier and happier than usual as they arrived in paradise.

Next was to manoeuvre through the immigration and customs and the madness of the airport. All without getting into trouble with any officials, which was another irrational concern of mine since the Schapelle Corby case. Luckily, I sometimes loved a bit of chaos, drama, heat and disorganisation diffused into my life to help me feel more alive.

This was followed by somewhat of a chaotic drive through the streets of Bali with traffic intermingling in a smooth yet frenzied manner. I noticed a whole family on a single motorbike with the driver checking out his iPhone as they were travelling along at speed. Holding tight to the armrests, the three of us finally arrived at the resort in one piece. We were greeted warmly and accompanied through scantily lit, uneven paths in the dark to our villas.

As I woke the next morning, the sound of the sea crashing below and the view over the sea seduced me. The warmth of the air against my body fully drew me in. I took the biggest stretch and allowed it all to settle on my soul. I was here. I was in Bali love.

I thought of the dogs briefly and then brought myself back to the present moment.

My morning outdoor shower was witnessed by two cows from the paddock adjacent to my villa. They had big cowbells swinging around their necks. After my surprise abated, I was cleansed of the flight and the foreign heat and humidity of the first night. Getting a small bag ready for the day, I enthusiastically headed down the path from last night that looked totally different in daylight to attend our 6am meditation.

This was followed by yoga and breakfast. Each day had something different – singing, group activities, painting, dancing, relaxing walks, delicious meals, pool time, community, comradery and massages. Funnily enough, Gloria from the Pink Peace Festival was at the resort and I finally had the privilege to experience her amazing massage and gong experience.

Over the five days and nights, we followed a fairly regular program and, wherever possible between sessions, I immersed myself in the coolness of the blue pool water. I had always loved the feel of the water against my skin, running through my hair and dripping off my body. It made me feel fresh, calm and rejuvenated in a miraculous way. I was a water baby at heart.

The retreat came with a sense of getting deeply in touch with myself, something I really wanted and needed. Questions were poised for contemplation and pondering. All the intricacies that made me a human, and all the imperfections and insecurities that resided deep, bubbled up to the surface to be dealt with.

This was exactly what the retreat had promised on the brochure. Some of my contemplations and beliefs were discarded and new healthier ones took their place. I noticed a sense of grounding and confidence in myself that became more profound. I was more connected. It was an awe-inspiring experience. A gift from the 'Island of the Gods'.

On the last night, I attended a spectacular fire ceremony where we chanted the Gayatri Mantra 108 times whilst throwing blessed rice into the fire. I wasn't sure I would make it through as droplets of sweat dripped down my face.

Soon after, I was brought back to reality when I casually turned on my phone to check my flight details. A little red number five appeared in the messages app — a confirmation of a dentist appointment, a message that Gidget's dental chews were ready to collect, my auntie wanting to know how the trip was going, Tommy asking for advice about some admin stuff and, lastly, Camilla asking me to call her urgently.

GIDGET

I cuddled up next to Charlie, nudging him so he would move over and give me some more room. I could hear Ernest snoring. It was so loud I couldn't sleep.

I replayed the day in my head. It had been a good one.

We went to the park and met Finn and Morty for a big play. Charlie was a bit naughty. He pushes the boundaries especially if he sees a duck. He goddamn loves those flying honking things. He was a hunter at heart and always had one ear cocked to listen for the honk.

We pottered around in the backyard while Camilla did some gardening. She didn't look like she knew what she was doing. She belted out some tunes as she danced around in between weed pulling so it was entertaining.

Charlie and I helped by eating the long grass, munching away like cows — sans the cowbell. When our tummies were full, we lay down, and I placed my head on Charlie's side and soaked up the sun with an afternoon snooze.

Later in the afternoon, Camilla was putting the bins out and the gate was open just a little bit. This is when Teddy secretly enticed both of us out. We took off full pelt behind Teddy up the street straight to the possum tree. Here we feasted on the little parcels of possum poop lying all over the ground surrounding the tree. So many sniffs! So much fun! Until Camilla and Ernest came madly running up the street. "Back inside NOW!" they yelled in chorus. I didn't understand what the fuss was about as we were a few metres clear of the traffic whizzing past on the main road. As we were dragged by our collars back home, Camilla said, "Your mum would kill me if something happened to either of you." She only calmed down when we were back on the right side of the gate.

After all the shenanigans and tell-offs, Camilla prepared a special doggy dinner. Dinner consisted of our normal dry dog biscuits and added to them we had a hardboiled egg, steamed veggies, a small piece of banana, a dollop of yoghurt and some awesome-smelling sardines. The juice spread over the rest of the plate. I looked at Charlie and lifted my lip just in case he had any sardine-stealing ideas.

After dinner we were all given a large carrot to finish the meal off. It was scrumptious. I licked my lips again and again. I was going to have to have a serious discussion with the chef of my household, Mum, and advise her of my new menu suggestions after this delicious spread.

It was strange being here overnight. We visited often but had never slept over. I was used to Camilla yet I felt somewhat confused as to where Mum was. She spoke of going on a plane to visit a faraway place to find her Zen.

I was just hoping that when she found this Zen she would bring it home with her and hurry it up. I needed my mum with me, always.

Tonight, I hoped I would dream of her. I repeated in my mind the words I heard her say every night: I love you Gidget girl. You and me always.

Slowly my third eyelids closed over and I managed to shut out Ernest's snoring and find some peaceful sleep.

Rogue ducks

GRACE

It was about 7pm. I frantically went to my favourites, chose Camilla and hit the number. My hands shook with fear, not knowing why she wanted me to call so urgently. My mind went through a whole host of what-ifs while I listened to the trill of the phone ringing, praying for her to answer... praying for my Gidget and Charlie to be okay.

"Oh, Grace, I'm so happy it's you. Now try not to panic but there has been an accident." I didn't say anything as I didn't want to delay the information that was about to be spoken. "I am with Finn and we are both at East Emergency & Specialist Centre with Charlie. We were all at the park this afternoon and Charlie was hit by a car."

My heart lunged into my throat and I couldn't speak. My beautiful boy. My perfect, innocent, happy-go-lucky, cheeky man. Gidget's brother. Only five. I felt sick. The tears welled and clouded my eyes, and the rest of my body felt frozen.

Camilla sensed this and kept talking. "He was with us one moment and the next he ran off after a duck. It was taunting him and playing chase for a while until it flew off overhead in the direction of the main road. We could almost see the situation unfolding in slow motion. We started running behind him calling for him but all we heard was a screech followed by a loud cry. When we arrived, he was on his side whimpering. Finn picked him up and carried him to the car, telling him what a good boy he was the whole way. I gathered Gidget, Morty and Teddy. They're all okay but I think they were a little rattled when they saw Charlie in Finn's arms."

I couldn't even speak.

"Grace, are you there?"

"What have the doctors said?" was all I could muster.

"He's been triaged and taken out to the hospital area so we're waiting for some news. They are going to run some bloods, take some x-rays, and give some fluids and initial pain relief while they assess the seriousness of the injuries. I'm so sorry and so scared, Grace, especially after what happened to Daisy all those years ago. Charlie had been so good all week and never left my side, even while chasing balls playing and racing around. It was those bloody ducks. I didn't realise he was such a hunter. I'm so sorry, Grace."

"I can't talk anymore, Camilla, I'm sorry. I'm on a plane first thing tomorrow. Please text me any updates or call if anything drastically changes. Whatever it costs, okay. I have to go now."

I hung up almost before Camilla could say goodbye. I was so angry and scared – a strong mix of both emotions – at her and at the situation. I was trying to see both sides like I generally do, not wanting to blame but to put myself in her shoes and understand it was an accident. But it was far too early to think compassionately. My emotions were running wild and just wanted to be felt first. I was in shock and in this space nothing is rational. I promised myself that I would try and put it into a rational perspective later.

The next twelve hours was a whirlwind of a trip home with turbulent emotions running wildly around my mind. Fred and his calming nature was by my side, holding my hand almost the whole way home. He even accompanied me to the vet hospital soon after we landed.

Gidget was with Finn and in his safe hands. But still I texted him to ask him to keep her on the leash if they went for a walk. He had responded, of course. I had numerous updates via texts from Camilla.

I think she was too scared to call. Charlie's bloods were average and he had broken a couple of ribs, one of his hips and his right leg. The main concern was internal bleeding and they weren't yet able to advise the severity. He wasn't stable but he was still alive.

As I walked into the hospital all I could think was that I had to call William. He would think I was calling to return his recent call and not be prepared for this bad news. But are we ever prepared for this type of phone call?

GIDGET

Charlie, are you okay? Wake up boy. What happened? Why are you so quiet? You love sitting next to the window in the car with the wind swishing your ears around.

Charlie, my brother, woof to me, please.

He was in the front seat on Finn's lap. I couldn't see him fully but he looked sad and a little lifeless. Why did he get the front seat? Was he playing a new game?

I didn't understand why we raced back to the car so quickly and why Charlie was being carried. He loved to run back to the car and wait for his treat before he hopped in. What was going on?

Next, I was sitting in the car at some strange place with a big red sign that had a picture of a dog on it. I couldn't read the words.

I was still with Morty and Teddy and it seemed like ages before Finn came back to the car and drove us to his house. Why are we here? Where is Charlie? I'm still confused. We were given a quick dinner and Finn left again. What... no couch snuggle time?

It had been a very confusing week. Where was Mum? Why had she left me? I didn't think she would ever leave me. Mum Suzy hadn't prepared me to be left alone without Mum. It was terrifying.

And now Charlie had gone as well. I barked for a bit but that seemed futile. So, I laid my head down on my paws on the soft bed. I huddled in next to Morty and his big ears and closed my eyes. I was feeling sad. I finally fell asleep dreaming of Charlie and me tussling and playing tug-of-war. I hoped we would get to do that again very soon.

Phone calls

Grace

Finally, after a few hours, they brought Charlie into the consult room to see me. It was different to the normal consult room, though, as it had a couch and more of a relaxed palliative feel. Fred had left a while back on my insistence that I was capable of being by myself – independent as always.

They offered me a coffee or a tea while I waited, but I declined. The girls on reception were lovely but they had this look that spoke volumes about how sorry they felt for me. They were talking softly, slowly and with care like you might talk to an old sick person. I had always been good at reading people, but on this occasion I wish I wasn't. This made me very nervous.

Two nurses carried Charlie in, his legs dangling towards the floor with his IV stand rolling along on wheels behind him. They placed him on a large fluffy purple rug on the floor in front of me. He was awake, his eyes were flickering but barely moving otherwise. He had various shaved bits, a catheter, some pink bandages with images of bones on them and dried blood spotted around his body.

I slid off the couch onto the floor and lifted his head so it rested in my lap. I looked into his eyes while telling him he was a good boy... the best boy. His ears pricked up a tiny bit at the sound of my voice, his mum's voice. My heart fluttered. I started patting him, swirling my fingers around the soft, beautiful fur on his head, ears and neck. As the door opened, I kept patting him.

"Hello, Grace, I'm Dr Edward Bernard and I have been looking after Charlie. I'm very sorry for the difficult time you have been going through, especially on the back end of your week abroad." Again, I seemed to have frozen so Dr Bernard continued. "We have done all we can for him right now but Charlie is not responding quite how we would have liked." He continued with a whole lot of medical guff that I tried to understand. He told me all the bones he had broken and discussed his blood results and his imaging. He explained how internal bleeding worked but it all just ended up like mush in my brain. I really wished Finn was here with me to interpret.

What I focused on though was his last statement. "Charlie has had a really traumatic injury and we need to wait a bit longer to see how his body responds to the treatment and if he improves. Sadly, I would prepare yourself for the worst just in case. We will know more tomorrow once we see how he goes overnight. He is getting the best care and we will do all that we can. We will keep you updated with any changes."

I was in shock and just said, "Okay, thank you." Questions swirled around in my head but my mouth couldn't voice them. He placed his hand on my shoulder as he opened the door to leave. The nurse returned and said, "Please feel free to stay a little longer but we should take Charlie back to hospital soon so we can monitor him and do further observations and testing. It may be a good idea to go home and get some rest."

I called Finn and asked him to come and pick me up. I wasn't as capable as I had initially thought. I nearly called Camilla but I felt

Finn would have more medical prowess and know the right things to say to help me get through this.

I couldn't do a lot to help Charlie here in the waiting room. I desperately wanted to get home to see Gidget and give her the biggest squish. I wanted to shower and be fresh for when the hospital called me back in to see Charlie again and give me more information.

It wasn't easy to leave Charlie and my irrational thoughts made me feel like I was abandoning him. My rational ones reassured me he needed to be cared for by the nurses and doctors in the hospital. Finn backed up my rational thoughts and held my arm as I stood up. He had spoken with Dr Bernard and was able to explain in layman's terms more about what was happening. The nurses said goodbye as he ushered me gently out of the room towards the car.

Finn turned off the car ignition as his car came to a stop in my driveway. He was truly a beautiful person and a good friend. "Finn, thank you so much," I murmured, "but I think I need to be on my own to call William and explain the situation. So I will speak to you later."

"Yes, certainly. Sorry, I didn't think. Just know I'm here if you need me for support or free vet advice, whatever you need. Morty is too."

Opening the door I yelled, "Gidget, my beautiful girl. It's me!" Gidget is normally so excited to see me yet on this occasion I was the one who overdid the enthusiasm despite my fatigue and overwhelming emotional depletion. It was fabulous to step inside, to be home and have her safe by my side.

I sat with her and let her jump all over me completely covering me in white fur. She was excited but seemed a little skittish. It was that animal empath part of me coming out that enabled me to tell she wasn't herself. The last week must have been stressful and no doubt she was wondering where Charlie was. Plus, I probably smelled of vet hospital, cats, dogs, all sorts of animals and animal paraphernalia. I got a total sniff down.

I allowed the water to run down my back as I stood in the shower. I placed my hands on the wall in front of me, dropped my head down and allowed the tears to flow. I was momentarily inconsolable.

Dogs were very sensitive creatures and Gidget had been through enough in the last week. I could see her sitting on the bathmat and licking the shower screen while looking at me sideways displaying the whites of her eyes. She was normally a little clingy but this was next level. Like Velcro attached to me.

I didn't want to upset Gidget with my emotional display so I pulled myself together.

It had to be done!

I was sitting on the edge of the bed, wrapped in a towel, feeling fresh and clean yet still shattered, hair wet and freshly brushed when I worked up the courage to dial his number.

The anxiety in my chest intensified with each ring that didn't get answered. He would hate me. On the fifth ring when I was nearly about to chicken out and hang up, I heard his familiar charismatic voice. "Hello Grace, I am so glad you called. What took you so long? There is so much I want to talk to you about."

"Hi Will, I..."

He interrupted me and kept talking. I didn't have the energy to stop him or maybe I just wanted to delay the inevitable. "I'll cut to the chase. I've been here for a while now and I still keep thinking of you, thinking of us, and I wondered..."

That was it. I had to stop him. This was not the time to discuss this.

"Will!" I interrupted.

"Yes Grace?"

"There is something I have to tell you. Please just let me get it all out."

"Sure, go ahead," he said, a little abruptly for my liking.

After explaining the whole situation in detail, I felt deflated, sad, nostalgic and confused. I even exhaled loudly over the phone.

"Oh Grace, that's so sad," he replied. "I wish I was there with you to help." He seemed to be more focused on my feelings rather than how Charlie was going.

Maybe Charlie was a bit out of sight, out of mind. Of course, he had shown compassion and concern but he didn't feel the situation as deeply as me and seemed to be just surfing around the shallows. Not that it should have surprised me when I thought back to him leaving Charlie with me without much of a second thought other than a pat as he flew out the door. Plus, he had initially decided to go to Paris without considering Charlie's needs in the first place.

Despite the seriousness of Charlie's situation, he returned to talking about me and him. "So, as I was saying, I have been missing you terribly and I think we made a big mistake not fighting harder for our relationship. Things have changed and I have another promotion approaching, one that will allow me to choose whether to stay in Paris or return to Adelaide."

This all felt a bit inappropriate considering what I was dealing with. I twirled Gidget's ears while I thought about how to respond. His voice and his desire for us to be together awoke something in me that yearned to be with him. Yet, my intuition was warning me quietly to stay away. There was an inner battle brewing. But all I cared about right now was Charlie. The rest could wait.

"Look, William, to be perfectly honest I can't really think about us right now. I have just returned from Bali. I have Charlie and his wellbeing to think about. I'm not sure he is even going to make it through the night."

"Of course, of course," he said. "How selfish of me. Let me leave you with those thoughts. I send all my love to you and Charlie and ask you to keep me updated on his progress. I must go to a meeting now so I'll speak to you soon."

And with that reply, he was gone. Was I exaggerating or imagining his abruptness or was I just tired? I felt an inner prickle at his tone. Clearly, he was being selfish. I was confused and needed reinforcements.

Within twenty minutes, Camilla was at my door with a bottle of bubbly and reached out for a big hug. Teddy ran straight past her almost knocking Gidget over as they flew out the back door tussling together. During Camilla's embrace, I scanned internally to see how I felt. I had definitely been angry when she called me in Bali. Now, I just felt loved and supported and very thankful for my dear friend. It was an accident, of course.

My mind continued to console me that she would never do anything to hurt me or the dogs, and I know she would have been extra careful knowing my helicopter mum ways.

Plus, Finn was there when it happened. He was even more responsible than the both of us put together. It really was just a tragic accident. Once my mind had rapidly processed all of this, swishing it around like soup in a Mixmaster, I knew we were okay. I drew her towards me for an extra-long stronger hug. I melted into it as I often did.

It was late when I received the call. The vibration of my wrist woke me. Camilla was asleep beside me. The bottle of champagne sat empty on the table. The dogs were sound asleep cuddled together in the same bed. Gidget lay with her four paws in the air and her ear flopped over Teddy's right eye. What a sight.

A late-night call was never good news. This one was no different.

I didn't wake anyone up. I just laid back down and curled into a foetal position, trying to pretend that nothing had changed. Then the tears came. I eventually fell into a pre-sleep state remembering Charlie. I thought of his love and his antics and the simple things like sitting in the park with him on a warm, sunny day enjoying the moment. If only. Bye my beautiful boy I mouthed as I dozed off.

GIDGET

Oh, Mum, you came back. I thought I would never see you again. I didn't think I could bounce this high with excitement. Oh, I feel a zoomie coming on. Couch parkour here we go! I thought you abandoned me. Here are some extra woofs and licks.

Did you know how worried I was? I learnt to whimper, you know. Teddy said I was being pathetic and kept telling me to be quiet. Charlie told me not to worry and that he was suppressing his whimpers as he didn't want to be laughed at. He was, after all, a macho boy dog.

He asked me to whimper for us both. Teddy was opposed to it but my sensitive soul couldn't resist. So much doggy peer pressure.

Every night when I went to bed I bowed my head and placed my paws over my nose as I said my prayers for your safe return. Camilla told me you would be back and she counted down the sleeps for me.

Ernest played with me a lot and took me (on the lead) to the infamous possum tree often, except the once when we visited on our own.

Teddy said that distraction was a good technique to quell sadness. But I learnt that only works for a while. At some stage, those furry feelings need to be dealt with as they can only be hidden for so long. Why would my mum go away or want to go anywhere without me? That I did not understand.

I will always remember this as being the time you went away and left me. I hope I don't suffer doggy stress from this experience. Promise me, Mum, you won't do that to me again. Promise? Lick, lick, lick.

Mum Suzy never explained this.

Morty told me at the park that often it's in the bad experiences that we learn the most and build inner strength and resilience. We grow, we mature, we build wisdom. He must have been picking up on Finn's insight.

For a millisecond, all I thought about during Morty's deep and meaningful was that it was bad luck you couldn't build longer legs so your ears don't drag on the floor. Using humour to try and deflect the situation briefly.

To top it all off, what I really don't understand is why Charlie isn't here and why he was acting so strange in the car. One minute he was chasing the ducks telling me to stay still as they were unpredictable and it could be dangerous. Like a big older brother. The next minute he was belly up being carried across the oval to the car. What the... woof!?

Mum, please keep patting me and help me understand. More than anything though I am just exceeding woofingly happy you are home.

I learnt from this experience that I never wanted to be away from my mum but if I had to I could cope.

Oh, and that Camilla had a secret.

The wake

GRACE

I took a deep breath and wiped my eyes before answering the door. In came Polly, Susan and Paula. I wondered if they met in the front yard before coming inside, fearing an awkward, sad and uncomfortable meeting. Their entourage of dogs followed, running madly down the hallway as usual, knowing no different. Olive, Snowy, Hudson, Shelly and Wilma, who was looking so much bigger now, immediately filled some of the emptiness. I felt sad, raw, shocked and very vulnerable. When I saw all their furry faces and those of my friends my spirits lifted slightly. I could breathe a little easier. I wasn't alone.

I had to make an appointment with Stephanie as I knew I was going to need help to move through this grief.

Camilla, Teddy, Finn and Morty arrived soon after. I was melting into the hugs and being propped up by having everyone together. Ernest had stayed at home. Camilla said he was stiff and sore from cycling, his latest love. "Lycra everywhere," she commented. I noted I hadn't seen a lot of him lately.

"Thank you all for coming today. We are here to celebrate Charlie's short but joyful life..." As I continued with my short eulogy, I was bereft and struggled to speak without crying. Sadness was echoed on the faces of everyone around me.

"Let's raise our glasses to having had such a gorgeous furry man in our lives. To Charlie. My boy, I will always love you. Rest now, my perfect boy, and run through the lush fields of Rainbow Bridge with your renewed strength, vigour and life. Look for Ernie, he will welcome you with open paws."

Charlie's ashes sat on the kitchen bench in a large royal blue urn with silver pawprints etched around the lid. Next to it sat magnificent purple and pink hydrangeas arranged in a big glass vase with a purple bow. From Polly of course. She had meticulously grown them herself.

Flowers were Polly's pride and joy. Her backyard in summer was almost like a mini Italian Riviera with open beach umbrellas in all sorts of patterns and colours set up in a row to protect her precious blooms from the sun. Just like little people sunbathing. She was always so thoughtful and on point with her gifts. Along with the flowers came a card I would read later. I needed to contain the tears for now.

The hydrangeas sat next to the most scrumptious cake. Susan said it was a pistachio and cardamon cake with whipped white chocolate ganache. Her baking prowess always exceeded our expectations. I didn't have any appetite whatsoever and couldn't remember the last time I ate.

Along with the cake came more stories of Bruce and Harry and the latest incident involving a go-kart they were building. They took it to the track to race it for the first time and the engine blew up right in front of them. Bruce, who was driving, was lucky to escape with only a minor burn injury on his forearm but a much more bruised ego.

She was forever telling us stories about the two numbskulls as she called them, and it really did lighten the mood today for a micro-moment. I welcomed the distraction. A moment of normal life amongst this sad tragedy. But I thought I sensed something behind her humorous charade that I couldn't quite recognise.

A memorial altar was materialising. Paula had placed a lovely silver photo frame with the most beautiful picture of Charlie and all his friends. What a wonderful memory. At the bottom of the frame was a small plaque with the inscription 'Charlie, the best boy'.

The generosity, the thought, the love. These people were my tribe, the ones who truly understood how I felt about Charlie, and they were here to share in the memories, the love and the grief.

Camilla opened her bag before the eulogy and pulled out six bottles of French champagne. I laughed. It was so typical of Camilla to turn a morning tea into another opportunity for a champagne. She always brought the party to any occasion and lifted the sadness of even this traumatic event. Somewhat.

Finn left his gift until last. After the champagne glasses were filled, the cake was cut and the eulogy read, he handed me a heavy box. I would have broken a toe or a paw if I dropped it. I looked at him before opening it.

Inside the box there was something covered in butchers paper. A note in pink texta on the paper read, "With love, Love Stones" with a love heart drawn underneath. Inside was a pale grey outdoor memorial river stone with a love heart and the name Charlie etched into it.

I burst into tears again and with that, Finn scooped me up in a big hug, a hug that felt more intimate than any others before. Maybe I just imagined it. I was pretty vulnerable, raw and open right now.

Gidget continually checked in with me. She would saunter up and do a little touch on my leg with her wet nose. A pat on her head and then she was off again to entertain her friends. She was a little more subdued than normal, but it was so subtle that only I would have noticed.

It was a lovely day honouring Charlie. As it slowly came to an organic finish, I was dreading them all leaving and being left alone with my thoughts, my memories and my emotions. I was wondering if I had chocolate in the cupboard. At times like these, a little comfort eating often helped. Healthy, probably not... soothing, yes.

"I'm not feeling that well. I think I'm going to head home," said Camilla. "Teddy, are you ready?" She was the first one to go, leaving two unopened bottles of bubbly in the fridge. "For next time," she said. Camilla was followed closely by Polly, Susan, Paula and their goldens. They all gave big hugs as they bid farewell.

Finn stood with me while everyone got themselves organised and departed, and then he turned to face me and took both of my hands in his.

He paused and looked down for a moment, lost in his own thoughts, then said, "Grace, my dear friend, I am so sorry about Charlie. He truly was a beautiful soul. You are strong and I know you will get through this in your own time. Honour your grief and share it only with people who truly understand the loss of a dog. The human–animal bond is stronger than most people realise. Life is a journey, and to truly and fully live and love means we experience loss and grief. The deeper the love, the stronger the grief. That is a life lived to the full."

He bent down and kissed me on both cheeks like an Italian farewell. I had always liked that cultural ritual.

"Today was a lovely farewell, Grace. Thank you for including Morty and me. Please know I am always here for you and you can call me anytime."

With that, Morty followed Finn out the door with his ears dragging behind him.

I finally had a moment to myself. Gidget was almost in my lap as I sat on the floor in the middle of the kitchen with a cup of tea next to Charlie's urn. What a rollercoaster the last few days had been. I looked into Gidget's eyes.

She looked sad, but then I wondered if golden retrievers always looked a little sad. She was exuberant all day with her little furry friends but would she feel something was missing? Charlie was missing and she would easily have picked up on my emotions as dogs are very astute and intuitive.

Amy and I had a conversation about this once. She had told me that despite not really knowing how dogs process grief, we do know they are capable of great love, so why wouldn't they also know grief. The difference is they don't get carried away by a myriad of thoughts that complicate the feelings and fixate and obsess on them. They don't run and hide and distract themselves with negative habits or blame themselves.

They most likely feel it and move on. It's more honest and pure. But grief can still create a behaviour issue for some dogs. One dog she knew whose mate died spent three months under the chair in the bedroom and only came out for dinner and toilet breaks. She explained others develop behavioural issues like anxiety, fear, reactivity and aggression, or they forget their toilet training or become clingy. Dogs are creatures of habit and routine so when things are upended, they can feel anxiety which can lead to a host of other issues. Others act completely unperturbed.

"Gidget, I promise you I will be there for you. I will observe your behaviour closely and assess any changes. If I'm worried about anything, we'll go and see Amy. I know you love Amy. I promise you that Charlie loved you with everything he had. He will be watching down over you as you journey through the rest of your sweet, long life. He would want you to live an extra special life as if you were living it for the both of you. Can you do that for Charlie?"

Gidget tilted her head as I continued.

"Gidget, I am so sorry you were not able to see Charlie one last time. I'm sorry if you feel confused. I am just so sorry."

I felt my tears welling and droplets falling into Gidget's thick coat as I pulled her in closely for a hug.

I pulled Polly's card out of my pocket and its simple message warmed me: "Dear Grace and Gidget, I love you both. Charlie loved you both. He is always in your heart. Just be still and quiet and you will see he is right there. You will feel his love. Love always, Polly x"

What a day. As I lay in bed drifting off to sleep, I could sense Ernie and Charlie curled up together woofing about me and getting to know each other. They had each other now and the important role of looking down over us and protecting us. They were family now.

As I drifted further towards sleep, a couple of other thoughts crossed briefly through my mind. Why hadn't I seen Ernest? And why didn't Camilla feel well? I was so deep in thought that I didn't hear the knock at the door.

GIDGET

Woof... woof... someone is at the door. Hey, it could be Charlie. "Mum, wake up!" I woofed.

Has he been locked outside? Where is he? He always cuddled up on the bed next to me and often interrupted my sleep. He liked to stick one of his legs out of his bed and sometimes kicked me in the face, or he would do his sleep upside downies and let out a stinker. I don't like being apart from my best friend, my brother.

I had heard my other doggy friends at the dog park talk about this happening. How one day their best friend just kind of disappeared. They were never told why and left to deal with a mass of confusion. They explained how they would look to their mums with questioning eyes but often no explanation was forthwith. Or it came out as a long ramble in human words that they didn't understand and couldn't interpret into woof.

Mum Suzy never mentioned this. She did elude that there were many lessons to be learnt when you live with humans and maybe this was one of them. I had to trust in her and in her words.

With all this running around my furry brain, I lay my head to rest on my pink floofy bed. I closed my eyes and said a little prayer that Charlie would come home soon. Wherever you are, I love you, Charlie. I miss you, my best friend.

♡ 159 ♡

The epiphany

GRACE

It was a bit of a long story with William. He arrived at my house late at night the day of Charlie's wake but I didn't hear his knock as I had been drifting off to sleep.

When he returned the following day, I invited him in. He was angry and rude about making the effort to come over to support me through the loss of Charlie and then I didn't answer the door. Quickly his mood changed and he was unrelenting on how we should be together.

He went on for ages, flipping from angry to loving and back again.

His charm and persistence didn't pay off this time. My rose-coloured glasses had slid off and I could clearly see his moods jumping between nice and nasty, loving and dismissive. Maybe his stressful new role had drawn out a side of him that had been dormant and buried previously. Maybe he was burnt out. Often, it's only when someone is pressured that their true self is revealed.

As I sat and listened to him it dawned on me that I had been much happier while he had been away. There were no fancy dinners and promises of lavish trips to Paris but there were no moments when I felt dismissed, left out or a low priority. I felt relieved I no longer had to defend myself for talking to my male friends.

That's when it clicked. That's when I knew. This epiphany changed things; it changed me.

He reminded me a little of Pierce, to be honest. Had I been repeating the same relationship with someone different? Stephanie told me it's not uncommon for this to happen. Until we learn the lesson, we will keep repeating the same mistakes. Until that time, the universe keeps gifting you the same predicament so you have another opportunity to wake up to it, learn from it and grow.

Once we learn the lesson we evolve and are no longer triggered by those things. Am I growing? I must be a late bloomer. I was in my fifties and I would have thought I had learnt all my lessons by now. Not so.

Both these two relationships were big turning points in my life.

I had surprised myself with how confident I sounded when I said to him, "William, I appreciate your good intentions to come back for Charlie's wake. I really do. But it's over between us. Really over. But thank you for your part in my journey. I am blessed that you left me with Charlie for the short time we had together."

Taking a breath, he had stared at me in shock.

We went back and forth a little more until Camilla knocked at the door to come and collect me for yoga. I was finally able to escape his clutches and leave feeling freer than I had in some time. I waved goodbye as we drove away. I left him standing on my front lawn looking perplexed with shoulders hunched.

Sometimes you never know how far you have come until you look back and reflect on what has happened – the good and the not so good – and your resilience levels, your strength, your inner peace and your ability to live in the present moment fully and happily.

This was one of those magical nights. Life is not how I thought it would be a few years back. But other than losing Charlie, I felt better, more myself, more powerful and more fulfilled. I was full of gratitude for a life well lived and amazing friends who really got me.

Gidget

"Hi William," I woofed while doing some little jumps. He gave my head a quick tussle but didn't seem that interested in me. I skulked away back to my bed to keep an eye on what was going on.

I wonder what he is doing here? Maybe he is looking for Charlie too.

I was mystified by the comings and goings of humans and the mix of disagreements, seriousness, laughter and tears they experienced. It was like a rainbow of emotions soiling their auras and disrupting their peace.

I kept close to Mum so she knew I was there with a soft head to pat if she needed. Although it looked like she had everything under control.

I couldn't have been happier when Camilla arrived to collect Mum.

I sat at the front window as I watched them leave. This is where I sat every time she left the house, keeping guard and waiting eagerly for her return home.

I noticed Will standing on the lawn for some time after Mum left, his head lowered towards the ground. I closed my eyes for a daytime nap, one of my favourite things to do. When I awoke, Will had left and my view out the window to wait for Mum was clear once again.

Romance in the air

GRACE

Finn was the best vet in town. He had just finished building a purpose-built vet hospital that would see his business grow and expand. He had been pretty busy finding new staff and equipment to fill the hospital. He was an altruistic soul living his passion project.

The community followed along on his social pages and Princess Park Vet was soon to be Princess Vet Hospital, newly renamed to represent the feel of the big hospital rather than the small practice.

He was so committed to his clients, his staff, all the animals and all my friends. He had been helping Paula recently as she traversed a tricky time with poor Shelly having been diagnosed with numerous malignant mast cell tumours.

He had been so busy but we always managed to make time to catch up and hang out together.

It was soon after the William fiasco that voila, along came the transformation of Finn's friendship into a relationship. He was completely different to William or Pierce. And the even bigger difference is that I felt completely different about myself around him.

It was one night that he and Paula came over for dinner that things changed. I had cooked a red curry – my favourite – and boiled a big bowl of rice. I didn't like cooking but on occasion it was fun, and cooking a curry for good friends was one of these times.

Once we had devoured the curry we sat talking about all things dogs. As usual, my conversations seem to revolve around dogs. It was getting late when Paula announced she was leaving as Shelly had an early vet specialist appointment tomorrow. She kissed us both on the cheeks and I walked her to the door to bid her farewell and good luck for her appointment tomorrow. I could only imagine how hard it was for her. If it were Gidget... I didn't even want to think about it.

"Grace, could I stay for a cup of coffee?" Finn asked, still glued to the spot on the couch.

"Sure, that would be great. Let me put the machine on," I replied. This is unusual, I thought, as normally he leaves early too with having a big busy hospital to run. He looked uneasy. His body language was different and he seemed nervous with one leg bouncing up and down on the spot.

I made the coffee – decaf for me or I would never sleep and double espresso for him. Clearly he had no problem sleeping. I carried them into the lounge placing the blue mug in front of him and my hot pink one next to it. I also brought in some almond bread and hazelnut chocolate.

I made myself comfortable on the couch next to him and we started chatting about nothing that interesting until he began sharing information about the challenges around his divorce.

I shared my insights from my experience with Will and the epiphanies that had arisen during that time. It was good to discuss them again, knowing I had made the right decision.

It was just an interesting conversation, sharing life experiences with a friend. Being a yoga participant, it didn't surprise me that he would be interested in contemplating and questioning relationships and life in general. I love a good D&M and this was a great basis for one.

"Grace, can you see yourself in another serious relationship?" he asked with a twitch in one of his eyes.

"I'm not sure. I was only thinking about that the other day. I am in a good place now. I know that a good relationship adds such value to your life, but I would be scared though. I would have to take it slow, I suppose," I replied.

"How about you?" I broached.

"Well, that's what I want to talk to you about. Would it be too much if I asked you to dinner?" he asked nervously, stumbling over his words as he wriggled around in his seat.

It was starting to make sense where he was leading the conversation. It kind of surprised me at first but then my mind started to piece the jigsaw together and I wondered why I hadn't seen it before.

"Finn, do you have feelings for me?" I asked. It came out quickly yet softly as I reached out for his hand, hoping to alleviate his nervousness.

"I do. I didn't say anything sooner as you were with William and I didn't want to ruin our friendship." He stopped and looked down, fidgeting while squeezing my hand.

"I would love to go to dinner with you," I responded quickly, almost automatically. And in that moment, I realised I did want to go to dinner with him – and in more than just a friend's way.

After another coffee, he opened up a little more and explained that he'd had feelings for me for a while but was too nervous to say anything. I found this hard to believe as he came across as a confident, successful businessman. But understanding matters of the heart is always complex and showing vulnerability is never easy.

He took my hand as I walked him to the door and any doubts I may have had were dismissed when I felt a flutter in my belly, something I hadn't felt for a long time. The feelings were mutual. I squeezed his hand to indicate my mutual affection.

For a long time, we were just friends or so I thought. My mind was clouded in William charm and I didn't see past that for a long while. When I was able to see more clearly, he was crystal clear in my vision right in front of me. He knew now was the right time to ask me out.

At the door, Finn said, "How about dinner on Friday night? I can pick you up and we'll go to a nice restaurant, but just us this time, no dogs. Morty can hang with Gidget if that's okay with you."

"That would be lovely," I said.

And with that he leant down towards me. I went to kiss him on the cheek but instead, he gave me the most beautiful soft kiss on the lips. My knees buckled.

The next few weeks were a bit of a whirlwind. We just clicked. Everything was wonderful — the long getting to know each other conversations, the romantic dinners, the delicious dog walks holding hands, the slow gentle kisses, the tight hugs.

Being with him was different to anything I had known before. There was a kind of enchanting comfortableness and a sense of safety, of peacefulness, of trust, of being myself, of being seen, of being heard, and of melting inwards instead of holding back with an inner protection. Opening up to being vulnerable and loved, and to hope and possibilities, just felt right with Finn. And not forgetting there was a whole lot of chemistry. He was hot! And his sidekick Morty was A for Adorable.

I was so ready for this new chapter bonding with Finn, Morty and Gidget and daydreaming about building our little family.

I was falling, for sure.

Gidget

Mum had been so happy lately. I wondered if it had anything to do with Finn as he seemed to be knocking on our door a lot more lately. And there seemed to be more touching and kissing.

Morty was always attached to Finn which was excellent as we were best friends now. We did so much together over the years but recently I saw a lot more of him. His ears still always get in the way. I would often step on one and he would let out a wince, but we were still best friends despite this.

Finn and Mum seemed very happy and their aura was peaceful and loving. I sensed a familiarity. It was how I had felt around Charlie. I think it was love.

I basked in the memories and the way Mum was feeling. Life sure was beautiful.

Happy tenth birthday

GRACE

"Happy birthday, Gidget!" It was Gidget's tenth birthday. Life was flying by.

The usual crew arrived to celebrate her birthday and simultaneously commemorate Charlie's life. He was never forgotten. Polly, Paula, Susan and their goldens arrived with big smiles and bags full of presents for Gidget. No doubt more soft toys that she could dismember in her own time.

Fred and Lilly brought along Tommy who looked even more tranquil than usual. I wondered secretly if he'd had a little chemical help to be so chill. Bert, always friendly and a clone of Tommy's relaxed mood, tagged along too.

Finn arrived with Morty who crossed the doorstep stepping on his ears. I had noticed he had slowed down a lot in the last few months. He was nearly fifteen now, which was old for a dog with such a long body and short legs.

Finn reached for my hand, leaned down and gave me of one his beautiful kisses. I melted.

Gidget was all done up and looking pretty with her hot pink bow wrapped around her collar. She jumped all over the arrivals as if to remind them it was her birthday. She still had spunk despite her age. Some might say she was a little crazy still, which was obviously part of her DNA. I kept wondering when she would calm down.

So much had changed in the last few years, I reflected, as Camilla filled my champagne glass.

"How are things with you, my beautiful friend? I asked as I gave her a big hug. I was always interested in her life's goings-on.

"Everything is wonderful. It's been hard the last few years since Ernest left but Freddy is turning four soon. It was weird giving up being a flight attendant but absolutely the right decision. I love being a mum," she said.

"And what about Antonio? Still going strong?" I enquired nosily. I loved Antonio. He made the best weak soy lattes.

"Yes, he is amazing. It's been nearly twelve months now. He loves Freddy and Teddy, and we love working together to make Penelope's the best café in the neighbourhood. We have added lots of gluten-free treats and books on loan for our hip clientele," she gushed.

"Well, I think motherhood suits you, just like all the beautiful, elegant black dresses you used to wear to parties," I said smiling.

Susan approached as Camilla turned to pick up a nagging Freddy before Teddy could get to him. He was covered in chocolate and tugging at her skirt.

"Hi Susan, it's so good to see you. How are you? I asked, waiting to hear a story. She always had a story to tell and usually it was pretty funny.

"I'm pretty good considering," she replied. "You know that Bruce and I are separated now? It was the final straw when I came home one day and he had driven our Mercedes through the front fence. It smashed through the loungeroom wall and we could even see the TV inside from the footpath. The car bonnet was completely crunched up like a closed piano accordion. His antics had been funny for so long, but I wasn't happy and I decided enough was enough."

"Ooh, that's brave. That must be tough for you,"

"Well, I think I had been hiding my true feelings for a long time just to keep the peace. I may have been using humour or sarcasm as a way of not dealing with the obvious," she said. "I feel kind of relieved, relaxed, happy and invigorated now. I'm not constantly on edge. Plus, I love having the dogs on the bed every night, something Bruce never let me do. Life's pretty good, Grace."

Polly approached the two of us as Susan excused herself to go to the bathroom. "Menopause," she said chuckling as she left. "I'm in there all the time."

"Oh, Polly, it's so good to see you. How's the plant business?" I asked.

"Well, I have expanded and I'm growing all sorts of different flowers now, even peonies and tulips. I also host community garden events and have been receiving lots of accolades. I recently won the 'Garden of the Month' award. Lovely Olive potters around helping me in the garden and occasionally chewing up the odd gardening glove. It's bliss." she said.

"Wow, that's amazing. Congratulations. How is Olive with her noise phobias?" I asked.

"Well, interestingly, she has got much better being out of the city. I bought her a pair of noise-cancelling headphones which work like a treat, so much so that on occasion I borrow them when the world gets too noisy," she said laughing.

Paula turns up and joins in the conversation.

"Hi!" we both chant, exchanging hugs.

"How is Shelly going with her mast cell tumours?" I ask.

"To date, she has had four removed and three lymph nodes to go along with them. One from her flank, one on the top of her head, one under her tail and one that took a few toes in surgery. It's been very stressful. As soon as they operate to remove one, another seems to pop up in its place."

Apparently, mast cells can appear as a lump in any size or form. They follow their own rules and can be small or large, hard or fatty, raised or flat. They are masters of disguise. They can be removed and pop up again in the same spot. It depends on whether they are high grade or low grade and a few other medical criteria whether you need chemotherapy.

"That's terrible. So is she doing okay now?" I asked quietly.

"All Shelly's have been low grade except the last one. Now she is on a round of chemotherapy, poor girl, and having a second dog has made this more difficult. They can't share food bowls or water bowls. All the poo must be picked up so as not to be eaten. I have to ensure Wilma doesn't ingest any of the chemotherapy waste or toxins for a week after her treatment.

"Well, I know she is in good hands being looked after by you. If there is anything we can do to help just let us know."

"You can thank Finn for helping me. Let's just enjoy Gidget's special day," she said.

"I can absolutely do that," I replied, turning to check that everyone had a full glass and that the dogs were behaving themselves. They weren't of course!

"Let's toast to Gidget turning ten," I said. "And to Charlie and all the changes that have happened since he passed," I continued.

"What changes? Nothing has changed!" Camilla yelled out, a little unsteady on her feet.

"Only a few small things," Susan chimed in.

"Nothing really," Paula chuckled.

"But a few things have blossomed since then." Polly laughed, thinking she was so funny.

"Life is an amazing journey and every moment is one to be cherished," Fred added gracefully as he reached for Lilly's hand.

"Only for the better, my gorgeous Gracey girl!" Finn said. Always the quiet charmer. Everyone loved him. They truly thought he was wonderful but then how could you not? If someone loves animals that much, they must be an outstanding person.

"You are all hilarious!" I shouted, followed by "Watch out!" Before I knew it, Gidget had jumped up on the bench and tipped the bottle of champers over onto its side. It was flowing down from the countertop towards the floor like a champagne fountain. Snowy and Hudson were on the other side looking like university kids tipping their heads upside down to take the shots.

"Gidget, surely you must be all grown up by now," I said, remembering I had said this on many occasions before. I was assured goldens normally grew up by the time they were five. Even Finn reiterated that, but no such luck in this family.

With that, we all sang happy birthday. Olive was the first dog to join in with her barking which enticed the rest to woof along. My Apple watch sent a notification saying 'loud environment'. I was used to that; it happened all the time.

Gidget

Mum, I'm going to rest my tired body. It's been a big birthday day. Thank you for the pink cupcakes and the chewy pigs ears and the bowl of vanilla ice cream. What doggy delicacies. I feel we should incorporate these into my daily diet.

I particularly liked the game we played with the treats hidden under the sports field markers in the driveway, and the go find it game we played on the back lawn. The doggy pool in the front yard with the colourful balls was a hit and more so the dunking for apple pieces.

What amazing fun.

You can take my pink bow off now and put it in the special Gidget drawer for next year. Put it back next to Charlie's blue bow. We don't want to lose his just in case he comes back one day. I keep praying for him to appear. I even prayed to Mum Suzy to help him find his way home.

I looked inquisitively at Mum, hoping she would understand me and explain again where Charlie was. I still didn't understand. But I had learnt to live with the new normal of the last few years. It wasn't a bad life. In fact, it was amazing. It would just be exceptional if Charlie were still here to enjoy it with me.

But a bond so deep never goes away and he lives on in my heart and my prayers. In my dreams, we run around the park together and sit in the creek hiding from Mum while we are engrossed in ourselves and our doggy world. We sit and while the world away with doggy talk.

Later, I heard Mum say, "Night Gidget. You and me always, beautiful girl," as she turned out the light. I woofed, "Happy Birthday, Charlie!" and then slowly drifted off to sleep surrounded by all my new birthday toys. I had placed one on the spare dog bed next to me for Charlie... just in case.

Freedoms

Grace

"Let's go, Gidget," I yelled down the hallway as I grabbed my hot pink treat bag and pulled it over my shoulder. I waited and then called again. It took her a minute to wake up from her snooze and make her way to me.

"Out we go for a wee and then off to work," I said as she followed me outside to her special wee spot, the same one every time. On the command "wees" out it flowed. Sometimes if she didn't feel the urge, she would do a little fake squat anyway and then look at me as if to say I'm done. She was such a smart and good girl.

I found it truly endearing how dogs always wanted to please their owners. There is this deep loyalty and devotion that radiates from them. They offer us unconditional love and if we are willing to accept it that love can outshine all others.

It's a love that can bring a grown man to his knees. One that can morph an empathetic, sensitive girl like me to wrack and ruin when we lose them. Those big eyes look at you so desperately, so patiently, for your approval.

We humans have full lives and we have people and family and jobs and hobbies and a myriad of stressors and out-of-control to-do lists. Dogs, well, they have us. They may be a big part of our lives, but to them we are their whole lives.

I believe we owe them the same devotion!

Our doggy friends are a big responsibility. They are like eternal toddlers who always need to be cared for. To give a dog a promise and commitment of love and parentship is to give them your heart and to receive a furry one back in return. It's no small feat and it is a lifetime commitment, not an impulsive purchase.

I see this a lot at Animal Aid where I volunteer, especially around the holidays. Dogs arrive and bound out of the car, excited to be out and about. But unbeknownst to them they are being dropped off at the rescue. Their human then leaves and the dog is led whining, whimpering, lunging, panting and barking all the way to the small concrete enclosure they now call home. Whether it's for one day or one year depends on how adoptable they are.

It is heartbreaking to think they left their home that morning thinking they were going for an outing like they had so many times before with their loving family only to find themselves facing a whole new kind of adventure in a strange place. They experience so much confusion and fear with all the unfamiliar faces and new smells and noises. Locked in their cage, their family, home and freedom are gone in the blink of an eye.

I often wonder what these abandoned dogs think and I do all I can to help them. I volunteer my time, I walk them, I talk to them, I wash them, I feed them and I tell them they are good dogs. I hope in each case they get a new family and a home where they are allowed inside and receive the basic dog rights and more – a nice warm bed, lots of cuddles, a bowl full of food every day, clean water, daily walks, vet visits and lots of doggy friends.

We follow the RSPCA five freedoms religiously at the rescue: 1. Freedom from hunger and thirst, 2. Freedom from discomfort, 3.

Freedom from pain, injury or disease, 4. Freedom to express normal behaviour, and 5. Freedom from fear or distress. Potential foster carers and adoptees have to agree to these and are put through a vigorous and stringent test before being granted adoption rights.

I added a couple of extras of my own: 1. Accept all life stages and adjust your own life accordingly to honour your joint life commitment, and 2. Accept their life is only so long and when the time is right be by their side, holding their paw as they transition over.

They love me at the rescue. I am like an animal interpreter paying attention to all the behavioural signs and the way the animals communicate. Observing their body language tells me a lot. Toe-tapping on the pavement means it's too hot, pulling to get somewhere may mean a good smell, and barking and lunging may mean fear.

I learnt a lot from Amy and continue to do so. Sadly, I can't bring Gidget with me to the rescue but she is normally home with a licking mat and having a good snooze once her tummy is full. She is a lucky dog. She has all the five freedoms delivered to her on a silver dog platter. Plus, she has me, of course, to love her.

With that, I pulled into the carpark at work and straight into Morty's Spot. I opened the back door for Gidget and out she jumped and ran straight in the front door wagging her tail.

Gidget was officially the mascot at Pink Peace Yoga and had been for a few years now. When she was about six years old, Fred had finally said, "Grace, she is ready." I was so thrilled. She now has a pale pink bed at reception, another one at my desk and a third in the actual yoga studio. They were all identical beds and she knew the command "go to your bed" by heart and was impeccably behaved, regardless of who requested the behaviour. She had perfected this over the years.

"Grace, do you think we could sneak Morty in to be assistant mascot," Finn asked pleadingly most nights. "He is super chilled and I hate leaving him at home on his own." But sadly, Fred had drawn the line at one dog or rather one set of fur – that was enough work for George, the Robo vacuum, he said.

Everyone loved Morty at the studio. Finn brought him in often to visit and everyone would come outside and smother him in pats and feed him endless treats. We even dedicated a parking spot in his honour. The words 'Morty's Spot' and a big pair of ears were painted in white on the bitumen.

Gidget had been a hit with all the yogis from the first time she came to work. They would often bring treats or toys and shower her with affection at the reception area, usually getting covered in fur at the same time. People would bend down to pat her and she would turn upside down and expose her tummy, turning her head to one side as her body followed in the opposite direction, twisting and turning. Or she would give them a love lick, which may have been more ick for some.

We had to invest in fur rollers everywhere throughout the studio. This helped with the hair and what wasn't absorbed into people's yoga pants flew around like tumbleweeds, gently landing and getting trapped in the corners and crevices of every room. George did a marvellous job of cleaning up the evidence a few times a day. He was our hardest-working employee and the cheapest to employ.

There is one particular yoga teacher Gidget loves. When Karen arrives, all Gidget's manners disappear and her excitement levels rise as she leaves her mat and runs over to get pats from her. Karen normally has treats stashed in her bag ready for the greeting. On one occasion Gidget went and licked her face before Savasana was even over. She is smitten with her.

"It's that time of year again, Grace. The Pink Peace Festival is coming up," Fred said as he meandered past my office. He never travelled at a fast pace – everything in moderation, everything in balance. He had time for everyone and did very little multitasking but still managed to get everything done. Lilly followed him, barefoot and skipping around like an adolescent gypsy. Her pink and purple flowing dress stirred up the tumbleweeds. George spun around at top speed to pick them up behind her.

Fred told me once when I had just started, "Grace, slow down. There is no need to rush. Did you know people rush around to avoid their feelings? Or that, for some, rushing makes them feel more important?" He continued, always wise yet slightly blunt. His filter occasionally needed a little attention.

He continued with more wisdom. "We are all important and all worthy just by being who we are. Slow down and listen to the messages that the mind and body send you. Deal with any that are past traumas or difficulties. Learn to just be and to be happy with who you are."

All I gulped in return was, "Well, that seems easier said than done."

His next wise words came quickly. "Just observe Gidget. That would be a good start. She knows all the lessons on how to live a full, loving, peaceful life."

Gidget

"**I**'m here!" I woofed on arrival. "Is Karen here today?" No one responded so I just went up to everyone individually and tapped my nose on their legs, my favourite method to get pats or treats.

My sticky beak tendencies had me diving my nose into all the yoga bags and pockets I could find to scope out all the stashed treats. My sniffer working overtime, hyping up my brain, sending messages to my drool. Mum called it being a stickybeak. I called it being smart.

Oh, liver treats in that one – not much imagination there. Lamb ears in that one – they're good and crunchy. Veggie sticks over there – no meat, not so tasty. Schnitzel roll, one of my absolute favourites, buried in that one. And chicken balls under a yoga mat here but a bit too small for my big hungry mouth.

Then voila, Karen arrived with the epitome of yummy treats – pieces of BBQ chicken wrapped in a piece of cheese stuck together with some peanut butter. My version of a bacon-wrapped filet mignon. Karen's special creation. I loved her.

Gulp! Down it went. I didn't even get a chew of that one. Looking back up at Karen, I waited for her to deliver another one, drooling on her bare feet to speed up the process. She always had more than one.

After she had deployed about five of these, the bag was empty, I knew the drill.

"Gidget, follow me, girl," she said and with that we sauntered off to the yoga studio.

I sat at the front of the class in my bed with a special toy she had given me: Barnaby the Beaver with his big pink tail. I proceeded to join in the yoga class by starting in my version of the Savasana pose, lying on my back with four legs in the air.

I could hear my tummy rumbling, digesting the food, making room for more treats after practice.

A sad farewell

Grace

I pulled out my to-do list as I prepared for the tenth and final Pink Peace Festival. It was getting more difficult each year to find artists and holistic practitioners who wanted to be part of this festival. Many had moved overseas or out to the country to escape exorbitant city rent or mortgages. Others had taken normal paying roles after not being able to survive on their creative lifestyle incomes.

It was a difficult decision but the studio was going strong and Fred said now that he was getting older he wanted more downtime.

Gabriel had arrived for a meeting to discuss the final set-up, followed by two furry attachments.

"Hi Gabriel, so good to see you. It's been a whole year. Do you remember Gidget?" I said.

"Yes, hi Gidget, gorgeous girl," he said as he knelt down to her level and rubbed her ears.

Gabriel told me the two attachments were foster Labradors – Arnie a cream and Rudy a black. Both were senior oldies just happy to have a place to call home.

Arnie and Rudy approached Gidget boldly and brashly as Labradors do. They all did the signatory butt sniff circling around each other like the merry-go-round that I loved as a kid in the playground.

They then lay a few licks on each other faces. Arnie, the playful one according to Gabriel, launched into a downward dog to initiate play. Not wanting to make a mess we reined the dogs in and asked for a polite sit. "Good girl, Gidget," I said as she sat on cue as always.

Gabriel filled me in on the last year. "I've been in Europe most of the year hanging out with friends from many years ago who I had reconnected with through Facebook. I always despised social media but I even have my own page now. It drums up so much business, you know."

I was a little gobsmacked observing his persona, which was more positive, more optimistic and lighter than I had ever seen.

He continued before I could get a word in. "Guess who else I have been speaking with on Facebook?" He noticed my eyes inquisitively enlarging. "Gloria!" he spurted out excitedly. I couldn't believe it.

Well, it appeared that Gabriel and Gloria had formed a mystical relationship. How they would cohabitate cordially with the sound of the gong during her treatments after his previous frustrations with the sacred percussion instrument, I didn't know.

But it seemed all the sounds, vibrations, intuition and holistic healing had been what drew them together. It had changed them both deep in their heart space. They were smitten kittens apparently.

The dogs love the chanting and the Tibetan sound bowls. They were super sweet, delightful and perfectly behaved as they remained in the sit position.

After we finished discussing all things festival, Gabriel said, "Play date soon please. They obviously like each other." He skipped out of the office. "See ya, Gidget!" he yelled as he left.

In his wake, I contemplated how different things could be in twelve months. I continued to work my way around the festival set-up to get things ready. I wanted to put in the time and effort to ensure that Fred and Lilly would have little left to do.

I was a bit of a people-pleaser. That seemed to be an endless item on the Grace personal development to-do list. It went hand in hand with learning to say no more often, and if I did say yes it should be because I would feel elevated as a consequence of the interaction or experience and not feel depleted as a result of sacrificing my own wellbeing to please others.

The phone vibrated about five times as did my wrist before I was able to find it buried under papers on my desk. I could have answered on my new swanky iPhone watch but I hated talking on that thing and ended up with a sore arm from having to have the watch face right up to my mouth. I also got sick of people saying, "Can you hear me?"

"Grace?" Finn said with a wavering in his voice. We knew each other well and others may not have picked it but I could. "Hi Finn, I..." He cut me off before I could finish. "Grace, he's gone. Morty's gone!" My breath caught in my throat as I listened to him continue. "I went home at lunch and Morty was lying on the back lawn in his favourite sunny spot but when I called him he didn't move. I ran to him but there were no breath sounds, no movement. I even checked with my stethoscope to be sure. Grace, I can't believe he's gone." The pain was evident in his voice.

"Oh, Finn, I'm so sorry. I'm coming over right now. Wait for me before you take him to the hospital, please."

"I'm already back at the hospital," he said. "Can you meet me here?"

Morty was like my own dog. I had spent so much time with this little pocket rocket with short legs, and he was truly Gidget's best friend.

We were going to throw a big birthday party next month for his fifteenth, a ripe old age for a basset hound. I had even ordered him a special blue and white checked birthday boy bandana and a matching hat, plus a new blue collar with his name on it in hot pink – my influence.

He had been off his food for a few days yet the blood tests hadn't revealed anything sinister. Finn was in the investigation stage delving deeper, working up his case and thinking about referring him to a specialist. And now this. It seemed so sudden.

As I got in the car, Gidget jumped in beside me. I felt like it was Charlie all over again. I was not going to leave Gidget out this time. I wanted her to see Morty so she had a chance to see what had happened to him and to say her own goodbyes.

We don't really know what dogs understand. But from my experience and seeing how dogs and all animals mother their young naturally, they just know what to do. It's nature. It's quite amazing really. This makes me assume that they would also understand death if they were allowed the opportunity to be present and smell the situation. And even if they didn't, I believe they should be given the benefit of the doubt to potentially make their own grieving smoother.

All the feelings and emotions I thought I had long since dealt with rose up from deep within. My legs started to shake in the footwell of the car as I tried to work the accelerator. This would often happen when I felt stressed or anxious.

Deep breathing was the antidote to still my body's shock reaction. It worked every time. Or at least it stopped the uncontrollable body shaking so I could drive safely to the vet hospital.

I explained what had happened in simple terms to Gidget in the car on the short trip there. She looked at me and tilted her head from left to right. The tears flowed as I pulled into the Princess Vet Hospital car park and parked in the 'Vet Only' spot.

We sailed past the reception desk saying hello to Donna – the client relations extraordinaire as Finn called her – on the way in.

Donna was able to multitask people, phones and admin tasks, and quell any client complaint with her kind nature. She had laser point focus on the client and outstanding active listening skills. She was also strong, blunt and took no crap, as Finn would say, but in a smart, assertive, wise way.

Finn had told me she had even worked out Mrs Sutton who was their most infamous complaining client. There was always something wrong with the bill or she thought it was too expensive or the reminders were incorrect or she didn't like how the staff greeted her.

When Mrs Sutton arrived, Donna would give her a warm welcome and go around to the other side of the reception desk and kneel down to pat Barney, her Maltese. Barney normally warned her with a growl that he didn't want any attention.

Then she would proceed to say, "So, Mrs Sutton, how is that lovely, handsome husband of yours doing?" Instantly, she was putty in her hands. Donna had found the magical button that transformed Mrs Sutton into a soft, mushy, eat-out-of-your-hand-style client. Needless to say, any time she walked in the door all the other staff ran and hid, waiting for Donna to magically appear and utter her transforming question.

Donna lowered her head when I appeared and tilted her head to the left indicating the door that led out to the hospital. On the other side of the door we saw all the nurses and vets standing around and Finn in tears. This was unusual for him yet completely normal given the situation.

I sensed that most of the staff, being so young, were a bit uncomfortable with their boss in tears but trying their best to comfort him. An almost audible sigh of relief reverberated through them when they saw me walk in the door with Gidget.

I went up to hug Finn, another unusual display of emotion in front of all his staff, while Gidget's tail wagged madly from all the attention the nurses were starting to give her. She started jumping up all over them with pretty ordinary manners, not that the staff, or even me for that matter, minded today.

Finally, Gidget saw Morty on the ground, lying lifeless on a red fluffy rug. She stopped, a little confused, somewhat perturbed. Her tail stopped mid-flight and she raised it high in the air as she slowly edged her way over, inquisitive yet unsure.

The whole hospital room came to a quiet standstill as everyone had eyes on her. She crept forward one tiny step after another. Once she reached Morty she lowered her nose to his head slowly and gave what looked like a big sniff. I wondered if that told her all.

As she turned to me, I said, "It's okay, Gidget," and she looked back at Morty. She did this a few times like she was asking for permission or reassurance. Her nose gave his shoulder a little nudge as if trying to stir him. Nothing.

Then she opened her mouth and out came her pink tongue with the three big black spots on it. She gave Morty the biggest lick on his head... and another... and another, until he had a wet, sticky mohawk to cross to the other side with. After her last lick, she lay down next to him, her nose inches from Morty's. She had a sadness in her eyes, a lethargy in her body and melancholy in her energy. I sat next to her as I patted Gidget with one hand and Morty with the other.

I was certain she understood. I was grateful I had allowed her to say goodbye. It was only right and fair. Respectful.

"Bye Morty," I murmured as I gently stroked his head. "Thank you, dear old boy, for all the entertainment over the years. The love, the laughter, the cuddles, the licking of my feet. You truly were the best boy. Those silky ears, that stellar personality, the little legs that carried you everywhere all the big dogs went. You were always there not far behind. I will never forget you. I promise to look after Finn and Gidget. Your parking spot at yoga will always be there in your honour."

Tears ran down my face as I glanced from Morty to Gidget and back again.

"Now run to Charlie and Ernie as you cross the Rainbow Bridge with all your health restored. Don't look back. Run, run, run forward, forever young once again. They will take good care of you. My special mission for you is to tell Charlie and Ernie that I love them and miss them both."

That night Finn lay with his head in my lap. Gidget was beside us and we spoke about the number of times Morty tripped over his own ears, how he tried to chase tennis balls but the ears again got in the way, and how he often didn't hear us and we wondered if the size of his ears lessened his hearing. We presumed not as he always heard the word 'dinner'. There was an empty spot on the couch tonight, and Finn and I fell into silence as we acknowledged it. We just looked at each other and as tears flowed, we remembered Morty in our own ways with the most enormous love.

GIDGET

"**M**um, what happened to Morty? He smells different. He smells like the possums we see in the park that have been maimed by foxes and lie half-eaten on the ground. You know the ones that I try to pick up and flick around. The ones you eagerly wrench from my mouth and place in a poo bag and throw away.

"Mum, what happened? He has no life left in him. He seems empty and I can't smell him. I kept hoping he would lift his head and come back to life. Then we could play and sniff all the trees, run through the creek and get all muddy. I could trip over his ears again when we went for walks together and then come home and snooze the rest of the day together."

This all came out in one big long woof. Mum tried to communicate back but all I really heard was "Gidget, you are such a good girl and I love you." Now those are words I understand.

Lying in my bed ready to go to sleep, I wonder again where Charlie is. I always wonder that. And now I wonder if Morty has gone to be with Charlie. I want to be with them. I can't bear being without my best friends. But that would mean I would have to choose between being with my mum or being with them.

An impossible choice.

Until I remembered back to what Mum Suzy always said: your purpose is to make your human happy and to give unconditional love. I had committed to that one big mission from day one, paw on my heart. I cannot get distracted from it. I accept that and feel honoured I have a mission so special. I feel equally privileged to have had good friends to share it with along the way.

So, I close my eyes and let Morty enter my nightly dreams. In those dreams, it was the three of us, the three furryteers: Morty, Charlie and me. We were wreaking havoc at the dog park, dropping, wriggling and rolling, chasing tennis balls, sharing treats and essentially loving our lives with each other.

Best furry friends forever. BFFF!

I furry love you guys. Sleep tight wherever you are, my dear Charlie and Morty.

A hitch

GRACE

The final Pink Peace Festival went off without a hitch... well, nearly!

Fred and Lilly were swanning around socialising with all the stallholders and were really pleased with how everything was going. They checked in with me regularly and, like always, my finger was perfectly on the pulse of each situation. There wasn't a lot for them to do but simply be in the moment and enjoy, which was their specialty.

Gabriel and Gloria were ecstatic to be involved in the event together. Their foster pups Arnie and Rudy slept some of the time in Gabriels's tent and every now and then would wander off to see Gloria in her tent at the other side of the festival grounds.

Gabriel and Gloria were constantly on the phone to see who had them in between clients, of course. Other stallholders had commented that the Labrador pups were hanging around at all the food stalls begging for food en route – sausages to be precise followed by a Mr Whippy, without the flake of course, from Stan at the ice cream van who had long dreadlocks, arms full of surfing tattoos and was always barefoot. Earthing, he said.

Gabriel commented, "Well, they are Labradors. They think that that's their job. Their stomach is a never-ending empty pit."

Gabriel wasn't too bothered about them wandering around aimlessly begging... or anything really. He had a pretty chilled persona. It could have been attributed to all the time he spent with Fred discussing all things spiritual and enlightening. Fred really rubbed off on others and when you were around him you couldn't help but feel grounded and calm.

Everything seemed to be going swimmingly until I turned around and noticed that Gidget, my sidekick who is normally like Velcro, was nowhere to be seen.

"Gidget!" I started to call, then yelled more frantically.

Even if I offered her a million dollars and a roast chook, I don't think I could get her to leave the house without me. She had never run away despite her crazies as I called them. The only time she came even close was one day when I arrived home to find the side gate open and her outside under the verandah shaking in her skin. I always wondered if she had gone out and got a fright or wanted to go but was too scared, so she just sat in her anxiety instead. I'd never know.

My first instinct was to stay cool as she was sure to be with people she knew. She was likely the third accomplice to Arnie and Rudy hijacking the sausages or somewhere behind the bleachers with ice cream saturating her muzzle.

I found Arnie and Rudy asleep at Gloria's feet while she was sounding the gong over a tent filled with young girls. It was then I started to get worried.

"Gidget!" I kept calling, trying to raise my voice over all the instruments, people talking and traffic whizzing by. It was a lost cause.

I rang everyone I knew and finally called Finn. I almost ordered him to come over which was unlike me. He had been working most of the weekend on call. Even as the owner he didn't break from weekend on-call shifts. He was so committed to his role, to his hospital, to the animals and to his staff that it made me fall deeper for him all the time.

"I'm on my way, Grace," Finn said. "Did you look at the sausage and ice cream stands?"

"Yes, of course," I said a little snippily. It was so unlike me to be like this with Finn. He was the perfect partner and surprisingly never irritated me which was unusual. Most men did. He was so easygoing, attentive, strong, wise and kind.

"I'm sorry, Finn, I'm just so worried," I offered as an apology and tried to curb my tone.

"I understand, Grace. Let's just find her. Keep looking and I'll be there in ten." He hung up before I could reply.

GIDGET

"Eddie, that ice cream was great. I'm going to try the chocolate one next."

"Gidget, you nincompoop you know you can't have chocolate. It's poisonous for dogs. Do I have to teach you what you can and can't eat?" shrieked Eddie, loud like a typical Jack Russell.

"I know," I replied, tipping my head downwards shamefully.

"Follow me!" he woofed.

I did as he asked. I had only just met him. Mum had told me all about this wiry-haired Jack Russell called Eddie. He was Stephanie's offsider and had helped her heal her broken heart.

"I feel so safe with you, Eddie, to leave Mum's side and explore a little. It's fun. She always says I'm so confident and often uses the word crazy but underneath I'm a bit of a sook. It's just hidden by all the furry bravado," I offered up to Eddie sheepishly.

"People do that too, I'm told. They cover their real true selves scared to reveal their imperfections and foibles because of what others will think. It's great to have a friend like you that I don't have to pretend with. I can just be authentically furry. I feel free! I feel happy!" I hoped Eddie would think I was smart, free and easygoing.

"I do just like to be with her cause she's my mum. It's my purpose to love her unconditionally and to look after her, you know. I promised my doggy mum Suzy I would do just that. But how about just for tonight we have an adventure? One to remember for always and bond us as blood friends... without any actual blood, obviously." As I woofed it, I thought, oh no, he probably thinks I'm a sook now. Us golden retrievers are very loyal and clingy, not like the courageous and adventurous Jack Russell breed.

I had learnt from Finn being a vet and an expert in all things animals that all dog breeds have certain predispositions to certain health conditions, and they often have certain temperaments or personality traits. For example. Jack Russells were bred to hunt so had lots of energy. According to Finn, they were usually hyper. They were also predisposed to luxating patellas, cataracts and a host of other things.

I heard him say to Mum that golden retrievers are social, playful, highly trainable and need lots of exercise. Tick, tick, tick, tick, I thought. That's me. Did someone say BANG? I lay on my side waiting for my treat.

He didn't mention loyal and clingy. Maybe that was not a golden retriever trait but a Gidget trait. He said that we were predisposed to atopic dermatitis, hip dysplasia and ear infections. Well, I do get itchy. Mum takes me to get a special injection a few times a year which stops the itch. So, I suppose it's one tick there. He was pretty spot on and intelligent, my friend Finn, Mum's special friend Finn. I liked him a lot.

I was getting lost in thought as I rambled on to Eddie.

"Absolutely!" was all Eddie said as he took off at lightning speed despite being an old boy with me loping along behind him trying to keep up.

It was getting darker now and I could see the festival fading in the distance behind us.

"Where are we going, Eddie?" I woofed. "Is there a plan? Will there be food?"

But he just kept running. Maybe he couldn't hear me because of the wind in his ears.

Finally, he came to a sliding halt. I nearly crashed straight into his backside. While I was there, I had a quick sniff.

"Here we are, Gidget," he woofed.

I looked around and there under a tree I could see a little scroungy dog, maybe a Jack Russell, I couldn't tell. She was filthy. Beside her were five puppies letting out little cries and jumping all over each other in play.

"Eddie!" I woofed. "Did you have anything to do with this?"

"Well, I might have. Mum told me I was finally going to get the snip and, well, I freaked out a little so I escaped through the hole in the gate and here is the rest of the story. My legacy."

"We all need family," I woofed to Eddie. "Did you know I lost my two best friends, Charlie and Morty? It's been really hard. Mum talks all the time about how your mum Stephanie is so wise and is really good at sorting through problems. Maybe she could help us with this little conundrum."

GRACE

I was a crying mess in Finn's arms, almost unable to get myself together. We had looked everywhere. The next step was to call around to the vets, shelters and the RSPCA, and slather posts on Facebook. One advantage of the crazy, time-wasting social media platform was that it was a really good space to reunite lost pets and owners. The more you flood social media about a lost pet, the more chance you have of finding them. Other people then get involved and help, and it's a lovely way to build community and connection along the way.

Recently, a dog was stolen outside the front of the local supermarket. He had been tied up innocently waiting. A water bowl had been placed next to him and he had his collar on with lead attached while his owner was inside doing some food shopping. You would expect it to be safe. But no, not these days! Well, not without a big risk anyway. She returned with her bags some minutes later but there was no dog, no lead and no people fessing up to seeing anything. Imagine!

The owners placed a post on Facebook and it spread through Adelaide like wildfire. One person shared and then another and then it multiplied exponentially. Before long, the dog was found tied up to a bus shelter in a shadier suburb further away. Obviously, the heat of the post made the person who took it panic and leave the dog for someone else to find it and hopefully take it to a vet to be scanned and reunited with its owner. Thankfully it was a happy ending. This time.

But this is not always the case. Other owners who posted are still reaching out for their family pet that went missing years ago, families still bereft and broken longing for their furry family member to return home. The not knowing would be the worst. Are they being cared for, looked after, safe, well, happy? Awful!

So, for me, I never leave Gidget anywhere out of sight... and I mean anywhere! You just never know who is around or what they may do. The consequence, being huge, far outweighs the tiny risk, an equation I learnt in the corporate world. It's called a risk assessment.

It was only when I was about to hit POST on the Facebook group Lost Pets Adelaide, hoping I would be one of the thankful ones, that I saw Eddie. At least it looked a lot like Eddie, racing around the corner on the left side of Gabriel's tent.

How weird. I didn't know Stephanie was here tonight. He ran straight up to me and I picked him up in my arms just like I had done at every counselling session. I read his collar and sure enough, it was Eddie. Sit tight Eddie, I just have to finish this Facebook post.

Then, just before I hit POST, not far behind Eddie and looking like she had run a marathon was Gidget. She was no elite athlete that was for sure. But she made a beeline for me and jumped up onto my lap, shoving Eddie off.

I was so elated and focused on Gidget, almost crushing her with my hugs, that I didn't see what else was going on.

"Grace, look!" Finn yelled.

With that, I released Gidget a little and looked up to see a dirty-looking Jack Russell and five tiny puppies struggling to keep up running towards us.

"Finn, quick, get them!" I shouted.

Finn and I gathered up the pups and mum dog. We breathed a sigh of relief and amazement while piling them all into the car. Eddie and Gidget jumped in last. As the pups jumped around frantically yapping, we took off to the vet hospital.

Fred got a call on the way, asking him to take over managing the festival while we sorted the puppy dilemma out. "Please tell Gabriel we found Gidget," I asked.

I then called Stephanie to ask her to meet us there.

"Hi Stephanie, it's Grace. You must be nearby as I have Eddie with me and you will never guess what he has been up to," I said. I knew he could get himself into trouble because Stephanie always made a joke about it.

"Oh, he is such a terror. What has he done now?" she replied with an emphasis on the 'has'.

"Well, I think he may have passed on his genes to the next generation," I said while Gidget was barking up a storm behind me, wanting my attention. It was like a comedy movie – Gidget, Eddie, scroungy mum dog, five puppies and the two of us. My perfect night really.

"Oh my... give me thirty minutes and I'll be there. Tell me more!" she said.

"Meet us at the Princess Vet Hospital and all will be revealed," I replied.

Gidget

"Oh Eddie, you're hilarious but you're such a bad influence. I have had a great night. Look how gorgeous scroungy mum dog looks now she has had a bath and a floofing. And your puppies are perfect and the spitting image of you with all their faded black spots waiting to poke through their white coats."

I sat down on the bed beside Eddie at the vet hospital. I really needed a snooze after all our fun.

"You know, Eddie, Charlie and Morty would have loved this adventure. Morty would have tripped over his ears and slowed us down. But he would have loved meeting you. You would have been welcomed into the furry pack," I said.

Then I whispered, "Will you be my new best friend? There's a space open."

Eddie lay down in the bed next to me and promptly fell asleep while Mum and Finn checked over all the puppies.

Stephanie looked on almost speechless.

Grace

"Gosh, guys, what are we going to do with all these puppies?" I said.

"Don't you worry, Grace," replied Stephanie. "I'm the best problem fixer and I adore Jack Russells, like really adore them. How about I take them all and look after the litter? Finn, I would need your help, though. And when they are old enough, I will rehome them. I would likely keep one for myself and possibly keep the mum dog too. I could call her Molly. I love that name," she said excitedly.

"You know, once you name them, it's all over," I said as I laughed.

"I'd love to help," threw in Finn. "How exciting."

Later, as I lay against Finn's chest ready to go to sleep, I murmured slowly and quietly, "I really thought I had lost Gidget. My heart feels a little bruised. Just the thought of not having my sweet baby girl here with me is torture. I think losing her would break me."

"I know, Grace. Losing Morty has broken my heart but I look to the paw prints he has scattered all over it. I remember all the fun times and know that all the tears and grief are so worth all the love and companionship he gave me. I truly hope that's not something you have to experience anytime soon, my gorgeous Gracey girl," he added. I loved it when he called me that.

I closed my eyes, and said, "Gidget, I love you. It's you and me always, beautiful girl." My nightly ritual of nearly twelve years.

Gidget

"Night Mum. I love you to the moon and back. So sorry for making you so worried. I love you, I love you, I love you absolutely unconditionally. My heart is connected to your heart, now and always. As you always say to me it's you and me always, Mum."

With that, I faded into sleep hoping that Charlie, Morty and Eddie would join me in my dreams for another adventure. I would surely not ever do that again and make Mum worry so much. The adventures needed to be saved only for my dreams with all my best pals.

Announcements

GRACE

Beep beep! It was Camilla collecting me for Friday yoga and coffee.

I looked forward to every Friday, my favourite morning of the week, hanging out in downward dog and other poses, or asanas as they were known in the yoga world.

Fred always told me, "Grace, it's very important to allow the nervous system a chance to rest. To restore, to rejuvenate, to calm, and to slow the fight and flight response caused by our stress-filled lives. An easy way to begin is simply to stop and breathe."

Now here I was heeding his wise words in Savasana, the first pose of today's practice, grounding myself and giving my nervous system a much-needed gift – the ability to reset, to calm, to open and to turn on the parasympathetic nervous system, otherwise known as the rest and digest function, and to step out of the fight and flight sympathetic nervous system where all the stress lives. I mimicked Fred's words in my mind to keep me motivated and centred.

Feeling lighter and refreshed after yoga, we walked into Penelope's. I waved to Antonio, and Camilla skipped up to him and planted a kiss right on his lips. They behaved just like teenagers in love.

Penelope's looked amazing. All the work they had put into doing it up had paid off. There would be a huge line-up for brunch on Sunday and you would need to wait to be escorted to a table.

Of course, we got the best table every time. Our regular table was reserved for us, surrounded by books both new and used. Antonio personally brought us our coffees and two gluten-free chocolate brownies. Our favourites! He planted another kiss on Camilla's cheek before he whisked himself off to attend to others. He left a cheeky smile in his wake.

"Guess what happened at the festival over the weekend?" I said, indulging in my weak soy latte. Aaaah, the best moment of the day.

"Tell me all," she said.

I proceeded to tell her what had happened and about the five cute puppies.

"Well, I was actually thinking about getting Teddy a friend. Do you think a small Jack Russell would like to live with an enormous Bernese mountain dog or do you think it would get squashed as they play and tumble?" We both laughed at the thought.

I knew a Jack Russell would absolutely be capable of taking care of itself. If all else failed, a high-pitched Jack Russell bark would shock Teddy into submission. The Jack Russell would be the boss, we were sure of that.

We talked about how well the festival went. Fred had done all the final wrap-ups while I was at the vet hospital helping Finn and Stephanie and the whole furry Jack Russell family. Gidget had looked on eagerly assessing the whole situation but mostly she was smitten by her new friend Eddie.

Stephanie as promised had taken all the dogs home with her. Finn was touching base with her daily with tips on how to look after them. Stephanie had decided to keep the mum dog and officially called her Molly. The other five were yet too young to be rehomed but it looked like one already had a home with Camilla. Being as cute as they were, the other four would no doubt be snapped up swiftly.

Before she left with the puppies, Stephanie said, "It's interesting, Grace. Things always seem to work out how they should. If we dwell too much in the past, we are at risk of falling into depression. If we dwell too much in the future, anxiety may occur. But, if we live in the present moment and deal with what arises with confidence and resilience, life travels more swimmingly. It's less stressful and simultaneously we take care of our health."

Like Fred, she was a wealth of knowledge. I was grateful to have selected people in my inner circle who were positive, optimistic and knowledgeable, and always lifted me up. The two-way interaction was mutually beneficial.

I used to think it was luck but now believed it was by design. Sadly, I had spent time culling my friends somewhat since my corporate job. This had reduced the number of people who caused me drama, were shallow, depleted me, put me down or were just mean.

Life had changed. I had changed. Life as a consequence was much sweeter. I seemed to spend much more time with dogs now too. They always provided unconditional love and companionship with no expectations or judgement. Perfect!

"Hello, it's Grace and Gidget," I said into my new flagship iPhone, still barely knowing all its functions and features.

"Hi Grace, it's Gabriel. Thanks so much for all your efforts with the festival. We had a wonderful time and gained some new clients and made lovely connections."

Before I could comment he continued. "Gloria and I have made a big decision that I wanted to talk to you about. We're going to head over to Europe for a few months, starting in Rome. She has always wanted to throw some coins over her shoulder into the Fontana di Trevi – most likely to wish for a bigger gong! We want to try working there while travelling around so we can immerse ourselves in the culture. We are looking forward to seeing the sights and eating lots of homemade pasta, crostoli and cannolis. But it leaves us with a small dilemma. The doggies. Do you know anyone who may be able to look after Arnie and Rudy while we're gone?"

"Ooh, hmm," I mumbled, feeling sad for the two Labradors who had fully fallen into their new routine with their fun and doting foster parents. I was a little shocked but not surprised.

"They are still legally listed under foster care but the rescue is inundated with rescue dogs. There are not enough foster carers to go around despite numerous marketing attempts. Apparently, it's a big issue for the industry. For all rescues. So they have asked me if I could try and find anyone to help out," explained Gabriel.

"We are likely to adopt them as we love them, but we haven't made that final commitment yet and decided to leave it until we return. That way, we can be sure that we're happy to settle down rather than continue travelling. As we know, it's important for dogs to have a stable forever home and it's a lifelong decision owning a dog, let alone two. We found it very hard to decide to leave them but it's what we need to do for us," he said.

"Yes, I understand it is so important. I know this dilemma personally because we have the same problem with overcrowding at Animal Aid where I volunteer. We are often at the point where we can't take any more dogs. I always worry about what happens to them then," I said feeling melancholy, always an animal empath.

"So, do you think Finn or you may be able to help us at all? I would love them to stay together being a bonded pair," he said.

"Leave it to me and I will put some feelers out," I said, feeling dangerously involved already.

I pondered a lot on how we could help. Maybe Animal Aid had some foster carers that could help. Or one of my friends possibly. Maybe Finn had a client who had a couple of spare spots in their home.

We had enough animal connections. Surely we could find a solution for these two beautiful dogs.

I didn't say anything to Gabriel or Gloria for a week about what was transpiring. They arrived for another play date on a Friday evening. Dogs and dukkah night we had called it. It was just our way of saying come over for champagne and some nibbles.

Gloria always brought a good dukkah. She had an obsession with it that was likely attributed to her Egyptian heritage. Once we had finished a bottle or two, pizza normally came next. Camilla, Antonio and Freddy were coming as well so we were not short on French sparkling that night.

"Hello everyone," Finn said when he arrived thirty minutes late with spots of blood on his collar. "Sorry I'm late. We had to do emergency surgery on a dog hit by a car. Luckily Morticia, the black cocker spaniel with long ears and extra-long fur hanging down like Morticia from the Addams Family, is going to be okay. The owner looked somewhat like Morticia too, with long black hair, long nails and red lipstick. Like animal, like owner," he said, trying not to laugh at one of his clients. He was too professional for that, but I knew him well enough that I could tell he thought it was funny. Everyone else was laughing but only after they found out Morticia was going to fully recover.

"Top up anyone?" Camilla said. Despite her interest in yoga and all things calm, I loved that she honoured both sides of herself. Party girl and yogi – it was a balance she always told me.

"Yes," I said, "top me up. I think I will need it for this announcement."

Gidget

Eddie and I had been spending a lot more time together, along with Molly the tag-along, as I nicknamed her. The little bossy one was much like Eddie actually. Honestly, I was a little jealous of Molly. Eddie seemed to love her and followed her around everywhere. Did he love me that much?

I wanted to be loved more. He was my special friend. Molly had come out of nowhere and commandeered all his attention. I wasn't always good at sharing. I would often nudge up to Eddie and push Molly out of the way – gently of course. She would give me a little snarl and I would shoot her a golden retriever clown smile in return.

Mum said it was a little strange us hanging out so much as Stephanie was her therapist but we had lots of play dates anyway. Stephanie often popped in quickly to drop Eddie off but she didn't stay too long.

I think she felt uncomfortable. She said something about mixing business with pleasure, or help and healer with friend. Mum tried to explain to me that it was a conflict of interest, but I didn't really understand as those big words didn't have a woof translation.

I couldn't work out the big deal. A friend is a friend as long as their butt smells good.

What is a therapist anyway, other than someone we tell everything to? It's someone we share our hopes, dreams and fears with. But that's just what I did with Charlie and he was no therapist. The difference, Mum joked, was that a therapist actively listened and wasn't busy preparing a response in their head before you had even finished talking.

But I was only a dog. What did I know? I couldn't even talk.

But then I did know things. I sensed them.

Like when Camilla was pregnant with Freddy, everyone ignored all my sniffing at her belly and hovering around her ankles in the first few months. Did anyone listen to me? No! Not until the doctor advised her she would soon be pushing out a little person into the world.

I could have told you that was going to happen months prior. But as my humans didn't speak Woof, I just quietly smirked and got on with life.

Mum said I was a wise one, just like Fred except furry. I had fur and lots of it, not like wiry-coat Eddie.

Mum talked about shaving me once until someone told her that when the fur grows back the coat can become different and more matted. The breeder told her we have double coats which protect us in all weather conditions and regulate our body temperature, keeping us cool in summer and warm in winter.

When I saw shaved goldens in the park I tried to explain this to them. But they just paraded around on tippy toes showing off, thinking they looked better than me all groomed to perfection.

Personally, I loved my flippy golden furs and my cowboy spurs, as Mum's friend Susan called them. They were the furs that ran down the back of my legs. Some people called them poo catchers. I looked beautiful unshaved. I was such a pretty girl. I knew this because Mum told me all the time.

I was practising the tippy-toe dance so I could go head-to-head with a shaved version when next I saw one at the park.

My friend group was growing. The regulars Olive, Snowy, Hudson, Shelly, Wilma and Teddy were still around. But lately Mum has also been having lots of play dates with Gabriel and Gloria's dogs, Arnie and Rudy, or the crazies as I call them. What characters those furries are. Despite their age, it seems they haven't ever grown up. It's hysterical actually. There is always something they are into – woofing silly stories, knocking things over, stealing toilet rolls (Oops! I do that one too), eating anything and everything, and barking about nonsense.

Dogs sure bring people together. Mum loved this.

I knew Mum's secret but I hadn't told anyone yet. I barked to tell the room of the upcoming announcement but nothing. No one was listening to me. They were too busy inhaling dukkah and swilling the bubbles while me, Teddy, Eddie and the crazies were left to our own devices. There could be trouble brewing. They were always trouble!

GRACE

"Can I have everyone's attention!" I shouted above the laughter around me. The conversation slowly died down.

"So, darling, would you like to tell them or should I?" I looked at Finn with a deep love that was growing day by day.

"Well," he said, "we put our feelers out to all our sources and we haven't been able to find anyone who has been able to help with Arnie and Rudy."

He paused, looking around the room to observe the expression on all the faces. Not to keep everyone disappointed for too long, he continued.

"But Grace and I have decided to foster Arnie and Rudy while you are away. We have grown to love them, their antics and the way they fill a room with love, humour and playfulness."

He again looked around the room at everyone's surprised expression.

"Now, obviously, we don't live together, so we thought what a perfect time to move in together. So, I'm going to move in here so as not to upset Gidget's routine. The timing is just right. Grace and I want to make a commitment to each other, and we couldn't think of anything better than to seal the deal with these two furry goofy loveballs to make our house a home. Right Grace, Gidget?" he said.

"Woo hoo!" Camilla shouted. Freddy looked up from his LEGO bricks to see what the excitement was about, while Antonio grabbed her and twirled her around like a teenager. He was always excited about any reason to be excited. He loved sharing his excitement with Camilla. They were a perfect match.

"So, Gabriel, Gloria, is that okay with you guys?" I asked, knowing the answer.

"Are you kidding me? That is so amazing!" Gloria almost sang with happiness. She did a little spin on the spot barefoot with her big hot pink flippy skirt. Gidget got caught up underneath and started doing her own little spins.

Everyone raised their glasses!

"So, when is the moving in day party?" Camilla asked, laughing. "I'll bring the bubbles."

GIDGET

"Woof!" I replied. Of course it was all right with me. I knew it all the time. Lucky I loved these crazies and Finn. Mum had asked me if I would be okay with it, but I had already known with my canine intuition. My sixth sense.

As I fell asleep, I invited Charlie, Morty and Eddie into my dreams as I always did. Then I sent a special invitation via telepathy to Arnie and Rudy. I was the happiest camper knowing I had two friends moving in. I would have to let them know they couldn't steal all Mum's attention from me.

So, let the adventures start.

Moving in day was two weeks. I had already picked the spots for their beds, right next to mine where Charlie had always been.

I heard Mum say, "I love you, Gidget. You and me always, sweet girl." My body jerked and my toes twitched as I fell into a deep dream state.

A senior consultation

GRACE

"Sit, Gidget," I asked nicely. We were at the vets for her yearly check-up. She loved coming to the vets. All the staff fussed over her. She knew that the treats lived above the scales and would eagerly pull on the lead to go straight there. As she sat perfectly still on the scales, she would look up, waiting for the treats to flow, as they always did. The scales showed thirty kilograms. Perfect, I told her.

Gidget was nearly thirteen and today we were booked for an extended senior consultation, ensuring enough time to discuss her health and retain all the information.

"Hi gorgeous Grace," Finn said, kissing me behind the closed consult door.

"Hi handsome," I responded laughing.

"Okay, let's get started. Remember you're a client here now, not my partner. Gidget deserves a full check-up and the same undivided attention I would give a client," he said in an unusually professional tone.

"Sure honey," I said, winking.

We were sitting in the consult room pretending to be good clients rather than family. He started with a chit-chat on how Gidget had been going in general with toileting, eating, drinking and all the standard stuff.

"Any concerns?" he asked.

"The main concern is she seems to be slowing down on her walks. She looks stiffer and her gait is different."

More questions followed concerning appetite, mood and behaviour, limping, difficulty in jumping or a reluctance to get up or down. Of course, he knew she hadn't experienced any of these things except for slowing down somewhat.

He got to the floor and performed a twelve-point physical examination.

Finn checked all her legs. He bent them, tucking them up underneath her belly and then stretched them out behind her, pulling them back and forth gently to check her movement. "A bit stiff," he said.

He then stood Gidget on all four legs. He took one paw and flipped it under so her top knuckles were on the ground and waited to see if she flipped it back to its normal position. A dog without a problem will flip its paw back immediately. This is to ascertain if there are any proprioceptive deficits as a dog's brain should know where its limbs are in space. It's also related to the sensory nerves and how they talk to the spinal cord and the brain. No issues there.

Atopic dermatitis was on the list of Gidget's ailments. The itch injection fixed her every time, sometimes for a month or more depending on her environment, time of year and how her body responded. No itching today, no injection needed.

Next, he took some blood before administering her yearly vaccination and heartworm injection.

"Grace, darling," he winked. "Gidget seems in pretty good shape. She is showing some signs of arthritis which would be expected at her age. I think we should start her on an arthritis regime."

"Sure," I said, feeling sad knowing she was aging.

Where had the last thirteen years gone? I thought back to the day on the beach when Charlie as a little fluff ball came running up to me. It all started with Will telling me about Charlie that day.

Imagine if I hadn't met him. Gidget would never have been mine. She is my life and despite how Will and I ended, without him Gidget would never have been part of my life.

Thank you, Will. He would never know how much I loved him for that. In hindsight, it was really only for that ... and Charlie of course.

One minute Gidget was a crazy puppy, then an exuberant adolescent and now a senior golden oldie. What an honour to have travelled this journey together. I sometimes thought about what would happen when the time came. You know, that actual time. Quickly I would put it out of my mind and continue to live in the moment. The moment when Gidget was here beside me — older but still as cheeky and beautiful as ever.

Finn prescribed Gidget a new diet that was specific for the joints. He explained it had therapeutic levels of omega-3 fatty acids and was enriched with glucosamine and chondroitin sulfate. Alongside the new diet, he administered an arthritis injection and listed some specific supplements.

"That's all for today," Finn said as he patted Gidget on the head.

We were ready to leave. She had many more treats at reception, we paid the discounted bill and left with arms full of stuff. Gidget was carrying a new green crocodile toy in her mouth. She had lifted it off the shelf quietly without my knowing yet once it was covered in slobber, I could hardly put it back.

It would come home to join the other toys with their missing appendages.

"See you at home, honey," Finn whispered in my ear as he opened the door for me to leave. "I'll get the hazelnut chocolate on the way home." Every day, Finn brought home a block of hazelnut chocolate. He had acquired the taste from my love of it. He had an addiction, I told him. He told me hazelnuts were good for you and offered several health benefits. He read an article stating just that in the wellness section of the Sunday newspaper, and I never heard the end of it.

"Sure, see you tonight," I said, more in love every day.

"Oh, I will have the blood test results to you in the next few days. We have requested a complete blood count and biochemistry panel to identify any red flags that would warrant further investigation, just in case," he said.

With that, he turned on his heels bending down to pat a hairless Chinese crested dog that had fluffy tufts of hair on its head, ears, paws, and tail. "Come through, Bruno," I heard him say as he escorted Bruno and his owner to the consult room. I exited the clinic, crocodile in tow, with Gidget eyeing off the lamb ear I had ready to get her into the car.

GIDGET

"**O**uch! Oomph! Ahhh!" I woofed. Even though it was Finn, I still felt a little violated.

A jab here, a thermometer up there, fingers all up in my mouth, flipping my ear flaps and inserting a scary black thing, lifting my eyelids and blurring my vision, and a whole lot of other unwanted attention.

I did like the treats. They could keep coming please. They were the only thing that made this epic disaster worthwhile.

I couldn't understand why Finn was being so serious. Mum told me health is a serious, serious matter, emphasising the second serious. Every six months we visited the vet, especially now I was older.

Finn explained one year in a dog's life is equivalent to about seven in a human, depending on the size of the dog. By my calculation that meant I was well into my eighties. Phew, I am old. I will be in a doggy pram having cataract surgery and getting hearing aids next.

I felt pretty good though, considering. I still wanted to chase the ducks and run a half marathon at the beach. Realistically, the ducks now chased me, quacking madly as they taunted me. Karma. And I only ran about one hundred metres at the beach now and not much faster than a tortoise.

My mind was full of stories and memories of my life. Some were funny, some sad and some dangerous. All with Mum, except my amazing adventure with Eddie that one time. The memories all came to the forefront of my mind and, momentarily, I felt what humans call melancholy.

I felt a desire to do it all over again, to live my life a second time. So many more ducks to chase, leaves and butts to sniff, butt wiggles to do, food to eat, snoozes in the sun to take, pats to get and licks to give. I would love never-ending youth or at least enough years to live as long as my mum. But, sadly, being a dog, that is just not to be.

Accepting I was at the shorter end of life wasn't always easy. Being a dog made it simpler as we didn't dwell on things that create unhappiness. We just get on with it and search for another pat, another sniff and another memory to create for our humans to hold onto when we are no longer around.

Living in the present moment as the humans call it always seemed a struggle for them. I hope Mum learns some of these tips from me. Us dogs don't complicate things like humans do.

And I hope Finn's arthritis potions will help me regain some of my youthful ability and flexibility. Time will tell.

Oh dear, I can see another needle heading my way. I duck my head and try to commando crawl to the other end of the consult room to avoid it. "Ouch!" Too late.

"All done," I hear Finn say to Mum.

Excellent. Let's get out of here, Mum.

A furry surprise

GRACE

"Good girl, Gidget. Great job! Now, I have a surprise for you," I said in a high-pitched voice. I did that often.

We got in the car and headed left on Statenborough to Gabriel's house, passing a koala climbing a gum tree. Only in Australia. It was the day to collect Arnie and Rudy and welcome them into our family while Gabriel and Gloria went overseas.

I secretly thought Gabriel would propose while they were away. Even though they were not conventional or traditional, they loved each other and behaved like teenagers most of the time. I could imagine him down on one knee on the floor at a food cart or a festival popping open a box with a vintage eighteen-carat red ruby solitaire ring in a filigree setting.

She loved rubies. The question would be met with a big yes. I knew that for sure.

Pulling up at Gabriel's, I reversed into the driveway to make it easier for the dogs to get into the back of the SUV. My lovely new black Subaru Forester was going to end up covered in even more fur. It was bad enough with Gidget who refused to sit anywhere except the back seat. I had a great seat protector but the sides of the seats remained uncovered and mopped up her slobber as she drooled en route to wherever we were going.

Now we had two extras to add to the mix so the slobber would be amplified. But love knows no bounds. There was no contest between a little slobber and fur versus no doggy love. The slobber wins every time.

"Hi guys," I said as I turned off the engine.

"Hi," they responded in a despondent tone. Gloria's eyes were red and Gabriel was trying to look stoic.

After some shallow conversation, the goodbyes began.

"We will be back soon. We love you. You will have a wonderful time with Finn and Grace while we are away," Gloria said in a baby voice. Gabriel looked at me and rolled his eyes while he walked over to hold her hand. That's love.

Arnie and Rudy eagerly jumped in the back as I opened the rear door. They were totally enthusiastic and tilted their heads, looking forward to an adventure. They loved to go anywhere in the car even if it were only up and down the driveway.

Packing the car amidst three dogs was tricky, especially with the dog beds they had amassed. But I tucked everything in somehow and, as Gidget tried to lick the other two from the back seat, I said bye to Gabriel and Gloria.

There were hugs all round. A lot of tears from Gloria. She was like a gypsy teenager most of the time but very in touch with her emotions. She never held anything back that needed to pass through her body as emotional energy.

Flooded in tears, she waved. "Go Grace. We will speak to you soon. Send lots of photos and updates. We will do likewise. Our first stop will be Fontana di Trevi to make a wish that dogs would live the total of our lifespan. Oh... and maybe that Gabriel will buy me the latest fifty-four-inch Chinese Chau Gong." Apparently they produce a full and sustained wash of musical overtones.

"Travel safe, you two. Don't do anything silly and have an amazing time. The boys will be looked after like they are my own dogs," I said, wondering somewhere deep inside if this would be the case.

"Let's go guys," I said to the three furries as we pulled out of the driveway, beeping and waving. The two Labs in the back panted excitedly. All I could see in the rear vision mirror was drool-like shoelaces dripping from their jowls towards the freshly vacuumed floor.

GIDGET

As we were driving home with my two new friends in the back, a memory popped into my brain.

I remembered fondly being at the park with Mum and her sister Gretel who lived interstate. We didn't see her often. Her dog Gilly looked like Eddie. She was fast and naughty and almost as wiry.

It was a bit peculiar that all our names started with a G.

Gretel was beautiful and she spread kindness around like confetti.

We were having a wonderful time at the park, playing in the creek, chasing the tennis ball, sniffing the butt of any dog that ventured over to see us. Just like any other park day and then... it happened.

Gilly saw a duck. She spun around almost mid-air and took off barking after it. Gretel took off after Gilly yelling for her to stop, and Mum took off after Gretel calling Gilly's name. I then started running after them all.

The odd-looking chase led us from the park onto neighbouring streets with Gilly in the lead. We passed dogs barking behind fences as Mum and Gretel continued yelling, "Gilly, STOP!"

The duck flew low to the ground, no doubt laughing at us all, as we continued the chase. We dodged cars and cyclists and got sworn at in the process. I was getting pretty puffed but Gilly looked like she could run forever.

Finally, the duck took flight straight up into the air. Gilly stopped dead in her tracks, jumping up, barking crazily. We all stopped, almost piling on top of one another like a cartoon reel.

Mum and Gretel grabbed us and put our leads on, and we all sat on the warm pavement trying to catch our breath. My big, pink, black-spotted tongue hung out the side of my mouth about two inches longer than usual.

Gilly was lunging and jumping. "I'll get ya, let me off, let me at it," she woofed.

Gretel kept telling her to calm down and the game ended as we were dragged home in disgrace.

I have heard Mum and Gretel laugh about this often after the event. On the actual day they were frantic. Gilly still says if she sees that duck again, she'll get it as she bursts into a zoomie. I'm practising, she would say.

I wish my legs were still that agile. I wish I was still able to run like the wind, up and down the beach, after Gilly and after ducks, and zoom around with friends and parkour all over the furniture.

I would sadly have to save it for my dreams now and continued drooling all over the seat.

Settling in

Grace

Arnie and Rudy settled in in no time at all. They took over on day one, and their antics became part of our daily routine. Dogs' beds littered the loungeroom, toys lost more appendages and stuffing lay spread everywhere, with the occasional squeaker hiding in a corner. Toilet paper rolls had to be hidden and socks kept high off the ground otherwise they would scoff them like a yummy piece of chicken. They were skilled at counter surfing so food could not be left on the counter.

They bonded with Gidget and us instantly and it was like a little senior furry pack following us wherever we went. True Velcro dogs. They knew nothing about personal space. Even the toilet was fair game. If you wanted to turn around on the spot to reverse your direction, watch out, because there was normally one or all three of them on your heels to somersault over. Such great tripping hazards.

Luckily, being yogis, our balance was excellent and helped us avoid any falls. We were aging too and I was getting close to the big six O myself.

Arnie didn't like the dog door so the back door had to be perpetually open. The house was constantly filled with flies. Gidget frantically ran around bailing them up in a corner and snapping them straight into her mouth. Always after a snack.

Rudy liked to bark. Sometimes a lot. He was either protecting us from all the scary people and dogs on the other side of the gate or he was just overexcited. He often spent time in the backyard waiting for Poppy the possum to arrive. Just like Gidget. He would body-slam the fence to scare her off. Also just like Gidget. It was a ridiculous behaviour but one that was impossible to untrain as we knew from experience.

Both loved water. This was great when you were at the beach but not so great when the water bowls you just filled in the laundry ended up as paddling pools, creating skid hazards from the cocktail of water and drooly slobber on the floor. Finally, I moved all the water bowls — or the pooch water station as I called it — outside.

But we all adjusted and the benefits definitely outweighed the frustrations. We absolutely adored these two goofy Labradors, and Gidget was smitten also. She was lonely no more and you would often find her waiting in a senior play stance, resting on her elbows with her butt in the air. The downward dog play bow would invite and instigate play.

Luckily for them, everything was at their fingertips. I was essentially bundled up as their slave, personal assistant, personal shopper, chauffeur, best friend, cleaner, chef, massage therapist, cuddler, groomer, entertainer, ball thrower, door opener, therapist and dog walker. With no income for any of my work, I joked often.

Gidget

I rose this morning feeling years younger, almost like a sprightly teenager.

I waddled from Mum to Finn giving their hands morning licks. It was an extra bullseye with Finn as I landed one on his cheek. Then Arnie and Rudy received wet good morning mohawks.

I looked over to my friends and gave them the 'you ready?' eye stare. Soon after, the three of us jumped up or rather walked up the specially made bed stairs onto the bed. We wriggled around, making it impossible for anyone to get any more sleep. Every morning. We had perfected it.

Mum and Finn would pull the doona over their head to escape the twelve paws and fifty-four sharp nails heading their way. They had learnt from previous unintended scratches that Labradors are pushy and not as ballerina-like as us golden retrievers.

This new arthritis regime seemed to be working wonders, I thought, as I barked to the whole room, "Let's go! I'm ready for my walk."

"Wees time," I heard Finn say with slight exasperation as he slowly swung his legs out of the bed looking half asleep.

We followed Finn out the door close on his heels. Mum always got to lie in for an extra ten minutes.

Happy thirteenth birthday

Grace

This afternoon was Gidget's thirteenth birthday party. I was so excited the whole crew were celebrating together at Susan's house. The girls and I often laughed at the sheer hilarity of a thirteen-year-old doggy birthday party, with all the senior golden oldies mooching around on the lawn with their party hats on waiting to devour the sweet potato cake topped with cucumber and blueberries. Hilariously cute.

Susan had finalised her divorce and, with the financial proceeds, purchased a lovely old bungalow on the east side of the city. It had a tennis court and a pool, where Susan spent a lot of time with friends – laps and chats she called these catch-ups. The bonus for us was that it also had a large grassed area she called the dog park paradiso. It even had a little wooden sign at the entrance.

Sadly, her golden boy Hudson had passed from kidney failure. Snowy was still going strong despite greying around the face. It looked like he had big Chanel-style sunglass marks around his eyes. In fact, most of the dogs looked like that now. I thought he looked a bit sad being on his own after being stuck like glue to Hudson his entire life. We knew dogs could experience grief too and Susan was good at keeping him occupied. I heard a whisper a new puppy may be on the horizon too.

Paula was thrilled that Susan was happy to throw the party as she lived in a two-storey townhouse with no room for all our big dogs. She had lost her golden girl Shelly not that long ago also. Paula had to make the difficult decision, one she still questions, wondering if the timing was right. We all wonder this, I said to her. The end-of-life decision is the worst. Is it too soon or verging on too late?

Amy told me that if you listen to your pet, observe their body and their behaviour, take advice from the vet and trust your gut feeling, you will just know. Unfortunately, that doesn't mean you will be released from the doubt afterwards or the horrendous grief that follows, for that matter.

Wilma, Paula's other golden girl, like Snowy, seemed sadder being on her own now. Maybe it was just me being an animal empath. We all anthropomorphise at times and project our emotions onto animals. I felt sad for Wilma so my inner mind translated this to mean Wilma was sad. This may not necessarily be the case, however, as we know animals don't feel feelings quite like us. But make no mistake, they do feel feelings, just differently.

Paula was also on her own, still forever single. She said men were just too much effort and she cringed openly at the online dating world. After a few hideous dates, she deleted her profile and focused more on her bridge game, thinking she was destined to be alone forever. She joked she would likely take up crocheting. Or, since she didn't like cats much, I suggested maybe she could adopt lots of small senior dogs, just like one of my favourite Instagram pages.

Polly lived in the Adelaide Hills in what looked like the prettiest B&B on the block. I loved visiting. I bought all my flowers now from Polly's Bloom. She still grew magnificent hydrangeas every year and still used colourful umbrellas to shield them from the sun. Olive would also take respite in the shade and guard the beautiful pink and purple flowers. So long as there were no thunderstorms, life for her was perfect.

Camilla and Antonio were able to attend being a Sunday afternoon and they left Penelope's in the capable hands of Saskia, their new team manager. I heard expansion to a second location was on the horizon and I wondered if their weak soy lattes would be as good.

Fred and Lilly had expanded the classes and the offerings at the studio and relied more on me for the full running of the business. I had to work a few more hours to achieve this but, thankfully, I was able to do a lot from home. I taught the odd class for them but focused more on the administration side of things and attending classes with other teachers.

Whenever I pulled up at the studio, I always parked in Morty's special car park spot. We had added a big red love heart to the bitumen under his name, and a pair of floppy ears and a plaque 'In honour of Morty' were added to the wall.

Morty had been an outstanding canine companion to Finn. The cutest boy ever. Each time we pulled up, I would say this out loud to Gidget and she would tilt her head as if to say, "I loved him."

Gidget still had all her spots at the studio. Karen, her favourite yogi, took her to all her classes and she just sat and observed. Lady Gidget, as Karen jokingly called her, was the best class mascot.

I was hoping to follow Fred's motto soon and slow down. I hadn't yet shared this with anyone except Finn. I was secretly hoping Tommy might step up and help out, but it was unlikely. He was still happy sitting on his verandah with Bert watching the sunrise and sunset, and not doing much else, besides surf of course.

Fred spent more time in his happy place meditating and Lilly continued her creative pursuits. Her latest hobby was painting, acrylics to be precise, and she continually asked Fred to be her model and sit for her. He said to me once, quietly, that he didn't think her amateur portraits were really shelf-worthy. But he loved her attempts and her persistence. He would do anything to keep her happy so he considered this as just another opportunity to sit still and meditate. Paint me with my eyes closed, he would joke.

Stephanie had retired from being a therapist. She had started to feel burnt out by everyone else's demands and issues. She wanted to brush a lifetime of stress off her shoulders and enjoy a life change to feel refreshed and lighter. Her own therapist had helped her arrive at that decision. I thought it was odd that a therapist needed to have a therapist. She reassured me that everyone needs to be held accountable.

In contrast, she opened a doggy daycare, which was poles apart from her previous role. She named it Eddie's Doggy Daycare. It was full of laughter, fun, playfulness and light-heartedness. Just what the doctor ordered.

Stephanie always laughed and filled the room with hilarious dog stories, most of which involved her own dogs, Eddie and Molly, who Eddie had seduced on that late-night adventure, and two of the five puppies conceived from their liaison, Lola and Spencer.

We were great friends now she wasn't my therapist and there was no longer any conflict of interest. She knew everything about me but the difference now was that Stephanie also shared her life and I was starting to know just as much about her. Being a therapist definitely doesn't make you perfect but enables you to hone your skills on how to actively listen to someone and allow clients to arrive at their own solutions.

Stephanie also loved catching up with Camilla as she got to see Bob, the little live-wire Jack Russell. Bob was the third puppy from Eddie and Molly's liaison, and it was always fun to unite the family for play dates. The other two puppies had been rehomed interstate but Stephanie received the occasional text and photo. They looked exactly like Eddie, that cheeky man who escaped and planted his seeds all over town that night long ago.

Bob was a little overenthusiastic. Definitely a Jack Russell! Amy, always the expert on all things dog behaviour, said he had doggy ADHD and he was overstimulated and hypervigilant. As much as this may seem entertaining to the humans, for the dog it is highly stressful being in a constant state of high anxiety.

A happy dog is a calm dog, Amy always said. After much discussion and resistance from Camilla, Bob was being trialled on medication plus behavioural training techniques to help his issues.

Dr Finn had chosen a selective serotonin reuptake inhibitor (SSRI) antidepressant. It helps with depression, panic, anxiety or obsessive-compulsive symptoms, he told us. It was a game changer for both Bob and Camilla as the medication did its job. Teddy also woofed a sigh of relief as Bob stopped constantly hanging off Teddy's jowls. Poor Teddy was so endlessly patient.

Gabriel and Gloria facetimed to wish Gidget a happy birthday and said they were having a marvellous time. They were going to be away for a few more months if that worked for us. Of course, we said, secretly happy. The Labs were part of the family and we knew we would happily adopt them if that ever became an option. We covertly hoped and prayed it may be one day.

And as for Finn and me, we had also settled into a great routine. I had lived on my own for a while and everyone had said to be careful as I would be so set in my ways. But this was not the case. It turned out to be so easy. We followed the three Cs – consult, collaborate and compromise. We had the same views and deeper moral values on most things, which was the foundation for a good relationship.

We did each stand our ground on a few things. I didn't do any ironing at all and Finn was fine with that. Finn often had to be called out with little notice for work emergencies and I was good with that. He was helping animals after all.

Charlotte and Oliver, Finn's kids, dropped by often and were the most easygoing kids, just like their father. They had accepted me from day one, thankfully. And of course they loved Gidget. I mean, who wouldn't? So there were no issues there at all.

It was one of those eras and chapters in life when everything was running smoothly. I would often sit in the backyard with the sun on my face and dogs at my feet, and close my eyes and smile. A poignant tear made up of sadness from past losses and excitement for future gains and experiences not yet realised would appear. Colossal gratitude for the right now would follow. Life was imperfectly perfect. Or was it perfectly imperfect? Maybe it was both.

I was aware not to take this for granted. I knew life could be fragile and, at a moment's notice, anything could change and uproot everything you knew as real with the potential to throw life into chaos.

Everything is a lesson to be learnt. Everything is an experience, be it good or difficult, to help you build resilience and strength simultaneously. So, I practised gratitude with fervour and passion and often said I love you to all the important people in my life... just because.

I greeted everyone with a warm hello as they arrived at the party. In came various gift bags full of treats and more toys to be dismembered.

Gidget was doing little senior jumps all over the place, happy to see both our furry and human friends. She had developed this little happy dance, where she would jump up and down at the same time that her head would be going up and down and her middle wiggling from side to side.

She always loved a party, so her dancing was apt and enamoured by both dogs and people equally.

Gidget

"**M**orning everyone! It's my birthday and I'm thirteen," I woofed "Where's my party hat and my hot pink bow?"

Mum and Finn sang happy birthday loudly, maybe not realising my hearing was one thing that hadn't deteriorated. The boys started barking. That was how this birthday day started.

The whole day went by in the blink of an eye. It was the best day. Another day gone and I was back in bed circling around to find the precise spot.

"Mum, Finn, thank you for the best day ever," I woofed.

The party went on for hours and lunch turned into pizzas for dinner. A pizza or takeaway order happened often as Mum didn't like to cook much. The only advantage of Will all those years ago was the doggy leftovers that Charlie and I would devour. They were amazing, especially the gnocchi ragu.

How amazing it could have been if we had celebrated our thirteenth birthdays together. I still missed Charlie. I felt nostalgic thinking that I lost my brother and best friend at such a young age. He had so much more life to live and love to give. He was still in my dreams every night.

Everyone fussed over the party girl – me – all day. It was awesome. I often looked over to check on Mum and she looked so happy. I had been through so much with her. The highs and the lows.

I remember vividly how sad she looked in that era when she broke up with Will and again when she lost Charlie. Things were different now. They felt lighter and happier.

You see, being a dog we are very – and I mean very – in tune with human emotions. We feel everything. We notice any subtle emotion or change. And as mum Suzy told me, it was my job to love Mum unconditionally no matter what she was feeling.

If things were really bad, I just lay my head in her lap and flicker her my sad eyes. I had done that often but not so much in this stage of her life. I hoped this happiness would last and the smile etched on her face was eternal. I clown smiled.

Some nights, just like tonight, both Finn and I had our heads on her lap. Not because we were sad, just because we were family and it felt nice. She would pat my head and stroke my fur telling me I was a good girl. The two Labs were at our feet. They had no idea about personal space. We had this big lounge room with a big modular white leather sofa, yet everyone was almost piled on top of each other. That must be love.

Mum took off my hot pink bow. It was starting to look a little scruffy around the edges after so many years. I think I should get a new one as there are plenty more special events and birthdays I want to attend and I can't go around town looking shabby. I was a classy dog, or at least, I thought so.

I actually owned a Louis Vuitton collar which Camilla brought back for me from one of her trips. Mum occasionally wondered out loud if it was the real deal or a knockoff from the markets. She never found out but it didn't matter to me. I didn't care much for material things. I only cared about being nurtured and loved by my family.

"Wees!" Finn said and the three of us shuffled outside. It was one of those few miracle nights when we all dropped and lifted legs, or Arnie to be more precise did a weird half-squat/lift manoeuvre, at the same time. "Triple wees!" shouted Finn.

Rudy did his business on the new life-size Buddha water fountain in the backyard. You're marked, I could imagine him woofing.

"Oh no, use a tree, Rudy, not the new Buddha," Finn said laughing a little. Arnie then squatted with his rounded and hunched back and pushed out a big steamy late-night poo. Probably from all the extra treats. He then proceeded to kick dirt up all over the place with his back paws covering Finn and me in the process.

I went running over to try and eat it but Finn beat me to it and scooped it up.

We played this game sometimes. Not sure why. Finn called it coprophagia when a dog eats dog poo. On occasion, I was known to eat poo and then proceed to throw it up. "DIS-gusting!" Mum would say. She would shun my doggy kisses for some hours afterwards and another worming tablet would be shoved down my throat. Urggghh.

Mum had investigated this strange phenomenon, using Dr Google before she spoke with Finn. He told her off for searching online when she had a live-in vet. There was nothing wrong with my health, he said. She tried all sorts of home remedies including adding pineapple to my food but none of it worked. It was obviously a myth or a mystery.

I knew why I liked to eat poo. It tasted good. The oldies had a special arthritis food that was packed full of omega fish oils and it smelt great, going in and coming out. Everyone else's poo was perfunctory and I'd wander past nonchalantly.

"Well done, guys." I knew what Finn meant as often he would have to wait outside for ages before we all did our wees. I would have to sniff everything. Rudy would have to check for the possum. It could take ages. Mum would often ask Finn what took so long when we finally made it to the bedroom. She had taken off her makeup, brushed her teeth, taken all her supplements and read a chapter of her book by the time we finished.

He didn't tell her that he often sat on the bench in the backyard under the stars. He loved this peaceful time of the day when the world was quiet. It was his own private moment to himself, to ground, to be conscious and to check in with himself. He showed gratitude for three things every night. I was often one of the things he was grateful for, but I didn't get a mention on the poo-eating nights.

Tonight, number ones and some twos were done and dusted in about five minutes. Finn hardly had time for his gratitude practice.

Instead, he just looked at us and said, "I am grateful for 1. Gidget, 2. Arnie, and 3. Rudy." He pointed at each of us in turn and then we were whisked back inside to bed.

We were all really tired. It had been a big day – a big, beautiful birthday day. Lights went out.

"Woof!" I barked at Mum to say I love you and thank you for the best day.

I heard back, "I love you, Gidget. You and me always, baby girl." And then she muttered something to the Lab duo, my buddies. I didn't hear it as I was still basking in her words and tucking them gently up into my heart.

I loved her voice, her words, her smell and how she made me feel special. In fact, I loved everything about her. My mum.

I closed my eyes and prayed as always to run free and wild with youth and vigour in my dreams with Charlie and any others that cared to join.

Happy birthday to me.

Blood results

GRACE

"Hello honey, I need you to bring Gidget in this morning. Does 10am work for you? Finn said quickly.

"Sure, but why?" I asked apprehensively.

"I need to give her a recheck, following up from last week's appointment," he said with a weird edge to his voice. Maybe it was his vet voice, possibly just on autopilot doing his follow-up phone calls.

"I'll see you at 10am," he said.

Before I could ask any more questions, the call ended, leaving me a tad befuddled. My iPhone wallpaper appeared with a picture of Gidget's face with her long tongue curling up to touch her nose. One of my favourites of about 10,000 stored on my phone.

Dr Finn is how I thought of him when he was being professional rather than just Finn or Finny. Clearly he didn't want to elaborate any further, unintentionally leaving me to worry instead.

It was 8.30am now so at least I didn't have to wait long.

"Let's get ready, Gidget. We have to go out," I said, smiling at her as I rustled the long thick furs that had grown on the back of her head in her older age. I loved how their coats changed as they aged and became thicker and sometimes curlier or denser. Such perfection. She was such an adorable senior lady – classy, spunky, cheeky, graceful, slower these days, looked great in a hot pink bow and totally lovable.

Arnie and Rudy looked at me as if to ask if there was any more food. A common occurrence. I laughed and ignored them as they looked pleadingly at the pantry door where all the treats lived. It was full of dog treats. And I mean full... a whole shelf full.

I was only at the vet last week as I had taken Arnie and Rudy for their health checks and vaccinations.

They got the all-clear besides Arnie weighing in a little heavy for his body shape at a whooping thirty-six kilograms. The lovely nurse Sally drew up a weight loss plan for him, calculating the exact calorie intake needed to get him to his ideal weight of thirty-three kilograms. An online food calculator had worked it all out. He would not be impressed that he had to cut back on the treats or reduce his breakfast and dinner allowance. There would be outrage. If Arnie loved anything it was his food, and we often called him Hoover Boy.

When he first arrived, he scoffed his dry food so quickly that he nearly choked. I could imagine it all sitting in a big lumpy obstruction in his oesophagus. I started to mix his food with water which helped prevent the gagging but he still hoovered it. Next, I invested in a special slow feeder bowl, which did the trick. His was bright orange. Rudy got a bright green one and Gidget, obviously, a hot pink one.

It was 10.02am and I was sitting in the consult room with Gidget waiting for Finn. Despite being still worried, I looked at Gidget and couldn't believe how lucky I was. A warm fuzzy glow ascended from my toes all the way up to my forehead and goosebumps slowly developed all over. I loved that feeling. It felt like a whole body orgasmic frenzy. I felt alive.

This happened a lot when I just sat, truly present in the moment and ready to receive. I thought about how unconditional and totally eternal the love I had for her was. Soon after, the tears pricked and threatened to emerge and just as this happened the door opened.

"Hi Grace," he said, and leaned over to plant a kiss right on my lips. He drew me in for the most warm, tight and solid hug. He didn't seem to want to let go.

I knew right then there was something wrong.

"What's happened, Finn? Why am I here? Why are you being weirdly professional with me and what's with that hug?" I rattled off quickly.

The tears that were prematurely stopped before now rose up and flowed down my cheeks onto his shoulder. As he drew me out of the hug, he looked into my eyes and placed a hand on my face.

"Gracey, darling, I got Gidget's blood test results back this morning and they're not looking good," he said with a gentleness I knew well.

I flinched and my whole body contracted tightly.

"She has raised inflammatory markers and concerning red and white blood cell counts. I would like to do some more comprehensive blood tests but I am worried she may have cancer. Leukaemia or lymphoma to be more precise." He drew a breath.

The tears engulfed me as I fell into another supportive and loving Finn hug. I could feel Gidget rubbing up to my legs, letting out little concerned whiney cries.

Gidget

I had been feeling more tired lately. At my thirteenth party, I didn't feel I could keep up with the others. I just thought I was an older doggy and this was normal.

But seeing Mum react like this, I knew something was seriously wrong. I tried to interpret her body language and sidled up to her and let my cheek touch her leg. I was letting out little whimpers to let her know I was concerned for her and for me.

I had eaten dinner last night eagerly as Mum added some marinated chicken leftovers to my special joint food. But this morning with no extra enticement I wasn't really interested in my breakfast. Since Mum was busy and distracted and whisked me out the door so quickly, she didn't notice that Arnie had wolfed down my bowl as well as his own.

Normally, when he tried this on, which he did often, I would give him a little lift of the lip – a gentle snarl, a warning only – and he would back away instantly. I don't like conflict. I'm definitely a lover, not a fighter. Rudy was much more of an obedient gentleman.

Arnie knew I was the pack leader but today I gave my food a sniff and then just stepped aside, essentially giving him permission to eat from my plate. He wasn't sure of my reaction so he sneakily crept in and gobbled it all up doing a little gag after. Did he take this as a sign that he was taking the pack leader role? I hope not.

It was now mid-morning and I noted to myself that I still wasn't hungry, but I really needed a drink.

Finn got the clippers out and turned them on to check they were working. My ears pricked with the noise that sounded like a bee. I was flung back into the past as a small puppy when that damn bee outsmarted me. Finn then shaved a little piece of fur off the front of my leg.

I wasn't quick enough to see the needle heading my way. "Ouch, not again!" I woofed. I thought we had done everything last week. More blood was drawn, straight into a tube labelled 'Gidget', and put into a plastic bag.

Finn applied a little gauze sticky tape over where the needle went. A liver treat was offered straight after but I just nudged it with my nose. I heard Mum say that I never refuse liver treats. I am worried now too. I proceeded to try and chew off the gauze.

I heard Finn say that he would do a more comprehensive blood test and gather some more information and we would make some decisions on how to proceed from there.

Grace

"Come on, Gidget girl, let's go home," I said, desperately trying to control my tears but knowing they needed to be expressed and not suppressed. Fred had taught me that, but I didn't want to upset Gidget with a big display of emotion. Dogs are so in tune with us and our emotions, but I didn't want to make her anxious. I would wait until I was out of Gidget's earshot before I fully let go.

There was a great lookout spot nearby with a magnificent view of the city. Despite discovering it years ago, I saved my visits for my emotional buildups. It wasn't frequented much, especially during the day, so it was a great spot to stop and yell as loud as possible to clear the energy, the tears, the anger and the frustration. Everything really... whatever arose.

After Charlie passed, I visited often and sometimes felt like an old Italian nanna dressed all in black. As the howling and wailing would ascend from inside, surprising even myself, I would roar it out into the ether. Another piece of myself healed each time as I journeyed through my grief.

I hoped I wouldn't be visiting the lookout sooner than I had expected.

It all happened so fast. Even though she was thirteen, I hadn't given myself consent to think about anything serious happening to her. It was inconceivable. Not acceptable. It can't be real. How could this be my new reality? In a heartbeat, things had gone from being beautifully calm and happy to traumatic and stressful.

Life doing what life does... again.

Fred and Stephanie's words reverberated around my head: expect the best but be prepared for the worst. I know, I thought to myself, but I was quite happy to remain in denial for a while longer.

Yoga and all the self-development had teflon-coated me somewhat over the years. I had built an inner strength and resilience to be able to cope with many life challenges. Now in my fifties, I could deal with struggles much easier than I had in my twenties and thirties.

I had grown and matured. I also had shelves full of personal development books that helped me. When I didn't have a specific title, Camilla invariably had it at Penelope's. They prided themselves on having all the up-to-date resources on how to be happier and healthier. It was almost their motto.

That night I knelt on the floor and like always I said to Gidget, "I love you. You and me always, baby girl." I held her a little longer than normal, taking in her smell, her love, her essence, and then crawled back into bed. Finn rolled over immediately to spoon me.

"Finn, darling, please hold on extra tight. I feel like I'm falling apart," I said with a shaky voice.

"Gracey." He started to speak but I interrupted him.

"Finn, just hold me. I don't want to talk. I just want to imagine we are all here, like every other normal night. Gidget, Arnie and Rudy, you and me for at least one more night before everything feels broken. But deep down I knew it already did and things would never be the same. Gidget would never be the same. Neither would I.

Gidget

"**N**ight Mum," I woofed. What a big day with bad news, needles and no appetite. Very weird. Then to top it off, Rudy slammed the fence to scare Poppy the possum and landed on my front paw while I was innocently sniffing a leaf. I winced and limped to the bedroom.

Finn had a quick look and said it was just a strain, thankfully. It appeared we had enough serious, serious, as Finn would say twice, stuff to deal with at the moment. I didn't need any more ailments or concerns.

I closed my eyes and prepared for sleep. I feared that it may not be long before I wouldn't need to dream of Charlie anymore and that I may actually be with him once again.

For tonight, though, I invited Charlie, Morty and Eddie back once again. As my third eyelids closed over, a field of green appeared complete with a free-flowing creek. I was sitting there with my ailing health and they were all running towards me full of energy and youth, woofing loudly.

I hoped that would be me one day again soon.

In sickness and in health

Grace

Everything changed. And not for the best. The next few months were demanding to say the least. One day Gidget would seem quite good, almost normal. The next she would be weary and not her usual self. And sleeping more.

Dogs mask pain really well so I needed to be extra vigilant and observant to note the extent of the changes to report them back to Finn. I started a notebook with all the signs she was exhibiting. I looked out for things like behaviour changes, lethargy and weight fluctuations, and the more obvious red flags like vomiting and diarrhoea. Finn said they are called signs not symptoms as dogs can't actually tell us what is wrong with them, so we just observe the signs.

She had a lot of digestive issues. One day, a perfect poo – a number four on the Bristol Stool Chart for humans. I would do a little jump of joy in the backyard, trying to convince myself, still in denial, that things would be fine, that she would get better or at least that we had time left. The next time, it could be explosive diarrhoea, just making it to the back lawn in time. Other times, she was unaware it was even coming and it would just flow out and drip onto the floor.

We accounted for this with special pads, mats and doggy diapers where needed. We kept her out of the carpeted areas where possible, but really who cared if we had to replace the carpet one day. She was way more important than anything materialistic. She still slept in our bedroom and as yet there had been no accidents there.

This was her time to be cared for and meticulously looked after. She had shown us absolute unquestionable, unconditional love and provided endless joy and humorous antics throughout her life. Now it was her time. Essentially she was in palliative care. Never knowing how she would feel from one day to the next, we adjusted our dog walks, our dinners and basically our entire lives to care for her. Our special Gidget girl.

Between Finn and I, we adjusted our work hours so someone was always with her. Failing that, she went to work with Finn to the vet hospital. She would sit with Ivy the practice manager who would keep an eye on her while all the nurses floofed all over her. Despite her illness, she was like a therapy dog who cheered up everyone's day when she was there.

There were health checks, copious vet appointments, specialist visits, discussions about CT scans and more blood tests. There was more observing. More noting in the notebook. More tears. More cuddles.

"How do I know when the time is right?" I asked Finn one night.

"You will know, Grace. You will feel it and she will tell you. Look for the signs. I will guide you medically as well."

Finn told me about clients who had left it too late, refusing the vet's strong recommendation, and ended up desperately running to the emergency clinic at 2am with a pet in terrible pain. They had so much regret afterwards.

Others make the decision but wonder if it is too early. They want their pet to leave with a quality of life and dignity and not suffer to the end stage of pain. We are lucky that we have the opportunity to make this decision for our beloved pets. However, this means that while we can remove our loved pet from their pain, we plunge ourselves into our own. That in itself makes the decision even more challenging.

It was an impossible, traumatic decision. Truly the final act of love.

My mind was thrown into a compulsive back-and-forth debate about what was right for her at this time. I contemplated how to prepare for the last kiss, the last cuddle, the sweet goodbye.

I felt like Gidget was a pin cushion with all the tests. She was so stoic throughout this time, being shuffled around from different hospitals and being tempted with more upmarket treats to appease her now picky palate. She would happily go along with whatever, never growling, never snarling, just being her beautiful self. But, sadly, a sick version.

It was about quality of life and once that was impaired, I knew I would consider her end-of-life plan.

The only important thing in my life right now was what was right for her, not me.

I asked myself constantly if it was that time yet.

GIDGET

Every day was difficult. My energy had lessened, my appetite vanished, my tummy was sore and my poo near-misses were embarrassing to say the least.

"Leukaemia," Finn had whispered in my ear while he lay on the floor with me half watching the Foxtel sports channel. He loved watching sport, much to Mum's displeasure who preferred binge-watching Netflix series.

"Gidget, we will do all we can for you to keep you comfortable. I promise you are in exceptional caring hands. When the time is right you just need to give us a sign. We will keep an eye out for it. In the meantime, we want you to live every day to its doggy fullest," he said. And that is what I intended to do.

There were so many more visits to see Finn at the hospital and so many more jabs – or ouchies as I called them. I heard Mum on the phone speaking to someone called Dr Sebastian Carter. Finn told Mum he was an excellent internal medicine specialist vet.

Sebby, as Finn called him, had gone through veterinary medicine at the University of Melbourne at the same time as Finn. They graduated the same year and were both working to give me the longest time as well as the most quality time for the time I had left.

Finn prescribed corticosteroids which helped perk me up a bit. It was a little blue miracle worker. Some part of me knew it was just masking an underlying, unfixable health issue. For now, though, my tail was wagging a little more, my appetite and energy increased, and I even did a butt wiggle. This made Mum happy.

Chemotherapy was questionable and was still being discussed.

I knew there was a timeline. I just didn't know what that looked like yet.

A woofy list

Grace

The woofy list, better known to humans as the infamous bucket list, became the most important thing on my agenda. I was determined to fulfil each and every one of the carefully selected twenty items I had placed on this precious list for Gidget. We were in no hurry. The last item, number twenty, was a sweet goodbye so we didn't want that one to arrive too soon.

It was very poignant spending time at our favourite beach. We would go often when Gidget was younger. She would run like the wind, ears flapping in the breeze trying to keep up with her body.

Her energy was contagious as she ran after the seagulls and up and down the sand dunes, zoomed around in circles and swam out to sea. She could go for at least an hour nonstop before she pulled up for a minute's rest before the whole routine was repeated. I ran behind her incessantly, trying to ensure she didn't run too far away, annoy anyone, jump on anyone, disappear, swim too far out or eat anything untoward like a puffer fish.

She had done this once when she was about four. She didn't eat it, thankfully, as that would have been fatal. But she picked it up, gave it a little lick then spat it out just as I yelled, "Drop it, Gidget!"

When I arrived at the East Emergency & Specialist Centre, Gidget started retching like mad, letting out a giant cocktail of seawater and puffer vomit throughout the whole reception area. "I'm here!" I could imagine her saying. "I'm so sorry," I said instead. They took one look at the photo of the fish and whisked her away, leaving me in bewilderment in reception.

She spent twenty-four hours in the emergency hospital while they administered activated charcoal to induce vomiting to remove any potential tetrodotoxin poison that was ingested and gave her IV fluids to help with hydration. In a case of severe paralysis, more life support treatment would possibly be needed but thankfully not in Gidget's case. It was a close call, nevertheless.

Now I tell everyone on the beach about her story to raise awareness. Most people, including the fishermen who throw the fish onto the beach willy-nilly instead of disposing of them responsibly, don't even know how fatal they are.

Now, though, she is a senior and she shuffled down the walkway to the sand. Gidget and I sat together as she nuzzled her head in my chest while the wind lifted her ears slowly up and down. They looked like they were hovering in space like Sally Field's Flying Nun habit. The tufts of hair that hung from her ears and chest swayed softly.

Once she had regained her energy from the walk down to the beach, I got out her hot pink water toy. This perked her up. It was the same one she had chased into the sea endlessly for years. It was as old as she was and it was worn out and tattered around the edges. Just like Gidget, I suppose. Now I just threw it about a foot away.

"Go get it, Gidget," I said.

Gidget did an old lady run with her back two legs operating together like bunny hops. She picked up the toy, made it squeak, then dropped it at my feet, looking at me as if to say, "Again Mum!" She threw her head in the air in a senior nanna excitement moment and let out a deep woof.

We got our paws wet in the shallows and we spoke about life and love – ours, of course.

Another of her bucket list activities was to visit the local artisan homeware store and get our photo taken for their Instagram page in front of a parquetry buffet. It was good and extra cute marketing, the lady in the store said. Her name tag read Posie, Artisan Connoisseur.

The one positive about Gidget being older was that her stubbornness had reduced. She would willingly get in the car now without needing endless bribery or without me having to recruit a stranger to help me hold her in while I quickly shut the boot.

I would have been happy to repeat any angst if only she were that youthful again. It wasn't that I didn't cherish the older age. The loyalty, soft nature and devotion had flourished over the years. Senior goldens are delightful, Gidget included, but I would happily do it all over again, especially if it meant not being at this final stage of her life, getting ready for the sweet goodbye at number twenty.

I wondered how this could even be possible.

The last one, number twenty, lingered in the wind, impossible to accept. I had no idea when it would occur, so I felt like we were in limbo land, betwixt the dichotomy of love and grief. And so we waited, with the heart-wrenching moments ticking by too fast.

We were ticking off one thing at a time from the woofy list. All with Gidget wearing her beautiful hot pink bow. I ensured I was fully present during each one and took endless photos to reflect on, for, you know, later. I felt like my heart was being torn into shreds. It was literally hurting, broken, bruised and cut.

I called Camilla often to talk to her and share my feelings. I knew I could cry, vent, laugh and go through the whole rainbow of emotions with her. Without her support, this situation would have been nearly impossible to navigate. She had been through this before as I had with Ernie. But every time, every dog, every situation is different and unique. None is easy. Camilla was always there for me and I was tremendously grateful.

This was my reality right now and I tried to live in the moment that was this. It was very hard but I did it for Gidget's sake. My sweet girl.

The doorbell rang. I opened the front door and saw the most stunning array of flowers materialise. Pinks, purples and whites, big and small, intermingled with what looked like leatherleaf fern and some spatters of myrtle in a clear crystal glass vase. It mimicked the Royal Doulton crystal range my nanna had given me on her passing. Stunning. I spied a little familiar lavender colour sticker. Polly's Bloom, it read. My spirits lifted momentarily.

I carried the flowers to the bedroom where Finn was sitting up in bed with Arnie and Rudy lying on either side of him. Finn was finalising his histories from his vet consults today, forever a workaholic. His eyes bulged and his eyebrows lifted all at once when he saw the bunch of flowers. "They are huge and simply stunning. Are they from Polly?" he asked.

"Of course, from all of them. They are such dear friends. I am very lucky" I said.

"Yes, you are, but you are luckier to have me," he said laughing, leaping out of his work professional demeanour into his cheeky Finn persona saved just for me.

The card read a simple, "Grace, we are all thinking of you and sending love. Polly, Paula, Susan and the doggies." It had a full row of Xs impersonating kisses at the end, and a woof following them.

Soon after, we turned out the lights.

"Night Finn, I love you. Thank you for everything you do for Gidget and me. Especially for Gidget during this tough time," I said cuddling him.

"Night, my sweet Gidget girl. You and me always, beautiful girl. I love you," I said, knowing this nightly habitual gesture would sadly have an expiration date.

And with that, my perfect family right here right now, was present and to me picture perfect.

GIDGET

Mum spoke to me while we sat on the beach. She has a softness in her voice that was loving and tender, a softness that touched on her vulnerability. As I nuzzled into her, taking in all her body smells blended with the salty air and seawater smells – what a concoction – I felt like I was in heaven.

It was paradise, just the two of us at my favourite place enjoying each other's company. For a moment it made me forget my pain and the uncomfortableness in my tummy.

A precious moment between Mum and me.

"Gidget," she said, "I have been the luckiest person to care for you during your life and to receive your never-ending unconditional love. You have taught me things about life that I would never have learnt if I didn't stop and observe your ways. I have taken in your energy, charisma, craziness, devotion and personality. I feel honoured to have loved you all this time, all these years, through thick and thin. I don't know exactly what is going to happen in the next little while but I think sadly it will be short." She took a deep breath and continued.

"I have decided, darling, not to do a CT scan as the doctors tell me the treatment protocol wouldn't be any different even with a concrete diagnosis. The blood tests and signs you are exhibiting give us enough of a diagnosis to proceed with treatment. I don't want to put you through an unnecessary anaesthetic. Not because you are too old. Thankfully, with vigilance and attention to detail, most older pets can safely undergo general anaesthesia.

Ernie had dentals every four to six months the last few years of his life and he lived to a ripe old age of fifteen," she said nostalgically.

"But you must know that any decision I make is with you in the forefront of my mind. It's all for you, my sweet Gidget. I love you so much," she said with a shaky voice as tears appeared.

The woofy list was fun but intertwined with being really emotional for Mum and me. I seemed to recover faster from the feelings than her. I was still excellent at being in the present moment.

Mum, on the other hand, tried hard but for humans it was more complicated she told me often. Her emotions carried through the whole day and sometimes at night I could hear her cry as the lights went out. Actually, most nights lately.

As Mum wrote about our woofy list in her new journal that she named Gidget's Life, I pondered quietly what had happened to my mum Suzy. Was she still alive or did she get sick like me? She was my first mum and I loved her endlessly also.

Mum and I really were connected and somehow she must have understood what I had just been thinking. As she wrote, she read out loud: Gidget born 1st May 2010 at 5.15pm to Mother Suzy (passed age fourteen, kidney disease) and father Chester (also passed age fourteen, heart issues).

Would Mum Suzy be proud of me? Would she think I fulfilled my purpose of giving unconditional love to my human mum? Could I rest knowing I did what she asked of me?

I then heard Mum say, "Gidget, you really are the best dog. Your mum, Suzy, and dad, Chester, would have been really proud of you."

That made my night. In fact, it made my life.

I love you too, Mum.

Sleep came quickly after that.

End-of-life ceremony

GRACE

One of the more moving and touching woofy list events was the end-of-life ceremony.

When Gidget turned twelve, I recruited Gabby, an animal masseur, to give Gidget monthly massages at home.

She would arrive in a scrub top patterned with cute dogs, carrying a box packed full of candles, a music dock, aromatherapy and acupuncture needles. She would sit on the floor massaging Gidget and placing needles in sore spots to assist her old and tired muscles. It was a hit. Gidget loved Gabby. I could tell by all the licks she offered.

It was at one of these massages that Gabby spoke about end-of-life ceremonies. I didn't even know they existed but it sounded like a beautiful way to honour a life. I asked Gidget her thoughts and she let out a muffled woof. Her woofs were a bit hoarser now she was older. Finn was concerned at one stage she might have been showing signs of laryngeal paralysis, but thankfully not.

"Hi Gabby," I said quietly, opening the door and letting her in past the ruckus of the two Labradors wanting attention and sniffing for food. Gidget slowly shuffled up the passage with her little black paw booties on her back paws.

Sally from the vet had suggested the booties and they had been a huge blessing to help her stay steady on her feet. One night I had come home from shopping and found Gidget splayed out on the floorboards gazing into the backyard with a big stinky poo lying next to her. I didn't realise right away that she couldn't get herself up off the slippery floor. She had either pooed because she had been there a while or from the anxiety of not being able to get up. Neither was ideal.

Amazon had the doggy boots to my front door two days later and from that moment she wore them on her back paws every day. Apart from a short adjustment period when she walked lifting her back legs one at a time high and out to the side, giving them a little shake before placing them back on the ground, she adjusted to the boots quicky and they miraculously prevented any more slips and embarrassing poo stories.

I was sure we would need to progress to four boots very soon. At night I would say, Gidget, time to take your booties off and she would sleep with her paws free to twitch, paddle and run like the wind in her dreams with her long-lost friends, as I imagined she would anyway.

"Grace, so nice to see you. How is our Gidget girl today?" Gabby said with less animation in her voice than usual. I felt an awkwardness emerging.

"Gidget is waiting for you. She loves your visits and I told her today would be extra special," I replied light-heartedly with a smile, trying to mollify any uneasiness.

Gidget lounged on her side in her big pink donut bed. Gabby, Camilla and I surrounded her in a circle while Gabby set up for her ceremony. She placed beautiful soft pink rose quartz crystal stones on Gidget's shoulder, belly, flank and hip regions, and oracle cards around her on the ground. Gabby started off with her normal massage, then some reiki, followed by a reading of the oracle cards.

Camilla and I sat just taking in Gidget's energy, the soft soothing music, the flicker of the candles and the aroma of the lavender essential oils. They induce calm apparently and were working their magic on me for sure. I felt an instant calm just being around Gabby and her beautiful caring nature. She was soft, gentle, genuine, patient and loving. The rest was almost periphery but welcomed.

"Grace, would you like to say a mantra?" Gabby asked. "Something pertinent to Gidget's stage of life. One that we can then use for a short meditation." I had done this a few times with our yoga class so was familiar with what she was inviting in.

Without even thinking, I replied, "I choose to go easily and effortlessly when the time is right. I will go with love and leave love." It just came to me. It was like I was a channel for something bigger than Gidget or me. The words just arose in my mind and spoke themselves out loud. They were perfect. The mantra was to become our anchor in a mini meditation.

Gabby then turned to Camilla. "Camilla, would you like to say any words to Gidget?"

"Aww, I'm not really prepared, I don't know what to say... let me think... Gidget, you make my best friend, Grace, so extraordinarily happy which makes me happy. Your mum loves you endlessly as do Teddy, Antonio, Freddy, Bob and me, of course. I have been there for all your adventures, all your years, your birthdays, your health, your friends and your illnesses. I feel privileged because of that. When that time does come, go easily, sweet girl. Go safely, and rest softly knowing how loved you are. Look for the others on the other side – Charlie, Ernie, Violet, Daisy, Morty, Shelly, Hudson and of course your mum Suzy. There is so much love waiting for you, dear girl," she said with love and a poise and a calmness I didn't see often in her.

The anticipatory grief was profound as we were guided through this end-of-life ceremonial meditation and ritual, with my mantra close at hand. We were all consumed in our tears, our grief and our joint love for Gidget.

Mine, though, was the deepest. Heartbreaking. Soulful.

I hugged Gabby tightly at the front door knowing it was unlikely we would meet again in Gidget's lifetime but still wallowing in denial. "I will see you next month. Maybe we can do another end-of-life ritual," I said.

She looked at me, smiled and lowered her eyes as a frown crunched up the skin between her eyebrows. "Maybe," Gabby replied.

Her comment jerked me out of my denial to awaken a pain so strong that I felt a tightness in my chest and a choking in my throat. The rawness of the pain sent me straight back to denial once again to avoid this oncoming barrage of hurt, grief and pain hiding just under the surface. Waiting.

I will save that for later I thought. I promise I will address you, grief. I will honour you, grief. But for now, it's about Gidget. I went back inside and sat next to her as she snoozed, releasing some little snores. She was exactly where we had left her. I curled up next to her and held her tight.

GIDGET

I was tired. It had been a big day. That massage was lovely on my old bones and muscles. That ceremony was so moving, and my doggy heart felt that sadness and melancholy again that I'd only really known when Charlie left. It was a reminder of him and of our bond. More sadness appeared for my mum knowing what was to come. How would she cope with all her human emotions without me?

I thought the mantra was pertinent, soothing and timely.

"I choose to go easily and effortlessly when the time is right. I will go with love and leave love." I repeated it with a woof.

I tried to have a little snooze in Mum's arms but really I was contemplating things.

Something had shifted during the ritual. I didn't know why or how but all I knew was that I felt an ending approaching. An era maybe. A chapter. Our chapter.

It didn't make me sad per se. I had an acceptance of a well-rounded life full of love, well lived and a full life cycle. It felt natural. Just like in all of nature, there is a beginning, a middle and an end.

I had enormous gratitude for having such a loving mum who always placed my happiness before her own. So much love. And I had enormous gratitude for living a long healthy life as not all dogs get to do that. I thought of my beautiful Charlie friend.

Maybe it was time to give Mum a sign.

And with that, I really did fall asleep in her arms, basking in her cuddles, her protection and her love for the short time I had left. I soaked it all up.

Blown glass Labradors

GRACE

It was the same day the Labs went home that Gidget sent me a sign.

I didn't expect it so soon. I tried to ignore it but I had to acknowledge it. I was attuned to listening for signs and I had asked Gidget to send me one when she was ready. I had made a promise to Gidget, and I wouldn't let her down despite the impending doom that was swilling inside me.

So, I accepted it was a sign and knew life was about to change unfathomably from that moment.

"Hi Gabriel, Gloria, welcome home," I said trying to sound enthusiastic as they arrived at the door spot on 2pm as promised.

They were never usually on time. They were a tad jetlagged, having only arrived back in the country the night before.

Arnie and Rudy bounded up the hallway and stopped in their tracks for a minute, unsure of who had arrived. They looked confused, then suddenly they took off so fast that their legs almost got caught underneath them. They almost bowled over Gabriel who had knelt on the floor to engulf them. He got the full sniff over, lick over, tail-wagging extraordinaire treatment. Legs, snouts and tails flailed around madly.

Gloria knelt down to receive the same welcome. I had never seen these two dogs so happy to see anyone, besides us of course. It brought a huge genuine smile to my face, lifting it from the frown that had been permanently etched on my face recently.

I briefly noticed something big and red flashing from Gloria's left ring finger. Eventually, she stopped cuddling the dogs long enough to hold out her hand momentarily before she was off again. Ahh, the ruby... magnificent.

We spent most of the afternoon together. Arnie and Rudy eventually calmed down and lay at our feet. Rudy rested his head on Gabriel's bare foot. Gidget stayed close to me, like Velcro, eyeing me often.

Finn and I heard all about the wonderful life-changing trip, the travels, the epiphanies, and the moments of pure ecstasy and joy. We enjoyed the stories while sharing a bottle of French bubbles, cheese and pate to set the mood.

The highlight was obviously the proposal at Fontana di Trevi, as well as a yoga festival in Milan and a visit to the glassmaking island of Murano. It was getting late in the afternoon when Gloria thanked us profusely for looking after the two Labradors. She opened up her colourful bag that was almost large enough to fit the Labs into it and removed a beautifully wrapped gift and handed it to me.

"There are really no words that I can communicate to you that will appropriately portray how much we are grateful for you caring for these two. I know it is likely tough for you to give them back after having them for so long. I'm sure you have fallen for them just like we did. It only took the first hello, really, for us and we were hooked. Mille grazie," she said with a seriousness she often kept to herself.

"Open it," Gloria said, breaking the pause.

Focusing, I opened her gift. Inside were two perfect blown glass Labrador dogs, one cream and one black. They were stunning and fragile, much more so than the real ones, even down to the tails displaying tufts of fur blown into the glass. How she got them back to Australia in one piece without losing an appendage or two was a mystery to me.

"Straight out of the streets of Murano, made to order, especially for you. The glass was blown while we watched and waited. Can you guess what we named them?" she asked, laughing softly.

GIDGET

"Check ya soon, Gidget," Arnie woofed.

"See ya soon, Gidget," Rudy woofed, giving me a bit of a lick across the eyelids. Yuck!

Arnie and Rudy were loaded up into the back of the old rusty red dual cab ute, always excited for an adventure. I tilted my head and wondered when they would be back and when I would see them again. Would I see them again?

Time was a mystery to me, so who really knew. To me, everything revolved around breakfast and dinnertime, the important stuff.

It was only after they left that Mum sat me down and explained they had gone back to live with their real parents, and that we were only looking after them temporarily. She said they would still visit. "What?" I woofed, "I thought we were their real family." I tried to convey to her with the head tilts and the loud hoarse woofs what an atrocity this was for me.

Why do all the friends that I love go away? I don't understand. I wonder if Mum Suzy thought the same thing when my siblings and I left and went away all those years ago. Did she miss us? I missed her, no matter how much time had passed.

It was too late in the day though to ponder too much. This was deep, I was tired and I had big things to do, mostly worrying about and loving Mum.

A sign

Grace

Hugging each other, Finn and I were in our own thoughts. There were no words. The Labradors that had wormed their way straight into our hearts had gone. A sadness permeated the house.

Another loss to deal with.

And another was on its way.

It was time to break the news to Finn.

Closing my eyes, I said, "Darling, the time is right tomorrow."

"Yes, darling," he said, holding me tighter than ever before.

I said to Gidget, "Night beautiful girl, I love you. You and me always." I knew it was the last goodnight, which was breaking my heart bit by bit.

She was already snoring. Little quiet snores. Peacefully sleeping. My sweet baby girl.

Gidget

It was earlier this morning I had sent Mum a sign. Or at least I tried to.

I was outside doing my business as usual and Mum was sitting on the outdoor sofa. It was covered in dog fur, nothing unusual. She was checking her phone again. That damn thing, Finn always says.

Once I was finished, instead of sidling up to her like I usually did, especially lately as I never wanted to be far away, I waddled over to the crepe myrtle tree. I slowly lowered my body to the earth.

There on the ground was the beautiful river stone that Finn had given Mum when Charlie passed. Sitting next to it was another stone with Ernie etched onto it, another surprise from Finn. Next to that one was another one, more of an oblong shape, that read 'Mortimer, Morty for short'. Obviously it was oblong to indicate the length of his body and to fit his long name.

All three stones sat next to each other under the crepe myrtle. I planted myself right in front of them sheltered by the overhanging branches filled with pink flowers and sighed.

"Okay Gidget, all done. Let's go back inside," she said.

I just sat there, my head resting on my paw and my nose almost touching Charlie's stone. I often saw Mum sitting by these stones and feeling those pesky but necessary human emotions.

She tried to rouse me and even tried to lift me up by my collar but I refused. I was a dead weight, all floppy, my body glued to the ground. I could be really stubborn if I wanted to be. I sat looking back and forth from her to the stones.

Finally, she sat on the ground next to me, giving in to my old lady tenacity.

"Gidget, what's up, girl? You okay? What is it?" she said.

We both just sat for a while with me continuing to look at her and then back to the stones. Finally, I placed my head on Charlie's stone, looking at her sideways showing the whites of my eyes, pleading.

Mum took some deep breaths and came back to the present moment. I could feel it. Her shoulders dropped, her body loosened, her face softened. She was slowly moving out of her busy head and was connecting to her heart.

She then took a sharp inhale. She had got it. It took a while, but finally it dawned on her.

"Is this your sign, my sweet girl?" she asked me, unable to stop the flow of tears as she placed her hand on my head, stroking it ever so gently. I woofed softly.

I just stared directly into her eyes for the longest time and then crawled into her lap and flopped.

"I hear you," were her last words as we sat together, the two of us, thinking of the memories and the love that the stones signified.

Later, dinnertime came and went. I still had no appetite but I did eat the good treats though.

The final day

GRACE

I woke up in a fog knowing that today was the day – 6pm to be precise.

Everything felt surreal. I felt disconnected and confused. A serious lack of sleep was taking its toll alongside a tsunami of emotions waiting to overwhelm me. I felt like I was motionless in time.

I pulled the quilt back over my head and tried to pretend it was any other day in the darkness that surrounded me.

I heard the soft little snores that had comforted me for years rising from the end of the bed. These normally created a sense of peace, safety and love, but today they shot like an arrow into my heart, reminding me of what was to come. I tried to ignore the lump in my throat and the nausea within as I got out of bed and lay down next to her, tucking her up safely in my arms.

I watched her chest rise and fall as it had a gazillion times since that first cuddle when I asked her if she wanted to come and live with me. When she had answered with a resounding yes. That was the moment I fell instantly in love.

So long ago. A lifetime ago. Well, at least her lifetime.

Eventually she woke and opened her eyes. Her eyes were glassy and grey but they looked at me with so much love as they had done every day for over thirteen years.

The whites around her eyes had changed so slowly over the years that I almost didn't notice. Sunglass marks. Her muzzle also showed the signs of old age, now speckled with grey fur all the way around to underneath her chin.

She was as beautiful as ever in her senior years – an exquisite, mature version of her youthful self.

Her old joints were a little rickety yet she still managed to get up and walk around slowly. A little trip over the edge of her bed, a senior stumble, wasn't unusual. Her legs had a stiffness to them that made her gait awkward. I thanked Finn in my mind for helping reduce her pain.

"Come on, Gidget girl, wee time," I whispered.

I had promised that when this time came it was going to be a happy day for her. I would save the tears and the endless grief for later. I would cherish today. I asked myself how I could hold on to each and every moment to keep me satiated for the rest of my life. It seemed impossible.

With a slow and surprisingly steady squat and only a minor sway, she relieved herself. The love I had in that moment threatened to crack my heart and cause a break so deep I feared it may never heal. The lump in my throat remained, the tears wanting to spill.

Although she had little appetite the last few days, I picked the best treats. My pockets were filled with them ready to treat her for everything she did today. I handed one to her.

I even located her training clicker to help her feel young and smart again. She was always eager to please. At the first click, her ears pricked and her head tilted. As I shouted, "BANG!" she looked at me while she manoeuvred herself slowly to a side-lying position on the floor. It was like she was two again. They never forgot. Everything was a miracle. She was a miracle. I handed her another treat.

"Good girl. You're such a good girl," I said for the hundred millionth time. "It's sniffari time."

A short while later, I gathered up our worn-out hot pink dog bag. It had aged just like Gidget and was tatty at the corners but still much loved. I flung it over my shoulder and we headed to the car.

"It's not easy, this part of the life journey, Gidget, but I am always by your side," I said to her. "Let's go and enjoy today."

I sang 'My Girl' by The Temptations in my discordant voice as we drove along. I was praying to feel happy for her today. Whilst a familiar sense of despair and grief invaded me, I noticed that gratitude and a love so strong and deep were right there also.

Where did all the years go? Whoosh... She went from a naughty puppy to a devoted senior nanna in a nanosecond. A dog's life was too short. I felt ripped off.

We had a deadline. It was looming like an out-of-control steam train threatening to roll me over. I had to stay one foot in front of the destruction, at least for today.

"Back soon, Gidget. Love you," I said as I had done over a million times. I closed the car door and flew into Penelope's to get a coffee.

"Hi Antonio, a medium soy weak latte, please." It rolled off my tongue like a mantra, not surprisingly as I had been asking for it every morning for years.

"Morning Grace, I know what you want. It never changes. How's Gidget this morning?" he asked knowingly.

Looking at him, the tears started to fall. He looked mortified and I just shook my head from side to side and said softly, "It's our last day together." He nodded with a sweet acknowledgement and held my gaze for a moment.

Shortly afterwards, he handed me my coffee and a soy puppacino and said in the most articulate and meaningful way, "Le mie condoglianze," followed by "For a life well lived and a love forever embedded in your heart. Take care, Grace, I will see you at Susan's." He finished with, "Ciao Bella, this one is on me."

We arrived at the park and I lifted Gidget gently out of the car. She toddled with her signature butt wiggle combined with a certain creakiness about her. Slow and stiff yet determined.

I offered her the puppacino and she licked out every last bit while I sipped my soy latte. I sat and observed her determined demeanour as she took off slowly and with each and every wobble that followed, I treasured her. We loved this park and had come here often over the years.

I observed the depth of love I felt for her while sipping my warm latte. I was amazed at how fully present I was considering how busy and unfocused my mind was.

I wondered if Gidget's paws felt the familiarity of the soil beneath her, the same soil she had felt with these exact paws when she was a little puppy, or if she recognised the familiar smells still lingering from all those years ago. I hoped so.

Finn texted me love messages on the hour. I felt sad that his part, the actual upcoming euthanasia, would be so difficult. I could hardly think about it.

"Let's go, Gidget. Next stop is to see all your friends at Susan's dog park paradiso." Sliding into drive and out of the present moment, we took off.

I was completely engrossed in my busy mind. Why don't dogs live so long? Why did they get sick? Was the time right? Was it too early? Could I postpone today? How would I actually go through with it? Had Gidget had a good life? Have we spent enough time together? Have I looked after her well enough? How would I cope?

Endless unanswerable questions.

What a waste of precious energy. It was what it was, it would be what it would be, and I would deal with it as it arrived, I chanted to myself as I arrived back in the present moment. The seesaw of emotions was arduous.

After all, it was life with a beginning and an end. We all knew that. There was no escaping it.

For me to honour her life there was really no other choice but to be graceful in the event of a life ending and to show eternal gratitude for our love story.

I knew none of her health issues mattered any longer. I was slowly comprehending that I would no longer need to attend numerous vet appointments. I would not need to decipher blood test results or imaging reports with Finn. No longer would I need to deliver daily meds in half a piece of light cheese single, eating the other half myself, or sit in on her monthly massage appointments because after today...

"Hi Gidget," everyone said in chorus. Instantaneously, a pack of excited senior golden oldies wobbled over in a creaking ruckus to greet Gidget. Their rears and their tails wiggled madly. She got an extra special greeting, almost as if they knew.

My friends, especially the ladies, were my lifeline right now. They understood me perfectly and knew me so well. Even though Finn was amazing and supportive, sometimes a group of girlfriends and their shoulders to cry on were unbeatable.

All the dogs wore bows, mirroring Gidget's fashion attire of late. Every day since her diagnosis she had worn a big hot pink bow tied to her collar. It had always been her signature stylish addition for all her birthdays or special occasions. And this was a special occasion. Life was a special occasion.

Olive was first, followed by Snowy who accidentally knocked her over. Polly raced to the rescue and put her back on all fours. It was like watching a group at the local senior retirement village shuffling around, except the furry version. The senior nanna brigade.

Wilma, Teddy and Bert followed right up their backsides, taking a quick sniff on the way.

Arnie and Rudy, the Labradors, came running fast and uncoordinated. Despite their age, they were still able to move reasonably fast with endless enthusiasm and brashness.

The Jack Russells came last. The young ones, Lola, Spencer and Bob, were yapping all around the place and instigating zoomies. Eddie and Molly, the parents, followed like a pair of hairy, dishevelled, in-love pensioner twins.

The lick fest began.

Everyone was fluffing over Gidget. I froze in time taking in her antics. I watched the slowness of her tail wag, the sinking down of her back legs and the greyness around her eyes. I was in awe of her love of life despite her health condition.

A picture of her as a young pup appeared in my head. Old memories bounced around that had been softly resting in deep storage spaces of my mind.

What I would give to go back and do it all over again, and relive every moment and every oopsie... just for a moment. I was taken back as I pictured Gidget doing a zoomie as a tiny three-month-old pup, wearing her first pink bow, chewing the coffee table edges and playing with Charlie. I saw myself waiting in the rain every night for her to do a wee, nursing her through her desexing and helping her manoeuvre the hallway with the cone of shame. So many moments to hold close.

"Please..." I begged internally.

I knew it was a step in the impending grief. I knew it was normal. I also knew that knowing it was normal didn't help. This was my head understanding the theory battling it out with my heart and the depth of the love. It was almost impossible to comprehend.

I couldn't keep up with the memories. Feeling shaky and dizzy, I was thrown back to reality. The images faded and were replaced with the beautiful, devoted nanna that stood directly in front of me.

I drew my gaze away from Gidget and looked up to the ceiling. My hand covered my face and I broke down into tears so engulfing I had to leave the room. I headed to the bathroom.

And the girls and the hugs followed!

As did all the dogs right behind us, all managing to somehow fit in one small room. They were never far away. I had to pull myself together. I had promised Gidget I would be happy today. These emotions would have to wait, but the few tears I shed had released the pressure valve somewhat and I was back in the present moment.

As I looked at my friends, it reminded me of the generations before and of my grandpa's first dog ever, way before he met my grandmother. His name was Geoff the Bitsa. "Bits of this and bits of that," Grandpa would say. He would tell story after story about how much he loved that first dog, how important Geoff was and what a good boy he was. His legacy lessons. He lived to seventeen years of age.

Maybe that's why my grandma's name was Gigi. He married a G, my mum's name is Georgia, my sister's is Gretel and mine is Grace. Gretel's dog was Gilly. To follow the tradition, maybe I subconsciously chose the name Gidget.

We were a G family and it all started with one special dog. Today we were here to honour another special G dog, Gidget.

Dogs really change our lives in big ways that we often don't notice.

Back outside, I asked for everyone's attention. Fred, Lilly, Tommy, Camilla, Antonio, Freddy, Polly, Susan, Paula, Stephanie, Gabriel and Gloria all looked at me in total silence. My beautiful friends. "To my sweet Gidget girl," I said and with that, we all raised our glasses. Nothing more needed to be said.

"To sweet Gidget," they all chanted.

Gidget

"Hello, my friends." I woofed happily, trying to be heard over the hullaballoo Olive was creating. I thought briefly of my few friends who were no longer with us.

Gidget & Grace

"My best friends, you all look so fabulous in your matching bows. Let's go and have a little tussle but keep it gentle please cause some of us are oldies now. Then we can beg for some treats."

Today's the day, my friends, to make one last play date count. To have one last tussle and roust each other up a little. It was time for one last scrinch-face fest and one final goodbye, I thought to myself quietly. But I woofed nothing out loud. It was my secret.

I started a zoomie. Well, a senior pace zoomie around the room. In my mind I was still a young two-year-old pup. I imagined my couch parkour of years ago where I was known to knock a champagne flute or two off the coffee table with my waggy tail.

I heard Mum say it was like watching a turtle trying to move at full speed. A turtle zoomie. The humans laughed hysterically. Mum loved turtles.

I think I have always lived my best life, even in my old age. What was age anyway? My mind was young and it was just my aging creaky body letting me down.

Did someone say chicken treat? Sniffing it out, I tried to do a slow sit and I waited. Next to me were all my senior furry friends and a few young ones. I clown smiled.

It was a great playdate, the best in fact. Leaving was terribly difficult for me. The others knew no different. I didn't share with them that the last play was our last ever play.

Would they miss me when I was not around? I know I missed my long-lost friends that I didn't see anymore. Maybe they would dream of me like I did of Charlie and Morty.

I thought with their aging bones it was likely I would see some of them sooner than expected in another realm anyway. I kind of selfishly hoped so.

I waited with drool dripping down my chest while Mum plated up my dinner. I noticed dinner was early for some reason. I took in all the aromas drifting around the room. A chorus of smells overwhelmed the hairs in my nose which were twitching uncontrollably.

A doggy degustation was being plated up: Scotch fillet, BBQ rotisserie chicken, anchovies, sardines, the strong cheddar cheese I like, and yoghurt. Ikkk yukkgghh, I snuffed. I never had the heart to tell Mum I hated yoghurt but I ate it up anyway. Always last of course unless all the good stuff was buried underneath it.

I sensed the sweet sadness oozing from Mum's pores. I could tell she was trying to keep it together yet failing miserably.

This just meant I had to work a little harder to keep her happy and to love her unconditionally. I would do this until my last breath. It distracted me from the inevitable.

So, I licked her leg while she was plating up.

Grace

"Wait Gidget," I said, as I had thousands of times, before I gave her the "okay" command. I did the same today, hoping she would not think anything was different. Although likely an early meal may have aroused her suspicions.

She gobbled it up. Despite all the issues her body was dealing with, her appetite was good today. I felt it was because of all the delicious-smelling food rather than her usual boring dog nuts that she had been rejecting for days now.

Watching her eat was always a moving experience and more so today. She was eating it all up quickly, leaving the yoghurt till last. I always wondered why she did that, despite personally hating yoghurt myself. Surely that was the best part for a dog?

Back in the lounge room, she toe-tapped with her front paws, the indication she was preparing to lay down. It was a slow process these days, especially on slippery floorboards. Her front legs slowly slid out in front of her and her bottom dropped to the floor in kind of a thud. Her back foot booties ensured she didn't completely splay herself out. She finally made it to a lying position.

I handed her a carrot. She loved carrots.

Then it was time for her to have another snooze.

I just sat with her and put my arm over her and stroked her smooth furs as she rested in her warm bed.

I tried desperately not to be cognisant of the countdown.

Waiting

GIDGET

My eyes flitted open as I rested on my favourite pink donut bed. Mum was sitting beside me. I let out the semblance of a little woof.

Mum jumped. My woofer still worked to some degree.

"Gidget, stay there. I'll be back in a sec," she said. I did as she said, like always... well, sometimes.

I did have some selective hearing. I would listen for chicken, but I wouldn't listen for dropping a banana skin I found in a bush. I would listen for a pig's ear, but I wouldn't listen when I found a dead bird at the park. I would listen for some bull chews, but I wouldn't listen for a chop bone I once found under a car. I would listen for some liver, but I wouldn't listen when I found a rainbow lollipop at a playground. I would listen for some beef jerky, but I wouldn't listen for a whole unpeeled carrot that lay in the gutter. I would really listen for some sausage, but I wouldn't listen for cat poo that was buried under a leaf.

Gidget & Grace

Get the drift. There were serious parameters and factors to be taken into account, decreed by no other than me, of course.

I sat looking out our pink front door and watched the world go by. I loved the smells from the garden as they drifted in from outside.

Two birds flew into the garden and sat near the door. Bravely they edged closer, likely sensing my inability to run and shoo them away.

When I was young, I chased all the birds and other wildlife with such gusto out of the garden with the help of my ferocious bark and the fast speed that my body could run back then.

Once, I alerted Mum to a family of blue-tongue lizards in the back wooden retaining wall. Mum came out dressed in what looked like protective gear. She had on pink rubber gloves and her pink glasses and held pink kitchen tongs. She proceeded to remove the wooden planks and gently pried them out of their hiding space before relocating them for their safety.

That was so long ago. I had so many happy memories. In my senior years, I enjoyed just laying around, resting, remembering events from my young days, and being with Mum.

Mum was back in a jiffy. My fuzzy old lady eyes thought she was carrying a stack of books. On closer inspection, they were actually photo albums.

She opened the first album while keeping one hand on my head stroking my furs. On the first page I saw a beautiful puppy as large as life.

"Gidget, that's you," she said. "I took that when you were so young."

I was curled up in a tiny bed on the kitchen floor, only a few months old, small as small can be.

I turned to look right up at her with my dark brown eyes and bored them straight into her soul. As always I was intent on loving her, just like Mum Suzy taught me. I had perfected this over the years.

The human–animal Mum and Gidget bond was now enormously deeper.

Colossal in fact.

Mammoth!

GRACE

I appreciated every single moment we had had together. Memories of Gidget were scattered through photo albums and spread throughout my heart. Looking over our journey together was so poignant yet so fulfilling. So full of memories and so full of love. I still yearned for a furry do-over.

The irrational thoughts still circled until one thought came that quelled the madness and soothed me.

I knew definitively I could never have loved her any more than I did. From the first moment and that first cuddle until right now, our last moments, it had just grown exponentially. I loved her completely and fully with all my heart.

This pacified my weary and tired mind while I soaked up all the moments of our love story. My heart felt full.

GIDGET

Mum continued to flip through the albums as she told me story after story of our journey together. I was enjoying every moment of our special love story.

I feel your love, Mum. I feel safe and happy and cherish all the moments of our life. Every memory a treasure. Every nap perfect. Every outing appreciated. Every hug enjoyed. Every park play a joy. Every beach run magnificent. Every blade of grass sniffed sensational. Every tree peed on, snack consumed, trick learned and snuggle before bed was amazing. There was nothing that could have made our love story more special, except if it had been longer.

I totally understood the cycle of life. I was at the latter end. Was it the better end, sweeter and calmer, or not, as that meant it was nearly the actual end? It was hard to know.

All I knew was the whole journey had been spectacular, like the grandest of extravaganzas, and we were reliving it with gusto.

I heard Mum ask for another sign. "Gidget, I need another sign just to be sure." Here she was doubting herself again.

Compliant as usual, I raised my front right leg and placed my paw on top of the album. Feeling quite exhausted, this was all I could muster.

I remember Mum telling me about Ernie when I was young. She loved Ernie stories and told me that every night in bed when she was reading a book he would lay on the spare pillow. He would proceed to place his paw on her book. It was like a game. She would remove it and he would put it back on the book again. Over and over every night.

I thought she would like it. More importantly, I knew she would get it.

It took a moment but finally she said, "Gidget, Ernie used to do that every night," and burst into tears.

I could feel that the tears came from a place so deep it was like she couldn't breathe. I started to worry. I didn't want to upset her. I only wanted to make her happy. Somehow, I found my strength to stand up and deliver wet licks all over her face, noticing the tasty saltiness of the tears.

"Mum, sit closer. I want to smell you beside me," I woofed softly. "Mum, pat me. I want to feel your soft touch on my fur. Mum, just be close. I want to take all these memories with me wherever I go because it's been a lifetime of devotion and love both ways. Mum, I love you endlessly and I will miss you enormously."

It really was a gift to be born and experience a life like mine. I was thirteen and I had lived what was considered a full life in the doggy world.

Mum often mentioned this special quote from *Winnie-the-Pooh* by A.A. Milne: "How lucky am I to have something that makes saying goodbye so hard". It was one of her favourites.

Yes, how lucky am I!

I really am!

We both are!

GRACE

Taking that as a second sign, I dried my eyes. I knew, finally, I was making the right decision. Well, I always knew, but this cemented it.

We sat there for some time, continuing to turn the pages to look through our life together with a myriad of "I love you's" and kisses in between.

And we waited.

Finn arrived just before 6pm. He walked in more slowly than usual with his leather doctor's bag.

"Hi Grace. Hi Gidget," he said and with that he knelt to the floor and gave Gidget and me the biggest hug.

A sweet goodbye

Grace

The love was palpable.

I felt Finn touch my hand.

I saw Gidget lying before me.

I tasted the salt of my tears.

I smelt her familiar doggy aroma.

Then I heard Finn say. "Are you ready, darling?"

My heart, begging for one more day, was screaming an alarming and thundering no.

Yet sadly, I knew better, and instead out came the quietest "yes" while another tear slid softly down my face. And I waited.

"I love you, baby girl. It's you and me always. Goodbye. Sleep peacefully Gidget, my beautiful, sweet girl."

I felt the heaviness of her head descend on me as the life drained from her body.

Gidget

"**M**um, I'm ready. It's time. Just hold me till my last breath comes and goes. All I need is for you to be by my side. Like you always tell me, it's you and me always. I love you," I woofed softly.

I knew I had fulfilled my purpose to the best of my ability. Unconditional love!

I placed my head on Mum's lap, nuzzled in and took in all her smells.

"I love you," I woofed.

And I waited.

My eyes felt heavy and they softly closed.

It was there in that moment I hoped for two things.

First and foremost, for Mum to be happy. To live and appreciate life without me physically present, to not mourn for too long, to fully live life and to love deeply again. To open her heart and her home to another dog that has its own purpose to fulfil, just like I did, when the time is right. To understand I am still by her side spiritually, always walking beside her and shelling out unconditional love in bucketloads in the form of signs and memories scattered as paw prints all over her heart forevermore.

Second, for me to enter the best and most realistic dream of my life where all my long-lost friends reside and have been waiting for me. Where my youth is fully restored and I am able to run wildly chasing ducks and tennis balls, swim in the sea, do parkour zoomies, take long leisurely walks, sniff every sniff on long sniffaris, eat all the best foods and do everything else I love. With plenty of naps in between. And with time for contemplation to remember my two mums – Mum Suzy who taught me my purpose of unconditional love and, most importantly, my most beautiful mum Grace.

It's you and me always, Mum.
Gidget and Grace, that's us! A true love story.

GRACE

"She's gone darling," I heard Finn say. The moment, the dreaded moment, the one you dread from the minute you first hold your puppy had come and gone. Just like that. Her last breath. Whoosh... a lifetime had passed!

The final act of love, the final gift I could offer her, was to remove her pain yet plunge myself into my own.

The love was palpable.

The grief excruciating.

A sweet life. A sweet goodbye. A sweet girl. I sobbed as I kissed her once more on her lifeless head.

"It's still you and me always, Gidget. I love you.

"Gidget and Grace, that's us! A true love story."

Paris at last

GRACE

"Yes," I replied.

"Oh my, I am so happy right now," he said, doing a little toe-tap dance under the table and nearly unbalancing the macaron tower.

We were sitting in a café right in the heart of Paris on the Champs-Élysées, apparently one of the top twenty cafés in Paris and well known for its decadent macarons, according to Finn's extensive online research. It was divine. It was one of those famous cafés that also has locations in New York, Los Angeles and London. The décor, the ambience, the floral arrangements, the lighting, the food display cabinets, the soft music and even the floors were stunning. Every aspect was impressive and so very chic.

I sent some snaps to Camilla. For inspiration, was all I wrote. She sent me back the bulging eye emoji depicting wow. And it really was a high-level wow.

Finn and I were sipping wickedly wonderful floral teas and indulging in macarons of every imaginable flavour – coffee, caramel, orange blossom, pistachio, strawberry candy and the yummy list went on. The colourful, sweet, meringue-based confection with succulent smooth ganache or buttercream centres melted in our mouths, arousing all our taste buds and inciting a foodgasm.

I was not an aficionado like Camilla and Antonio but, if I were a food inspector and it was my job to critique, this surely was worth a Michelin star. That is if it didn't have one already.

And now Finn had just asked me the big question.

It had been a tough six months and looking forward to this trip had helped provide some much-needed distraction and pockets of normality from my unrelenting, incessant grief. The grief still bowled me over sometimes, actually a lot of the time. I was becoming expert at navigating unexpected tears in all sorts of inappropriate places.

But I was doing better.

It's not like the first few weeks when I needed to ask Stephanie for a referral to a good pet counsellor. She told me I needed to speak with Jane so that is what I did. Jane walked me through the five-step grief process and explained how pet grief is a form of disenfranchised grief. This means it is not openly acknowledged or accepted by society or seen as worthy of grief.

Finally, thanks to Jane and all my supportive friends who did understand, I was at the point of being able to share in Finn's suggestion of this trip. It had always been a dream of mine, even before Will, to visit Paris. And doing it with Finn made it even more special. He organised everything and it was perfect.

The question came during a bite of a strawberry candy macaron.

"Grace, I love you and I see our futures together. I know it has been a rough six months for you, but I was hoping that you would do me the honour..." he paused "of pet parenting with me."

I paused.

"Are you kidding me?" I replied. "That's a resounding yes from me, of course. Abso-yappy-lutely to be more precise!"

"Yes! That's what I hoped you would say," he said.

And with that he pulled out his phone, flipped to his photos, and turned it to face me. Two picture-perfect golden retriever puppies were staring back at us with those familiar big brown loving eyes and puppy clown smiles.

"Which one is ours?" I asked, looking at him excitedly.

"Well, I thought we could take both, one boy and one girl. Everyone deserves a best friend," he said hesitantly.

"Really? Yes! What a terrific idea. I'm so excited," I said, almost bouncing out of my skin.

We do need to choose names but we have plenty of time. The breeder said we can collect them the week we arrive home."

"I know what I'd like to call them. How about Suzy and Geoff, after a couple of dogs who changed my life?" I said with a cocktail of extreme happiness and a touch of poignancy. I noticed I was breaking the full G tradition but I was okay with that. "What do you think?"

"Perfect. I'm happy if you're happy," he said, always eager and easy to please.

Then he looked at me strangely, with his thinking face. "Grace, did you think I was going to ask you something else, like another big question?" he said worriedly.

"No, of course not. This question is so much better!" I laughed out loud.

Secretly, though, I was hoping the other question was not far behind. Before my birthday would be ideal. One week away. Maybe at the top of the Eiffel Tower where we were going for a special dinner celebration. I visualised it.

Manifestation essentially is focusing your thoughts on your desired goal. It is achieved by immersing in such things as visualisation, mindfulness and meditation. You think it, you believe it, you picture it, you open your mind to it. You harness the vibrations and send them out into the universe. Your desired outcome then appears. Hopefully one day.

"If only..." I stopped myself mid-sentence.

I didn't want to lose my grip on the present magical moment. This was special. Gidget would want me to enjoy every second, just like she would have. She would have loved imminent puppy arrivals. I could feel myself balancing at the precipice, about to plunge into the dark depths of grief again.

But then, words appeared, out of nowhere, in my mind: Fully live life and love deeply again, Mum. Don't let your grief halt your life. I am here always, forever with you, residing in the form of paw prints all over your heart. But your heart has so much more love to give to more doggies who want to be part of your family. Give them that honour. Every tear will be worth all the unconditional love they will share with you. Be present. Don't miss a second of your journey. It's too special. P.S. I love you.

It's like Gidget was woofing at me loudly. Whoooaaa, I thought. So true. Still teaching me, sweet girl.

"Thank you, Gidget," I said as I smiled softly.

So, with that, I continued to sip my tea, looking fondly at Finn, and fell into silence to honour my wise and beautiful Gidget. He knowingly respected the silence. He understood. Maybe he was appreciating his own moment with Morty, here in the captivating, picturesque and romantic city that is Paris. It was truly awe-inspiring... formidable even.

Then, we smiled at each other, he took my hand and life continued. The smells and sounds wafted back, tantalising my senses. I was in Paris with the love of my life and I needed to be fully present for that as Gidget taught me. Be present for everything. Miss nothing.

I wondered if Gidget had engineered these pending arrivals from beyond.

Just like that, another new love story was about to begin.

And I couldn't wait!

From over the Rainbow Bridge

GIDGET

"Charlie, slow down! Come on guys, keep up!" I woofed to the others. 'I'm So Excited' by The Pointer Sisters was stuck on repeat in my mind. Mum loved that song. She always played it in the car and it was now forever stuck in my head, one of many memories of her.

It had been a difficult day for me... a dog... me... saying goodbye to my second mum, seeing her so sad, closing my eyes, forcing myself to let go and to fall into the abyss, the unknown, to prepare for my next journey, a solo one this time. Most challenging.

I felt a kiss on my head.

I didn't know where I was going or what would happen. I didn't know how I would ever cope with no one there to hold my paw and no one to Velcro myself to.

I heard Mum say goodbye and I was engulfed with a haze of different colours surrounding me, swirling around and creating a rainbow. I looked around as I transitioned through the rainbow. I could feel the heaviness of my body and the stiffness of my legs alter. There was a transition to a lightness, an exuberance and a youthfulness that had been long lost but still felt familiar. As I kept moving through this exquisite array of colours all my ailments melted away. I suddenly felt like I was two years old again.

As I emerged from the rainbow, there staring straight at me was Charlie, sitting tall and proud, chest out and ears pricked. "Hey sis, what took you so long? I've missed you. I have waited every day and finally you are here," he said, racing over to lay a big lick on my face. "Let's go! Follow me. I have some furry friends you will want to meet."

I looked around as I followed Charlie. The sun was shining and the temperature was perfect. Large open spaces appeared. There were beaches, sand dunes and lakes. The grass was a deep green and the water a bright blue. There were no clouds and no sign of rain. I saw full clean water buckets everywhere and help-yourself food stations called snacky stops that were stocked full of treats. Donut beds of all different colours were placed at every corner. There were grooming pods that you walked into and voila, you were perfectly groomed with no tangles, no ouchies. Big toy baskets full of colourful clean toys and troughs full of tennis balls were scattered around. And there were electronic ducks that flew! Trees galore provided shelter and shade. And there were special business spots that automatically cleaned after you were finished.

Everything here was nirvana. I had never envisaged the beyond to be so beautiful, so serene and so specially concocted just for a dog.

It was enormously peaceful. There was no traffic, cars, loud garbage trucks, pesky posties, sirens, horns, beeping stop lights, noisy air traffic, fireworks, uber bikes or obnoxious people.

There were no neglected or abandoned dogs. And no fear, reactivity, aggression or anxiousness. All seemed to be stripped on arrival.

There were no vet clinics either. No jabs, no medicine, no cold things up the butt, no weight shaming on the scales, no poking and prodding, because no one ever got ill – ever – according to Charlie.

It was a blissful utopia.

"Gidget, it's a special day today. You have arrived at your final resting place and we get to be reunited and have fun. Let me introduce everyone," he said, running towards a group of dogs wearing pink bows and pink party hats, even the boys.

"Oh Charlie, what have you done?" I woofed, laughing. I'd so missed my brother.

First, I saw Hudson and Shelly. They were floofed and beautiful just like I remembered them. "We went through the grooming pod just for you, Gidget. So good to see you," they woofed together. Then came a bombardment of questions about Snowy and Wilma, and Susan and Paula. After I filled them in on all the furry details of their families on the other side, they ran off woofing.

Then two chocolate Labradors barged through the group, causing a ruckus on the way, much like Arnie and Rudy did on numerous occasions. They spoke quickly with excitement. "Hi Gidget, we are Violet and Daisy. Camilla is our Mum."

I remembered Camilla speaking of these two crazies as she called them. I didn't tell them that though. I did tell them all about how she had grown her family to include Antonio, Freddy and her two current furry family members Teddy and Bob. And I told them how Bob came to be with us, which meant explaining Eddie's runaway night of passion, which they thought was hysterical.

"So happy to hear all that. Thanks Gidget," they woofed. "We can't wait to play together more and get to know you and hear more about our mum." They ran off doing bucking broncos, causing more carnage on their way, just as Camilla had described them.

Next Charlie woofed, "Do you remember these guys, Gidget?" I looked over and there was an enormous Irish wolfhound and a pug with a smooshed-up face. I looked intently and had to search my memory.

"Oh my god, is that you, Winston? Wally?" I woofed in surprise. "It's been forever. You have got so much bigger than when I knew you. I always wondered what happened to you guys after puppy school. I wonder what happened to Audrey and Sammy too."

Once the crowd had parted a bit, I could see a short, extra-long dog standing on his ears while nibbling on some grass. He looked up slowly and, once he had untangled himself from his ear predicament, we raced towards each other.

"Morty, my man," I woofed. "My favourite shortest dog ever. How the woof are you?"

In return, he woofed, "No more ear infections here, Gidget. It's so good to see you. How's Finn?"

With that, we burst out laughing and did a play bow before I filled him in on all things Finn and Mum.

I turned to see a large, deep-chested golden retriever approaching. "Hey kid, nice to meet you. I'm Chester, your dad. I look forward to playing together."

I lowered my head in total surprise and awe. "Wow! Hi Dad!" was all I could woof.

How awesome it was to have so many of my favourite friends here. I soon realised I wasn't alone.

Charlie was still excitedly arranging the reunion and the introductions. I noticed a calm black Labrador with a lush velvety coat sitting patiently. What a gentleman. The pink hat and bow looked particularly stunning against his black, shiny coat. Could it be, I wondered. We locked eyes and Charlie said, "I would now like to introduce you to Ernie, a very special friend of mine."

I went up and sniffed his butt.

"Ernie? Not THE Ernie? Is your Earth Mum called Grace?" I woofed.

"That's me, Gidget. I sent you to Mum many years ago, especially handpicked after I passed. I knew she needed another furry soul to heal her heart and love her unconditionally. Thank you for doing just that. I couldn't have chosen better. I have been watching you both for all those years sharing a true love story, just like ours had been," he woofed. I knew instantly I had another best friend in my heart.

"There's one more to go, Gidget," Charlie woofed.

I turned around and she didn't need an introduction. She was a clone of me, or rather I was a clone of her... her baby. It was Mum Suzy! I ran to her so fast and gave her the biggest lick... and another one... and then started jumping around, turning upside down, woofing, just like I would have when I was a pup.

"Darling girl," she woofed to me. "Hello. You're here. Sweet girl, you fulfilled your purpose so much better than I could have ever hoped for. Thank you for being a sterling example of what a dog can teach humans. I am so very proud of you. And now we are reunited, never to be separated again. Charlie, you and me together again. The other siblings are still on their earthly mission and they will come home to us one day. But we don't ever rush them or wish the time away or waste time waiting. We just live in the moment and truly enjoy it."

I stood in awe of this beautiful place with these beautiful souls and knew I was going to be okay, actually more than okay. I had my mum Suzy and a whole new family.

Of course, though, there was one thing missing. My mum Grace.

I looked down and where I once wandered around the garden on her heels, there now rested a new beautiful river stone etched with Gidget 14.8.2024, a love heart, and the words 'A sweet life, a sweet goodbye. You and me always!' It was sitting next to all the others, the biggest stone of all. Mum had wrapped my pink bow around it.

I hoped one day she would be fully at peace. If only she knew how peaceful and happy I am here with all my friends in this park paradiso, the true paradiso, much better than Susan's version. I would watch out for her from here.

I was only a woof away from sending her a sign when she needed one. The first one I would send would be in the form of two golden retriever puppies needing a home. I knew she wouldn't be able to resist them or resist journeying through another love story.

One day was never the same as the next. Our little pack zoomied around the green fields and swam in the lakes, forever running wild, playing and frolicking. We were youthful and energetic, happy and present. We put ourselves through the grooming pod when we got stinky. We were fed and watered. We were happy, joyful and peaceful.

Charlie was normally the leader of the pack. He directed different activities and I was always happy to follow. Age was not a concern here. We all had the same youthful spirits, so I could run wild with Mum Suzy like I never could down there on the earthly plane.

Sometime after – time of no concern here – I looked down to see Mum sitting in the garden watching two young puppies racing around. She was sitting under the crepe myrtle in full bloom with a lovely new bench seat nearby.

She placed a hand on each stone, enjoying a quiet moment to herself. Next moment, the puppies raced full pelt towards her and started biting her madly with their little sharp teeth.

"Ouch, Suzy, Geoff, watch those teethies," I heard her say.

I woofed, hoping it travelled to Mum and the puppies. "Mum Grace, you are wrapped all over my heart. I will love you eternally. Never forgotten. Enjoy the pups. I will check in again soon." I saw her look around behind her like she was acknowledging something mysterious.

Our love story was the best love story ever and it continues, just on a different realm, I thought.

Then I looked to the group of dogs ahead of me, with Charlie in the lead and Mum Suzy looking back waiting for me. "Let's go!"

they woofed in unison at me. "It's a beautiful day and we have more adventures to fulfil."

And with that, I woofed back, "I'm coming!"

Go Gidget, I woofed to myself, and off I went, running youthfully, wild and free.

Thank you for reading my book!

I appreciate all your feedback,
and I love hearing what you have to say.

I would really love your input to help
make my future books better.

Please leave me a helpful review on Amazon,
letting me know what you thought of the book.

A big PINK Thank you!

♡ Lara Casanova ♡

Contact me

Web: www.lifeinthepink.com.au

Email: lara@lifeinthepink.com.au

Facebook: www.facebook.com/InthePINKxx/

Instagram: www.instagram.com/lifeinthepinkxx

Read about Lara's other books

Loss, Love and Lessons:
Healing pet loss and grief

Allow Lara, a heart-centred grief counsellor, to accompany you as she shares from her personal and professional experience and knowledge on pet grief. An array of tools, insights, reflections and exercises, interwoven with Lara's own grief love story, are designed to help you on your healing journey.

A heartfelt story of love, grief and loss – yours and your pet's – as you follow the 'paw prints' on your heart, enabling you to *heal* your loss, *feel* the love and *appreciate* the lessons.

Grief, Grace and Gratitude:
Transforming through your grief journey

Grief is an opportunity to open your heart. Opening yourself to an understanding of grief will open your heart to heal. Opening your heart to heal ultimately opens your heart to love again.

Lara will teach you how to transform yourself and find love, truth and purpose through the gifts and lessons of grief. You will walk through the stages of grief and return home to your true nature with a zealous desire to live a rich and full life in your loved one's honour.

Heartbreak, Healing and Happiness:
Flourishing after a heartbreak

Do you feel as if your world has crumbled around you? Is your physical, mental, emotional and spiritual life sprawled like rubble on the floor, with you in the middle of it, lost and scared? Are you hearing a resounding YES coming from deep inside?

Redesign and redecorate your life and heal any old lingering hurts forever. Emerge feeling healed and happy with oodles of energy, eager to embark on your new, fun and exciting life adventure.

Acknowledgements

This book was a joy to write because it's similar to many of my own love stories. Many people and dogs helped create the inspiration to put down on paper these words that live in my heart just like all my dogs. The biggest thank you to all those souls, furry or otherwise.

A special mention to:

My immediate family – Dad (deceased), Mum, my sisters, Dail, Becky and Nicole, my dad's partner, Pat (deceased), and my adorable nieces, Samantha, Charlie, Chloe, Imogen, Anna and Claire. And all your furry kids, of course. You all inspire me to be a better person and follow my dreams. I love you all.

My extended family – My aunties, uncles and all my cousins. I am blessed to have an amazing extended family.

My late family – My darling dad, grandparents and all the generations that were here before me, a lineage I am very proud of.

My friends – Thank you. I wonder if any of you can pick your traits from the characters in this book. You all may find yourself somewhere in here. And if not you, your furry family members.

Alex and her team at Author Support Services – Without you, I would not have been able to bring my fourth book to fruition. Biggest thanks ever.

My mentors and other authors – There are so many who have transformed my life.

Pippy, George and Sonny, my three current fur children, who stick to me like Velcro wherever I am. Like Gidget, always a tripping hazard and teaching me endless lessons about life and love.

All their furry friends and their owners, my doggy friends.

Lastly, all the dogs that came before – Maxy, Suzy, Chelsea and Charlie – and all their friends too. Especially Suzy to whom this book is dedicated. My beautiful sweet Suzy girl.

I feel unconditional love resting as paw prints on my heart from those I have lost and from those present with me now.

I look forward to meeting those I have not met yet. And thank them in advance.

I cherish my own love stories!

Thank you.

THE END